Guarding Her Heart

BlackThorpe Security
Book 1

Kimberly Rae Jordan

THREE**STRAND**
P R E S S

A CORD OF THREE STRANDS IS NOT EASILY BROKEN.

A man, a woman & their God.

Three Strand Press publishes Christian Romance stories

that intertwine love, faith and family.

Always clean. Always heartwarming. Always uplifting.

1

THAN Miller stared at the report on his screen and managed—just barely—to bite back a curse. Aggravation rode him hard these days. Everything annoyed him, and his teams' latest security job was no exception. If he thought it would make a difference, he'd fly to Europe to give the snotty rich kid a piece of his mind.

As it was, they had two groups of guys on the kid who was determined to try to slip away from her bodyguards at every opportunity. She knew about the main team, but they hadn't told her about the ghost team that was also in place. Than wondered briefly if her father would consider tagging her with a GPS chip. It would make it a whole lot easier to keep track of her.

But then they weren't in this business for the easy assignments—which is what these babysitting-type jobs *should* be. They got hired because they were the best, and this girl's father was paying the big bucks to make sure his little princess stayed safe while she and her friends romped through Europe during their spring break. He had a funny feeling his guys were going to be asking for raises after this gig.

A knock on his door drew his attention from the report. Surprise shot through Than when he saw Lucas Hamilton standing in the doorway. Though he looked an awful lot like his twin brother Lincoln, Lucas's more reserved appearance was always a dead giveaway to which twin he was dealing with.

Than pushed back from the desk and walked around to shake the man's hand. "Afternoon, Lucas. This is a bit of a surprise. Everything alright with Lincoln?"

"Lincoln is doing fine as far as I know." Lucas unbuttoned the jacket of the light gray suit he wore and smoothed his hand over his paisley blue tie. "I'm actually here about Lindsay."

Than's eyes widened. Well, that was even more surprising than seeing Lucas at his door. He motioned to the chair in front of his desk. "Have a seat."

After sitting back down, Than pulled his chair forward and leaned his arms on his desk. "So how can I help you with Lindsay? And does your sister actually know you're here?"

Lucas shook his head. "Nope. But at this point, it doesn't matter."

Than frowned. It sounded a bit like Lucas was going to try to force his sister to do something. That boded well for pretty much no one involved in the situation. From his rather limited experience with the woman, Than had still managed to pick up on the fact that Lindsay Hamilton let no one call the shots. "Does Brooke know about this apparent death wish you have?"

Lucas grinned at that. "Yeah, and it's been our first major argument since getting married, but hey." The man's broad shoulders lifted in a shrug. "I'm a big brother, and my protective streak is well documented when it comes to those I love."

Being a brother himself, Than understood that streak. "And now you want to drag me into this mess?"

"How do you know it's a mess?" Lucas asked with an arched brow.

"Oh, let me recap. It involves telling Lindsay to do something. You've had a fight about it with your beautiful new bride. And now you've actually resorted to coming to me for some part of this. I'd say it's officially a mess. And that's the polite term for it."

Lucas laughed as he slouched into the chair. "I really do need your help. I know there's stuff between you and Lindsay but, from what I hear, you're the best person to help me out."

"Okay." Than let out a long sigh and settled back, intertwining his fingers across his abdomen. "Lay it on me."

Lucas sat forward. "Lindsay has decided to go on a mission trip with a group from our church."

Than wondered if his eyebrows had completely disappeared into his hairline at that comment. "A mission trip?"

Lucas nodded. "They're going to go to the Philippines for two weeks."

"The Philippines? What are they going to do there?"

"The plan is to help a small mission with a school and orphanage. Do some building and help them with whatever else they need."

Than let the information sink in. Just going on his own interactions with her, it didn't seem like something Lindsay would be interested in. However, he'd seen a different side to her while on the island for Brooke and Lucas's wedding. She'd been more relaxed and had clearly doted on her nephew, Danny, and even Brooke's niece, Sarah. It had been an interesting view of yet another side of her personality. One of these days, he might have the complete picture of the woman who'd intrigued him to no end.

"So what is it you need me to do?"

"I want you to go with her."

Lucas's direct statement had Than straightening. "Go with her? On a mission trip?"

"I am not comfortable sending her halfway around the world without someone to keep an eye on her."

"Wouldn't that be the responsibility of whoever is heading up this trip?" Than asked.

"Someone whose *only* job is keeping an eye on her. I know the Philippines is a relatively safe country, especially where they are going, but that doesn't mean there's no risk involved. After what happened with Lincoln, Mom is a little reluctant—make that *extremely* reluctant—to let any of us too far out of her reach. I've told Lindsay that if she's determined to do this, then—for our mom's peace of mind— she's going to have a bodyguard go with her."

"And she agreed to that?"

Lucas hesitated. "She's coming around."

"So do you want me for the job or one of my men?" Than asked, pretty sure he already knew the answer.

"You. Even mentioning to Mom that I'd send a bodyguard with her wasn't enough. It was only when I said I'd try to get you to take the job that she finally relented."

Than gave an exasperated shake of his head. "Lincoln has no problem with me. Your mom trusts me—and apparently so do you since you're here—but you're asking me to trek halfway around the world with the one person in your family who definitely does *not* like me."

"Yep. That's about the sum of it." Lucas leaned back in his chair, apparently at ease now that he'd gotten it all off his chest. "I'll pay whatever it takes to get you to do this for us."

"Will that include funeral expenses and a trust fund for my family when Lindsay sends me back in a body bag?"

Lucas chuckled. "If I didn't think you could hold your own against her, I wouldn't be here. And this is what you do, after all, right? Deal with people who don't always want to be under the watchful eye of a bodyguard?"

Given the report he'd been reading earlier, Lucas was right about that. But was he willing to risk it and spend two whole weeks with this woman? He was pretty sure Lucas didn't have any idea exactly what he was asking of him. No one did. Than wasn't one to tout his failures when it came to women...especially the one that he just couldn't seem to get out of his mind.

He'd gone on three dates since that memorable evening with Lindsay eight months ago. But he'd finally tossed in the towel and stopped asking women out. It wasn't fair to the women when he spent most of the evening comparing them to his date with Lindsay. Inevitably, his thoughts would drift to why she had turned him down for a second date. And then he would wonder why he even cared... It was a vicious cycle that had gotten worse with each date, so he'd just stopped trying.

"Is the mission team okay with me coming along?" It wasn't like he was a regular church attender, even though his parents were. He always seemed to be able to find more important things to do on Sunday mornings than drag himself out of bed to sit in a pew.

"I've spoken at length with the mission team leader about the situation. He was a little concerned that having you along would upset Lindsay but seems to understand where I'm coming from. Obviously, if the worst should happen, Lindsay would be the most valuable person because of her potential worth from a financial standpoint, so the guy understands my concern. And while I don't like using my money to manipulate situations, I'm not above doing it for my sister's safety. A good portion of the money needed for this trip is coming from the charitable arm of Hamilton Enterprises." Lucas paused. "Anyway, Mark—the mission team leader— said he'd pray about it. He called me this morning to let me know that he'd also talked to the people at the mission center in the Philippines and it would be fine for you to accompany Lindsay."

Lucas seemed about to say something more but when he didn't, Than asked, "Have you run my name past Lindsay yet?"

Lucas shook his head. "I wanted to make sure you'd actually do it before I dropped that little bomb on her. No sense in riling her up if I didn't know for sure you'd take the job."

"What are the dates?"

For the next half hour, the two of them hashed out the details of the trip including what Lucas expected of Than.

"You've been to the Philippines before?" Lucas asked when Than revealed more than just a passing knowledge of the country.

"I'm actually half Filipino." Than turned around a family picture he kept on his desk. "My mom is from the Philippines."

Lucas picked up the picture and examined it. "Really? How did your folks meet?"

"Dad was stationed at Clark Air Force Base back before it closed. He attended a church outside of the base where my mom also went. The rest—as they say—is history."

"Well, now I feel even more confident in my decision to send you with her. Plus, it gives more weight to why you're the best man for the job. Do you speak the language?"

Than nodded. "Mom made sure I learned at a young age. All us kids are bilingual. Although, to be honest, English is spoken pretty much everywhere there."

Lucas set the picture back on the desk. "You have a lovely family."

"Thanks. They're a pretty decent bunch."

As he pushed up from his chair, Lucas said, "Thank you for being willing to take this on. I know Lindsay can be...difficult at times, but I hope this trip will help her see there's more to the world than the sphere we tend to operate in because of our wealth. I know that my trip to Africa with Brooke was an eye opening experience. I'm hoping it's the same for Lindsay."

Than stood and walked around the desk to join Lucas. "I'll talk with Marcus and Alex about the timing of this just to be sure they have nothing on their schedule for me. As long as I have some sort of internet and cellular connection, I should be fine."

Lucas stuck out his hand. "Thanks again, Than. I appreciate all you've done for our family, and even though Lindsay might not say it, I know she does, too."

After shaking the man's hand, Than stood for a moment with his hands on his hips, staring at the doorway Lucas had disappeared through, marveling at this latest turn of events. He had to admit, he was doubtful that this was actually going to happen. Once Lindsay got wind of what her brother was planning, Than was fairly certain she'd veto it all.

As he walked back to his desk to give Alex a call, Than realized the thought filled him with more disappointment than it should.

"You hired *who*?" Lindsay stared at Lucas. She'd known from the minute he'd walked into her office that she wasn't going to like what he had to say. She just hadn't known exactly how *much* she wasn't going to like it.

"You heard me." Lucas settled into the chair across from her desk. "And before you get all twisted out of shape, there are some pretty compelling arguments as to why it should be him."

"Really?" Lindsay crossed her arms and glared at Lucas. "Do tell."

"First, Mom finally backed down on her objections to your plans when I suggested we approach Than about going with you. Knowing he'll be there with you will give her peace of mind."

Lindsay gave him that point. Her mother had been anything but supportive of her decision to go on this mission trip. She'd thrown every argument in the book at Lindsay, so hearing that her mom had dialed it back when told Than would accompany her was rather surprising.

"Second, Than is actually half Filipino—his mom is from there—which means he knows the culture, the country, *and* the language. With that knowledge, he'll be able to analyze potential threats much more quickly and easily."

"I still think you're overreacting," Lindsay murmured with a frown. "Do you really think the church would send a group of its people into a dangerous place?"

"No. I'm sure they wouldn't, but there are pockets in that country where extremists are known to be. And things can turn on a dime. I just want to know that should things go bad, you've got someone by your side to help you and give you the best chance to get out safely."

Lindsay really thought Lucas was just being overprotective and controlling. More understandable was her mother's concern. Sylvia Hamilton had endured a lot in the past year and even though Lincoln was technically safe now, she'd still lost her son. When the news of Lincoln's death had reached them, the grief had been immense. Discovering that he had survived the crash had been welcome news, even though it had been overshadowed by the realization that he'd lost his memory, so Lindsay understood why her mother worried about something happening to her and Lucas. She hadn't been all that pleased that Lucas and Brooke had decided to go to Africa as part of their honeymoon, but after Lucas had promised to check in each day, she'd relented.

So if taking Than along was what would ease the fear her mom had for her safety, well, Lindsay would just have to accept that. She still wasn't one hundred percent sure why she was going on this mission trip. The first time it was announced at church, she'd felt a strong urge to join the team. Initially, she'd brushed it aside. After all, she would be the first to say her faith wasn't what it should be. Going through the motions was more her style. But she'd felt the pull to be a part of this mission trip, unlike anything she'd ever experienced before.

Convinced that they'd laugh at her request to join, she'd still taken the time to speak to the team leader to feel him out. Surprisingly enough, he'd been more receptive than she'd thought he would be. And Lucas, too, had been supportive for the most part. The roadblocks had come primarily from her mom. Once she'd heard of Lindsay's plans, her mother had demanded that she back out.

"Okay. If that's what it will take." Lindsay let her brother enjoy his win for a moment then said, "But on one condition."

Lucas's brows lifted at her comment. "And what's that?"

"He has to be part of the team. And by that I mean he needs to do what all the rest of us do. If we're painting a wall, he's right beside me with a paint brush in his hand. I don't care if he has a gun in the other one, but he's going to have to pull his weight. And actually, I'd rather he not be visibly armed while we are at the mission. I'm sure some on the team already question my ability to adapt and do the work, so I don't want them to see me as some pampered princess who has to bring along her muscle."

"Even if that's exactly what you are?" Lucas said, a corner of his mouth lifting.

Lindsay flung a pen in his direction. "Shut up."

With one last grin, Lucas left her office. Though she had a stack of files to review, Lindsay sat staring into space. Two weeks with Than. She'd done her best to avoid being alone with him since their date eight months ago. After meeting him for the first time, she'd seen pretty quickly the type of guy he was. A consummate flirt. A skirt-chaser. A serial dater. None of those things had appealed to her in the least, so she'd accepted his invitation for a date for one reason and one reason only: to show him that there was at least *one* woman on the planet immune to his charms.

The problem was that it turned out she hadn't been as immune as she'd thought. One on one with him during their date, he had drawn her in with his gorgeous smile and warm chocolate brown eyes. She'd been able to resist his attempts to make her laugh—but just barely. Though it had been hard not to allow his compliments to go to her head, she'd managed to keep from blushing.

With any other man, it might have been the perfect first date. Only she knew that while Than did first and sometimes second dates, it never went much beyond that. She was so not interested in becoming just one more in a long line of women he wined and dined. And she'd come pretty close to joining that line when she'd realized that beyond her assumptions of him, there were several things about him she found attractive. However, none of them outweighed his history with women and the knowledge that even if he did decide he wanted more than a handful of dates with her, there would be no happily ever after with him. Her father and even Lincoln had shown her that there were some men who believed that it was their right and privilege to enjoy the company of any—and every—woman who grabbed their interest.

Fortunately, thanks to Lucas, Eric, and Trent, Lindsay was also aware that there were men in the world who wanted just one woman to love and cherish. Somehow she had to just wait and see if there might be one of those men for her. Or if it was her lot in life to be an aunt, a daughter and a sister but never a wife or mother.

Strangely enough, until Brooke and Danny had come onto the scene, she'd been more than happy with the roles of daughter and sister. But somehow, seeing the love between Brooke and her son had brought something to life within Lindsay. And then when Lucas and Brooke had fallen in love, well, that had also awakened something inside her. A desire for more than she'd been willing to settle for.

But that *more* would never include a man like Than. No, she'd wait for a man who was willing to treat her the way Lucas, Eric, and Trent treated the women they loved. And not just for a date or two but forever.

So while the prospect of spending two weeks with Than close by was rather daunting, she was just going to focus on why she was going on this mission. To experience life outside her little bubble and to help the mission however they needed it. Than was there as a means to an end. Without him, she wouldn't be able to go, so she'd accept his presence, but it didn't mean it had to be anything more.

2

As HE packed his suitcases the night before they were scheduled to leave for Manila, Than had to admit he was surprised that Lindsay hadn't stormed his office demanding he tell Lucas he couldn't come with her. The past two weeks had been full of meetings and preparations for the trip in addition to all his normal work.

He'd met with Lucas and the team leader to go over the details of the trip so he was aware of their itinerary and where exactly they were going to be located. He hadn't been able to attend any of the team meetings though because he'd also had a ton of stuff he needed to do for work before he could leave. That meant he hadn't seen Lindsay since all this had been arranged. He sure hoped Lucas wasn't saving that little surprise for the airport.

"*Anak.*" His mother walked into his bedroom and shoved a bag into his hands. "You take this for your *lola.*"

Eyeing the package and hoping he could find a spot for it, Than asked, "What is it, Mama?"

She shrugged. "Just some clothes and beauty products. You know she likes that kind of stuff."

Yeah, he did. Almost one whole suitcase was full of gifts—*pasalubong*, as they called it—for his mom's family. "I'll see if I can squeeze it in with the rest of the stuff."

His mom flitted around the room, tugging on the bedspread to smooth out any wrinkles. She picked up the T-shirt and shorts he'd left on the floor earlier and with a *tsk* she dropped them in his dirty clothes basket.

Rosa Miller was a tiny woman whose only job since the day she'd married his father had been her family. She would no doubt be heartbroken when his youngest sister finally moved out of the family home and she had no children left to take care of. She'd survived the departure of both of his older siblings when they'd gotten married, but only because his two youngest sisters still lived at home. However, his mom didn't understand why he wasn't living there anymore as well, since it was often customary for adult Filipino children to stay with their parents until they got married.

Perching on the edge of his bed beside one of the suitcases, she cast him a sly look as she ran a hand over the stack of clothes he'd just packed. "Your *tita* said she had someone for you to meet."

Than pinned his mother with a firm look. "Not gonna happen, Mama. I know it worked for Steven, but I'm not interested."

"Not interested in having an *asawa*?" She arched a perfectly plucked jet black brow. "You plan to just have girlfriends for the rest of your life?"

"I'm not interested in having a wife right now, Mama. And when I do decide I want to get married, it will be to someone I've spent time with and chosen for myself."

"You're not getting any younger, *anak*. You're in your thirties now. You need to be thinking about having a family."

Than put the last of his clothes into the suitcase and leaned over to grasp the zipper tab to pull it around to the front. "Dad was older than I am when you married him. I think I still have a few years."

They had this conversation on a fairly regular basis since he'd turned thirty, and he always presented the same argument that she couldn't refute. She was definitely a tenacious thing, his mother. A bit like a dog with a bone when it came to his relationship status. He didn't bother to introduce her to any of the women he dated. That was just asking for trouble. At this point, he didn't think she'd even be that picky about the woman. She just wanted him married to *someone*.

"Well, at least meet the woman *Tita* Merlina has chosen. She said she is very *maganda*. She has competed in beauty pageants."

Recalling his mom's own experience with those pageants, Than just nodded. She'd won more than her fair share and had even gone on to represent the Philippines at an international pageant. Though she hadn't won, there was no question that she was a beautiful woman. And even now, coming up on sixty, she really didn't look like she was that old or that she was a mother of five and a grandmother of three.

Than bent and pressed a kiss to her cheek, inhaling the scent he would always associate with her. "*Mahal kita, Mama.*"

She patted his cheek. "I love you, too, my boy."

"Want me to bring you back anything?" he asked as he zipped up the last suitcase. He set it on the floor beside the other one. All that was left was to finish packing his carry-on.

"*Mahal?*"

His mother perked up immediately at the sound of her husband's voice.

"We're in here, Dad," Than called out.

Steve Miller appeared in the doorway of his room, a smile on his tanned, creased face. "Have you finished telling him about the woman your sister has lined up for him?"

Than grinned as his mom punched his dad in the arm. "She's tried, but I've already told her it's not going to happen."

"Well, you never know, son. I never expected to meet the woman of my dreams in a small church in a country on the other side of the world. It might be your destiny, too."

Than smothered a laugh. He sincerely doubted he would find the woman of his dreams on the other side of the world. Particularly since he was traveling with a woman who was far more intriguing than any he was likely to meet there.

Lindsay crossed her arms over her stomach, trying to contain the bundle of nerves that had taken up residence there. It had seemed like a good idea a few months ago. Now she wasn't so sure. What if she wasn't cut out for this? Maybe she *was* the princess her brothers thought she was.

"It's not too late." An arm slid around her waist, and Lindsay glanced over to see her mom beside her. "You could still come back home with me."

No. That wasn't an option. Too much work had gone into making this happen for her. There was no way she could back out—even if that's what her nerves were demanding she do. "I'll be fine, Mom."

"Ready to fly, Lindsay?"

His voice washed over her, at once creating a whole new set of nerves and yet, surprisingly, soothing the ones already in place. Than was there to make sure she was okay. No matter what happened once they stepped onto that plane, it was his job to take care of her. She'd never let anyone know how reassuring that actually was, especially not Than, but she couldn't deny that just seeing him helped settle her.

She looked at Than, always surprised by just how attractive she found him. He was dressed in a pair of jeans and a white polo shirt. The color of the shirt set off the tan of his skin and his dark hair and eyes. He wore a watch with a thick black band on his left wrist and a bracelet with a leather strap on his right.

"Yes. As ready as I'll ever be."

"Let me get these taken care of," he said as he gestured to her luggage. He and Lucas took charge of her bags along with his and headed for the airline kiosks.

The other members of the group were milling around. In total, there were twenty-one of them traveling including the team leader, his wife, and Than. They were an interesting mix of people. There were two retired couples who had been on a few mission trips before—together, if the familiarity in their conversation was any indication. A middle-aged couple had brought their teenage daughter and son along, and there was also another young couple who had only been married a few months. Apparently, they'd decided to use the money they would have spent on a honeymoon to go on the mission trip. The rest of them were single—five guys and three ladies—ranging in age from early twenties to late forties. Lindsay was pretty sure she was the only millionaire heiress in the bunch.

It took less than fifteen minutes for them to get checked in. Her mom was still hovering around offering her every manner of escape from the trip, but Lindsay managed to resist them all.

"Hope you have time for some fun," Lincoln said.

"There is some sightseeing time in the itinerary. Not sure what we'll be doing though."

"Will you bring me back something, Auntie?"

Lindsay smiled down at Danny and ruffled his hair. "I'll see what I can find. Make sure you don't grow too much while I'm gone."

They shared a grin, and Lindsay felt a pang. She'd definitely miss the little guy. They spent two weeks together while Lucas and Brooke had been on their African honeymoon. She had been sad when they'd returned, and Danny had gone home with them. She knew she'd probably be bringing back quite a few things for her nephew.

"We should head through security," Than said as he glanced at his watch. "They'll be starting to board soon."

Lindsay's nerves returned in a rush, but she kept a smile on her face as she hugged her mom and Danny.

"Please don't make Than's job too difficult for him," Lucas murmured when she gave him a tight hug after she'd finished with Lincoln and Brooke.

She stepped back and grinned. "I'll try not to. For sure I won't be trying to ditch him so I can run off to shop or anything."

Lucas tilted his head, his expression serious. "We'll be praying for you, sis. I hope you see God in a new way during this trip. It could be life-changing, if you let it."

Lindsay nodded, not sure what to say. Even amidst all the nerves and worries, the underlying feeling she had was that this was what she was supposed to do. "I'll be sure to tell you all about it when I get home."

She felt a touch on her back and turned to see Than beside her. He gave her a small smile. "Ready?"

Taking a quick breath, Lindsay nodded.

With a final wave, they joined the line for the security check and soon they were walking toward their gate on the other side. Than had taken her carry-on once they were through security even though she'd protested. He wasn't there to make things easier for her, just to make sure she was safe. Lindsay was fairly certain that rolling her own bag wasn't going to bring her to any harm—even if it was a bit heavy.

"We can sit here." Than motioned to a section of seats that weren't already occupied.

Lindsay settled into one of the chairs, anticipating that Than would join her, but after setting the carry-on bags at her feet, he headed in the direction of Mark, the team leader, who was standing there with his wife. The men shook hands and then Than shook Mel's hand, too. As he stood talking to them, the attendant behind the counter made the announcement that first class passengers were boarding.

Lindsay started to get to her feet then remembered...she was flying economy this time around. She was going to get her first "new" experience without even having left the country. If the Hamiltons weren't flying in their own private plane, they always flew first class. This was definitely something new.

The first of many firsts to come, she was sure.

Than made his way back to Lindsay's side when passengers began to line up to board the plane. She was perched on the edge of the seat, her back perfectly straight and shoulders square. He wondered if it had finally sunk in what she was doing and where she was going. At least she was dressed well for travel. She wore a pair of black pants and a loose fitting green blouse with small cap sleeves along with a pair of flat slip-on shoes.

She glanced up at him as he stopped next to her. Her gray eyes were wide, but he could read no other expression on her face. If he hadn't seen a few other sides of her for himself, he would have thought she was emotionless and in total control. But he had seen those sides, so the face she was putting forward now was a cover for emotions that went far deeper. If he had to guess, he'd say she was likely more than a little worried about was to come.

"They're going to call our rows next," Than said as he took out her ticket and passport. He handed them to her, then pulled the handle up on her carry-on and set his on top of it.

She stood up and slipped her purse strap over her shoulder. When the attendant called their rows, he touched her back and moved her toward the entrance to the jetway. Once they were on the plane, he noticed her looking to the sides as they moved through first class into economy. He bit back a grin as he realized that Miss Lindsay Hamilton was going to be flying coach for what was likely the first time. Though he wasn't looking forward to it himself, at least he had flown that way many times before. For the short jaunt to

Detroit, it would be okay, but the thirteen hour trip to Tokyo was likely to be a killer.

Once they got to their row, Lindsay slipped into the middle seat while he lifted their bags into the overhead compartment. They had just settled into their seats with him on the aisle when the person with a ticket for the window seat showed up. As the man looked at Lindsay, Than saw a spark of interest in his gaze. Oh, she was so not going to like this.

He stood up and drew Lindsay into the aisle with him to allow the man in. There was no way he was going to let the man climb over her. She shot him a look before settling back into her seat, but Than didn't miss that her arm was pressed up against his more than it had been just minutes ago.

"You headin' for Detroit?" the man asked as he pinned his gaze on Lindsay.

"Yes."

Than looked away so she wouldn't see the grin on his face. He was almost positive that wasn't the response Lindsay wanted to give him, but she'd been raised to be polite. No doubt she would have liked to point out that since the plane's destination was Detroit that was, in fact, where she was headed.

As he had his head turned away from Lindsay, Than noticed a woman across the aisle struggling to get her bag into the compartment. He stood up and said, "Let me help you with that."

He easily lifted it into the opening for her.

The young woman beamed at him. "Oh, thank you so much."

"Glad to be of assistance." He sat back in his seat as more people came down the aisle.

"You going to Detroit for business?"

Clearly the man wasn't giving up in spite of the waves of frostiness coming off Lindsay. Than thought about stepping in, but she needed to learn to deal with this kind of stuff. He had no doubt that she'd garner at least one marriage proposal during the mission trip. Being an American was a big draw to a lot of the Filipino men. The young ones were going to be all over themselves trying to tell her how *maganda* she was. Lindsay would have to be able to just take it all in stride.

"No, not strictly business," Lindsay murmured, her head down.

"Well, you want to meet up for a drink?"

Than jerked around to stare at the man. What on *earth*? The guy hadn't even been sitting beside her for five minutes and was already making a move. He was an idiot if he couldn't read the disinterest in Lindsay's body language. Than had no problem interpreting the *leave me alone* signals that she was sending the man. They were similar to the ones she'd sent his way on more than one occasion.

Though he'd originally planned to let her handle the situation, if this was how far south it had gone in less than five minutes, the ninety minute trip to Detroit was going to be miserable.

Resting his hand on Lindsay's arm, Than leaned toward the man. "We'd love to meet for drinks. Where do you suggest?"

The man's eyes widened as his gaze dropped to where Than touched Lindsay. "Uh, on second thought, I'm not sure if I'll have much time. Business stuff, you know."

"That's a shame," Than said with a grin as he lifted his hand from Lindsay's arm and settled back in his seat. She didn't look at him or say anything, but he could feel the tension ease from her body. Oh yeah, this was gonna be a fun two weeks. Not only was he going to have to protect Lindsay from kidnappers and terrorists, he was going to have to ward off lecherous men as well.

Lindsay wasn't all that keen to be invading Than's space, but it was definitely the lesser of two evils. And given how he'd just come to her rescue, she hoped that he understood *why* she was scooched right up against him and not read anything into it.

She let out a quick breath as the plane lurched and began to move back from the terminal. The flight was only ninety minutes. Hopefully, the dude would just keep his nose buried in his phone or stare out the window or something. As long as it wasn't trying to engage her in any more conversation.

And please, God, let whoever I'm sitting next to for the thirteen-hour stretch be someone nice. Preferably a woman.

Because their group was large, they hadn't been able to get seats together. The team members were seated in groups of two or three throughout the cabin. She still wished she could have flown first class. Then it would have been just her and Than in that row and she wouldn't have had to invade his space in order to get away from the dude by the window.

Lindsay wasn't a nervous flier, but take-offs and landings were not her favorite parts of a flight. Even on their private jet. She leaned her head back and closed her eyes as the plane gathered speed and then lifted into the air.

As the aircraft continued to climb, Lindsay heard Than say something. She opened her eyes and turned her head toward him only to realize he wasn't speaking to her but to the pretty blonde woman across the aisle. The one he'd helped with her bag earlier.

 Good grief. Five minutes on the airplane and all she got was hit on by an idiot who clearly didn't understand that coming on that strong just wasn't a good way to start a conversation. Less than fifteen minutes on the plane and Than was having a good ol' time chatting up the beauty in the seat across from him.

If nothing else, it served as a vivid reminder that he was not the man for her. Women loved him, and he loved them right back. How could a woman ever feel special with a man like that?

Now that she had nothing to occupy her, tiredness began to overtake her body. They'd had to be at the airport by seven which meant she'd been up at five after barely sleeping four hours. Closing her eyes again, she tried to block out all the noise and let herself just relax. In first class, she would have been able to comfortably recline her seat and rest, but she wasn't so sure she'd ever be able to fully relax squished in between two large men.

"Lindsay."

She felt a soft touch brush across her cheek.

"Lindsay. Time to wake up."

As recognition of the man's voice sank in, Lindsay's eyes popped open, and she quickly realized that she had, in fact, managed to doze off. Her cheeks flushed as she also realized that Than's upper arm had become her pillow. Straightening, she kept her head bent as she tried to pull herself together. Between her position and the warmth of his touch, she was feeling more than a little vulnerable in that half-asleep state she was still in.

"We're going to be landing in about ten minutes," Than said. He held out a bottle of water. "I asked the flight attendant to give me a drink for you since you were asleep when they came through. I hope water is okay."

Coffee would have been better, but given how dry her mouth was, she wasn't about to turn down any liquid. She took the bottle from him and unscrewed the cap. "Thank you."

"We're only going to have about forty-five minutes between flights here, so we'll find the gate first and if you need to use the restroom, you can do it then."

"Okay." She took a long drink of the water, grateful it was still on the cold side. "Is that going to be enough time for us?"

"Should be. Plus, we're a big enough group that they'll wait for us, I'm sure." He paused then said, "You doing okay?"

Lindsay glanced over at him in surprise and then wished she hadn't. His chocolate brown eyes held concern as he looked at her. He must not think too much of her if barely ninety minutes into this adventure—and without even having left US airspace—he was already concerned about her.

"Yep. I just didn't get much sleep last night. A bit of nerves and an early morning."

"You'll have plenty of time to sleep on the next leg. Though you should probably not sleep too much near the end of the flight. We're arriving around ten o'clock at night which means we'll likely be at the mission house by midnight. You'll want to be able to sleep so as to get over jet lag as quickly as possible."

Since the only time differences she'd ever dealt with were the ones between Minneapolis and places like London and Paris, the jet lag from a thirteen hour time difference was going to be a whole other ball of wax. Particularly when she wasn't going to have a few days of leisurely rest to get over it. They were arriving Sunday night and by Monday afternoon they were supposed to be heading out to the mission center where they would be staying for the bulk of their time in the Philippines.

Once again Lindsay prayed her way through the landing, her tension easing only when the plane taxied toward the terminal. As soon as it was stopped and the seatbelt sign went off, Than stood up and opened the overhead compartment. She stood as well and stepped into the aisle when he motioned her ahead of him. He put her bag down, and she reached for it this time, pulling up the handle. People from the rows in front of them had spilled into the aisles as well so they would have to wait before moving toward the exit of the plane.

"Thank you again."

Lindsay glanced over her shoulder to see that Than had once again helped the woman across the aisle from them. He smiled as he motioned for her to step into the aisle in front of him. Lindsay knew it was stupid to let his helpful nature rankle her, but it was hard to deny that if the woman had been eighty instead of in her twenties, she'd be finding his actions a lot more noble.

"Are you staying here in Detroit?" Lindsay heard the woman ask.

"No. We're catching a connecting flight to Tokyo."

Lindsay let out a breath and tried to block out the conversation. She was glad when the passengers ahead of her began to move. Without looking back, she moved forward and breathed a sigh of relief when she exited the plane and began the long walk up the ramp. Remembering that they didn't have much time, Lindsay moved quickly up the jetway, passing a few of the slower people as she went.

Than could take his time and chitchat with the blonde, but Lindsay wasn't going to be the one to hold them up. As soon as she entered the terminal, she looked for the departures screen to confirm the next gate they needed to be at. She glanced around and saw the other team members straggling into the terminal area. They headed toward where the team leader and his wife stood, so Lindsay moved in that direction as well.

"Let's head to the next gate," Mark said. "We don't have much time.

She noticed that Than was standing off to the side, still in conversation with the blonde. Well, it would be on his head if he missed the plane. Keeping a tight grip on the handle of her bag, Lindsay moved with the group as they followed the team leader.

Thankfully, they made it to the gate with time to spare so she slipped into the restroom to take care of business. Thirteen hours on a plane meant that she'd have to use the facilities onboard at some point, but she wasn't going to start out having to use them. Once she finished washing her hands, she took a moment in front of the mirror to smooth her hair and make sure it was still secure in her french braid. She resisted the urge to touch up her makeup. Although, she didn't have much to touch it up with.

She'd made the decision to bring only the bare necessities when it came to her makeup. Though she was used to wearing makeup every day and rarely went anywhere without it, she knew this trip wouldn't allow for that much pampering. Instead, she'd packed tinted moisturizer with a ton of SPF, concealer, mascara, and one palette of eye shadow.

As she exited the bathroom, Lindsay immediately saw that Than had joined the group. His brows were drawn together in a frown as he looked around the waiting area. When his gaze fell on her, his scowl deepened. Hoping this wasn't a sign of how the trip was going to go, Lindsay lifted her chin and made her way to a section of vacant seats. She'd barely sat down when Than reached her.

"What on earth is going on?" he asked.

3

LINDSAY glanced at him. "What do you mean? You said we needed to get to the gate quickly, so when Mark left, I just followed him. And then went to the restroom once I got here...as you suggested." She blinked twice, keeping the innocent expression on her face though she was fairly sure Than didn't buy it for a minute. "Did I do something wrong? I thought I was just following your instructions."

Than's brown gaze hardened as his lips thinned. It was tempting to look away, but Lindsay didn't. She kept her expression pleasant as she waited for him to respond.

"You need to wait for me. I can't keep you safe if you're running off on me."

"I was hardly running off. I was with the rest of the team. I was where *I* was supposed to be." Even she heard the snark in that last sentence, and when Than's eyes narrowed she wished she could take it back.

Before he could say anything, the attendant announced that the economy section was going to be boarded by rows. Lindsay glanced down at her bag and pulled out her ticket to check her row. It was as good an excuse as any to avoid Than's gaze.

As the rows were called, she said, "I think that's us."

She grabbed the handle of her carry-on and stood up. Though she didn't look to see if he was following her, Lindsay was pretty sure he was. She showed her ticket and ID to the agent then moved quickly down the jetway to the plane's entrance. It was time to remember why she was on the trip. She didn't need Than telling her what to do and where to go. She didn't need him carrying her bags and acting all gentlemanly with her. He was here to make sure she was safe, but that was it. *He* needed to keep up with her, not the other way around. If he wandered off, it was not her responsibility to go find him.

When she reached their row, she snapped the handle of the carry-on down into place and had it up and into the overhead compartment before Than could take it from her. A look at her ticket revealed that she was in the window seat. She stepped into the row to be out of the way while she rechecked her ticket. If she was in the window seat, did that mean Than was in the middle seat since there were three seats?

This was a bigger plane than the one they'd just gotten off of. Instead of just two sections, this one had three with each of the side sections having three seats and the one in the middle having four.

When she felt Than move into the row, bumping into her back, she quickly turned and sat down next to the window. When he settled in the aisle seat, Lindsay realized that she didn't like the idea of anyone sitting between them.

Than had pulled his phone out and was rapidly tapping out a message on it. When he finished, she said, "Am I in the wrong seat?"

He glanced at her briefly before looking back down at his phone. "No. Lucas took pity on you since you weren't flying first class and booked an extra seat for this portion of the trip."

"Oh." Lindsay sank back into her seat, relief coursing through her. She hadn't realized how much she had been dreading spending thirteen hours squeezed between two people—one of whom would be a stranger to her.

Lindsay looked out the window as the plane began to reverse away from the terminal. This was it. There was no going back now. Next stop was Tokyo and then Manila.

Than fought to keep his frustration at Lindsay under control. After all, he'd dealt with clients who were far worse than she was when it came to being demanding and making his life miserable.

Had she really been irritated that he'd stopped to help that woman? If that was the case, she was just going to have to grow up. He'd been taught from very young to help anyone who needed it. Be they one or one hundred, he offered his assistance. True, it was usually women who ended up being on the receiving end of his chivalry. But if it had been a really short man trying to get his bag up into the overhead compartment earlier, he would have offered his help to him as well.

Lindsay seemed to be under the impression that he purposely went out of his way to attract female attention. The reality was, it just came naturally to him. His mom had told him from very young that he'd always drawn people's attention because of his friendly personality and his cute looks. As he'd gotten older, he'd found out that being nice got him more friends than being mean, and he'd liked having friends. So he'd been nice to everyone. The nerds. The jocks. The popular kids.

Yes, he'd been blessed to inherit his dad's broad shoulders and height as well as a more masculine version of his mother's beauty queen looks, but Than liked to think that people were drawn to him more because of his personality than his appearance. The only person of late who didn't seem to be drawn to him on any level was the woman sitting one seat over from him.

Why that bothered him so much, he didn't really know. He just hoped she realized that she was going to have to let down that guard of hers if this trip was going to be a good experience for her. When he'd questioned Lucas further about Lindsay's participation in the mission trip, her brother hadn't been able to give clear answers.

"To be honest, Than, I'm not sure why Lindsay has chosen to do this. She's never shown much interest in spiritual things outside of attending church on Sunday."

"Isn't there some sort of spiritual requirement in order for her to join?" Than asked, not at all sure how things like that were supposed to work.

"Yes, and I went to the team leader about it. Interestingly enough, Mark said that while that was usually the case, in this situation, he felt it was okay to allow Lindsay on the team in spite of her low level of spiritual maturity. He said that often these trips can be as much about receiving a spiritual blessing as giving one. When I talked to Lindsay about it to make sure she knew what she was doing, all she'd say was that she felt this was something she had to do." Lucas shrugged. "Apparently God is at work in ways I don't really understand right now."

While Than didn't pretend to understand the faith that Lucas had or how strongly Lindsay did or didn't follow that same faith, he was curious to see how things would unfold over the next couple of weeks. He knew he'd be getting a taste of that faith up close and personal since he was going to be with the team each and every day.

His parents' faith was important to them and though he'd been raised in the church, he'd stopped attending in his mid-teens. They had been upset at his decision, but in the years since, even though they always told him they prayed for him, they'd stopped pestering him to go to church.

And they weren't the only ones in his life who had a strong faith as part of their lives. He knew that both Trent and Eric were also regular church attendees. He was pretty sure the Thorpes were too but had no idea about Marcus. It really hadn't been something he'd thought much about until the last few weeks.

When the plane began to gather speed as it moved down the airstrip, Than slid the phone into his pocket and leaned back, lacing his fingers across his stomach. He glanced over at Lindsay and saw that she had her eyes closed and her hands clasped together in her lap. With her hair pulled back in a braid, her profile was clearly visible to him. He noticed that she wore simple gold studs in her ears. She'd probably do well to just leave them in for the entire trip.

She had a soft profile with a rounded jawline and dainty nose. Than had a feeling that if he ran his fingertips across her skin, it would be satiny soft. His hands curled into fists, and he dragged his gaze away from her. He couldn't deny that one of the reasons he'd taken this job was in hopes that Lindsay might see him in a different light and give him another shot.

As frustrated with her as he'd been earlier, he knew that she wasn't always like that. Their trip to the Caribbean island for Lucas and Brooke's wedding had shown him that. He'd wanted her to smile at him like she did when she'd interacted with Danny and Sarah. Or laughing like she had with Alicia and Victoria, Eric's sisters. But as soon as she'd noticed him, she would withdraw as if afraid to let him see that side of her.

He could only hope that by the time this trip was over, that prickly attitude she had toward him would have mellowed. One thing he did know was that they couldn't go for the full thirteen hours without talking.

Once the plane had reached its cruising altitude and they were allowed to use their electronic devices, Than opened the side pocket of his laptop bag and pulled out his tablet. After clicking on an app, he tapped the screen a few times then glanced over at Lindsay. She was gazing out the window, her hands resting in her lap.

He held his tablet out to her. She must have seen the movement in her peripheral vision because she turned her head toward him. She looked at the tablet and then met his gaze. She reached out and took it from him. After a glance at the screen, she looked up, an eyebrow arched.

"Scrabble? You want to play Scrabble?"

Than shrugged. "Sure. It will help to pass the time."

She seemed to consider that for a moment before she looked down at the screen and tapped it to start the game. When she handed the tablet back to him a few minutes later and he saw that she'd used all her letters to make the first word, Than had a feeling he was doomed to lose.

"Affably? Really?"

One corner of her mouth lifted, as close to a smile as he'd ever managed to get out of her. "Hey. It's a word."

Than grunted as he bent his chin to his chest to survey the letters the game had given to him. If he couldn't win—which it appeared he wasn't going to be able to—he was going to at least make it fun.

He reshuffled the letters a few times before he spotted the word he could play using the top A.

DATED

Yep, he liked that one. He pressed play and watched as it added up his points. Definitely getting left in the dust. Keeping any expression from his face, he handed it back to her. He watched as she read the word.

She bit her lower lip, and he could see the muscles around her mouth twitch. He did grin then. After sitting there for a minute staring at the tablet, she tapped the screen a couple of times and then handed back to him.

Though she didn't smile, he caught a glimpse of a twinkle in her gray eyes before she looked away. He glanced down at the board and couldn't help but chuckle.

SEDATED

So that's how this was going to go. Suddenly, the game was no longer about points but just outdoing each other with words. He'd put a word down and she'd play one that when put with the word he just played would make a phrase with a completely different meaning.

When he played *PRETTY*, she played *DUMB*.

When he played *LOVED*, she plunked a *G* at the beginning of it and then added *ROSS*.

And so it went until they were down to just a handful of letters and were forced to make words like *IT* or *IN*.

"I win," Lindsay announced, the corners of her mouth edging up as she handed the tablet back to him.

Yeah, she had handily whooped him. He was about to ask if she wanted a rematch when the pilot came on the intercom and announced that the attendants would be coming through the cabin with food and beverage service.

He waggled the tablet at her before setting it on the seat between them. "We *will* have a rematch."

She arched a brow. "You think you'll be able to beat me? Ever?"

"Are you calling me dumb?" he tossed back as he stretched his legs under the seat in front of him.

"Well, not dumb. Just not as good as me. Scrabble happens to be my mom's favorite game, so I've played it a *lot*."

"Too bad we couldn't play it in French or Spanish. I'd kick butt for sure."

Her eyes widened slightly. "You speak French and Spanish?"

He nodded. "I speak them fluently along with Filipino. I can also get by in Russian, Arabic and Italian."

At his revelation, her brows both rose high on her forehead. "Good grief! How do you keep them all straight in your brain?"

Than shrugged. He'd been asked that before but really had no answer. To him, it was like his brain was a computer with each language as a program. He loaded the one he needed until he didn't need it any longer. As long as he was in that "program", that particular language came easily for him.

"I just have always had a gift for languages. I don't know if it was because my mom spoke to us in two languages from the time we were born."

"Do you have brothers or sisters with the same gift?"

"I have one brother and three sisters, but only one of them has shown any interest in languages. Not to the extent that I have though."

"I guess that's why you're so valuable to BlackThorpe," Lindsay commented.

"Yes, it was one of the main reasons they hired me, but right now my primary responsibility is organizing security for individuals."

"Like me?" she asked.

"Sort of. Generally, it's not just a one-man team though. I usually set up three to six-person teams for people who feel the need for security. It could be a singer on tour. Or someone who has a reason to fear for their safety. People thrust unwittingly into the spotlight for whatever reason. I have two three-person teams over in Europe now on babysitting duty for some heiress and her friends. They keep trying to ditch my guys, so we had to put a ghost team in place as well."

"A ghost team?"

"Yeah, one they don't know about. They blend in and keep an eye out for escaping heiresses and then report back to the main team." Than shook his head. "That girl's dad is paying handsomely to keep his baby safe, but she's making it challenging."

"I feel like I should apologize on her behalf," Lindsay said, a small smile teasing her lips.

Than lifted an eyebrow. "Why's that?"

"I seem to remember one year when my dad paid to have a security team with me and a couple of my friends when we insisted we didn't need our parents along for a trip to London. I think we spent a lot of time trying to ditch the bodyguards, even though the one guy was quite cute."

That made Than laugh. "We have found that the cuter the bodyguards, the less trouble the girls are likely to give them."

"As long as you realize that really only applies to the teenage girls."

"What's that supposed to mean?" Than asked.

"Well, I have no intention of trying to ditch you, but it has nothing to do with how cute you are."

Than grinned at her. "You think I'm cute?"

Pink swept up Lindsay's cheeks, but she didn't lower her gaze. "Don't even try to tell me you aren't aware of your appearance."

"Oh, well sure. I just didn't think you were." He chuckled as exasperation showed on Lindsay's face. "Well, for the record, I happen to think you're cute, too."

The pink in her cheeks deepened, but he had to give her credit, she never looked away from him. "Flattery will get you absolutely nowhere."

"Ah, but that doesn't mean that I still don't derive some sort of pleasure from flattering you, sugar."

"Would you like something to drink?"

Than looked up to see a flight attendant leaning in to their row. He glanced over at Lindsay. "What do you want?"

"Could I have orange juice, please?"

"Certainly. And for you, sir?"

"Coffee, please."

Once they had their drinks and a small bag of pretzels, Lindsay said, "Do they actually feed us a meal on this flight?"

Than nodded. "I would imagine we'd get at least one, maybe two. I remember one time when we flew to the Philippines to visit my mom's family and on our way home, we ended up having breakfast three times because of how the time zones worked out. I was sure ready for a hamburger when we got home to Minneapolis."

"Well, at this point, I'd settle for just one breakfast." Lindsay pressed a hand to her stomach. "I was too nervous to eat before we left the house."

Than grinned. "Well, you're in luck." He reached into his laptop bag where it sat on the seat between them. He found the plastic bag his mother had handed him the night before and pulled it out. "Pick whatever you want out of there."

Lindsay took the bag he held out and looked at its contents. She glanced up at him. "You certainly travel prepared. I packed some but they're in my checked luggage."

"That would be my mama's doing. She packed that for me."

As she opened the bag and reached in, she said, "Are you her baby?"

"Not really. I have two younger sisters, but I *am* her favorite."

That got him another look from Lindsay. "Seriously?"

"Nah. Not really. She doesn't play favorites with us five kids. Although I could say I'm probably her most frustrating child."

Lindsay handed the bag back to him. "Now *that* I can believe."

"It's only because she's upset that I'm not doing what she wants. My older brother and sister gave in too easily, so she expects me to do the same."

"Gave in?" Lindsay took a bite of the protein bar she'd chosen.

"Yeah. She is determined to see me married off sooner rather than later. And to that end, she arranged to have my aunt introduce me to a potential bride while I'm over there this time."

Lindsay choked on the bite she'd just taken and quickly reached for her orange juice. After taking a sip and clearing her throat, she looked at him. "A bride? Does your family believe in arranged marriages?"

Than shook his head. "Not really, but that doesn't stop my mom and her sister from trying their hand at matchmaking. It doesn't help either that it worked out with my brother. He met his wife on a trip back to the Philippines. They've been married for almost ten years now."

Lindsay's eyes widened. "Did they love each other?"

"I would imagine that love looks different for every couple. They're not over the top affectionate with each other, but they seem happy. My brother is fairly reserved. Being he's the eldest in our family, he's the responsible one. Juliette is also fairly reserved, so they go well together."

"And your sister? Did she meet her husband in the Philippines, too?"

"No. Max is a family friend. His parents are like mine. His dad was in the military and met his mom over there, too. Our moms met when they both joined an organization for Filipinos in the Twin Cities."

"So your mom prefers you all marry someone with Filipino blood?"

Than shrugged. "I'm sure she has her preferences, but they're certainly not going to dictate my life—even if the woman she wants me to meet is a beauty queen."

"A beauty queen? Seriously?"

"Yep." Than lifted his coffee and took a sip. "Given that's what my mom was back in her day, she's partial to those types."

"Yeah, and aren't most guys," Lindsay muttered before taking another bite of her protein bar.

Did he hear a tinge of jealousy in her voice? Why, he had no idea. To him, she was as beautiful as any beauty queen. Though by definition, those women were usually statuesque and super slender with features that society deemed were beautiful enough to move them ahead of other women. Lindsay was of average height and slender wasn't how he'd describe her. Curvaceous was the word that came to mind. Definitely all woman. He quickly pulled his thoughts from the direction they were going.

He'd always been a man who appreciated the female form, but for some reason, it didn't sit well to analyze Lindsay in that way. Through her reactions to him, she'd managed to set herself apart from the other women he'd come across in recent years. Without saying a word, she'd demanded he treat her differently. Of course, at the moment, she was a client. He'd do well to keep that at the forefront of his thoughts.

It wasn't long before the attendants were back to collect their empty cups and pretzel packages. Than had planned to ask Lindsay if she wanted a rematch, but before he could, Mark, the team leader, appeared next to him.

"Hey, guys. How's it going?" He looked at Lindsay. "You doing okay, Lindsay?"

Lindsay smiled at him, her gray eyes warming. "Yes, thanks, Mark."

"Good. Be sure to let me or Mel know if you need anything, okay?"

"I will."

Mark looked at him. "I got an email from my brother and he said it looks like a tropical storm is forming in the ocean to the east of the Philippines. Its current path seems to indicate it is moving toward Manila, but we'll likely feel some of the effects."

"Guess we'll have to keep an eye on that. Those storms can change paths as they strengthen."

Mark nodded. "So far it's just a storm, but it can morph into a typhoon fairly quickly."

"That would certainly add some adventure to the trip," Than commented.

"Well, a little adventure is fine. All part of the joy of venturing into the unknown."

"I'm going to hook up to the internet here in a minute, so I'll have the guys back at BlackThorpe keep an eye on it for us and let me know if anything changes that we should know about."

"Thanks, man." Mark clapped him on the shoulder. "I know your role is mainly to be with Lindsay, but I appreciate your willingness to help with the whole team."

"Not a problem. Lindsay has promised me she's not going to try to ditch me, so I should be able to keep an eye on her and still help out as needed." Than felt a light punch on his upper arm.

"Well, if looks could kill, you might be a dead man right about now, my friend," Mark said with a laugh.

Than turned to see Lindsay glowering in his direction. He grinned at her. "Well, that *is* what you said."

Mark laughed again. "I'll leave you two to sort that out. Let me know if you hear anything more about the storm. I'm just a few rows back with Mel if you need anything."

When he saw Lindsay pull her tablet out, Than picked up his own and quickly went through the steps to purchase an internet connection while in-flight. "Did you want internet access, too?"

Lindsay paused and then shook her head. "I think I'll be okay. I downloaded a bunch of books to read and most of the games I like I can play offline."

"You don't want to get in touch with your brothers or mom?"

"Actually, I think I need a little separation from them. If you're in contact, they'll know that I'm okay. I need this trip to...re-evaluate some things in my life."

4

REALLY?" Like what?" Even as he asked the question, Than was pretty sure she would brush it aside.

Her brows drew together as she stared down at her hands. "It kind of all started when we first got the news that Linc's plane had gone down and he was declared dead. You know, the realization that life is short."

"But Linc isn't dead. He's back home now," Than pointed out, surprised that she'd answered seriously.

She looked up at him, her gray eyes soft. A small smile lifted the corners of her mouth. "Yes, he is, and that was the first real answer to prayer I'd ever encountered. I mean, beyond things like *Please, God, let there be a parking spot close to the store.* Or something dumb like that."

Yeah, Than knew about those kinds of prayers. He'd muttered more than a few over the years. "It was amazing when he showed back up."

Lindsay nodded. "And then there was Brooke. And Danny."

"She is quite a woman," Than agreed. "I met her through Eric, and she shot me down just like you did." And yet...her rejection of him hadn't intrigued him anywhere near what Lindsay's had.

"I always knew she was a woman of taste."

Than placed a hand over his heart. "Ouch."

"Oh please." Lindsay rolled her eyes. "Anyway, I saw the kind of life she lived, very simple but doing what she loved. Painting and taking care of her son. He was...is her world. She would do anything to protect him and yet managed to raise him to love life and just to be an all-around great kid." Lindsay paused. "I love my mom, but I wish she'd been a stronger person. More like Brooke."

Than thought about Mrs. Hamilton and didn't understand what Lindsay was saying. "Your mom seems to be a pretty strong person."

"She is now. But it took my dad's death for her to realize the strength she had. She should have found that strength years ago and left him."

Because Lincoln, the person he was closest to in the Hamilton family, had no memory of the years prior to his accident, Than really didn't know much about the family dynamics when it came to her dad since he'd been dead for several years. "You wanted them to get divorced?"

"Yes. She deserved so much better than how my dad treated her."

"Your dad...abused her?"

"Not physically. Emotionally. Every time he decided to spend the night with the sweet young thing he'd met at a business dinner or at a party—often dropping my mom off at home first—he stabbed her in the heart. Woman after woman paraded through his life. His excuse was that he'd chosen to marry my mom and he provided well for her, but that sometimes he needed variety. Lincoln was no better. Thankfully, Lucas is nothing like either of them."

Than listened to her talk and suddenly pieces began to fall into place. *Woman after woman paraded through his life.* He had heard the disgust and anger in her voice as she talked about the way her dad lived. No doubt she'd looked at Than's life and seen the same thing. Goodness knows he was teased often enough about his serial dating and the revolving door when it came to women.

It definitely explained her reasoning for not accepting another date invitation. She had no interest in joining the women parading through his life. And she apparently thought that every woman he paid attention to was someone he wanted to date. Or that every woman he *did* date was one he became intimately involved with.

His gut clenched to think she would have such a low opinion of him, but was she wrong? The women he'd dated all knew it wasn't a long term thing. He was pretty good at judging a woman's character and could usually tell if they were someone up for a good time or something more serious. He only went for the good-time ones, and he'd try to make sure their one or two dates included something they enjoyed doing. He'd taken a few to concerts they were dying to go to. Others had been dinner and a movie. He never asked for the second date—if he wanted one—at the end of the first. He'd given it a few days to see if he felt the same, and then he'd call them up for another date. For the most part, when they parted ways, they'd stayed friends. He had a *lot* of friends.

Actually, when he'd first asked Lindsay out when they'd been at the Hamilton cabin the previous summer, he'd been certain she'd say no. But his judgment had been off with her because she'd accepted. Something told him that she knew he'd expected her to turn him down which is why she'd accepted. Of course, it seemed to have kind of backfired on both of them. He'd actually asked her for a second date when he'd dropped her off at home. And she'd said no.

He still wanted that second date, but Than had to admit that the conversation they were having had revealed more to him than any date could have.

"Anyway, I realized I've become a bit...jaded. Mom and Dad never encouraged us to look beyond the world we'd been raised in. Lucas was really the only one who did anything like that. He started up the Hamilton charitable foundation and is more active in the church than any of the rest of us. He's twice the man my dad was. And frankly, than Lincoln was."

Than could hear the admiration in Lindsay's voice for Lucas. What would it be like to hear her speak about *him* like that? The thought came out of nowhere and took Than by surprise. Why should it matter if she admired him or not? Sure, he wanted people to like him, but it didn't have to go so far as admiration. And yet...that thought suggested that he wanted to be a man worthy of Lindsay's respect.

He gave his head a shake. "Well, you've certainly taken a huge step outside your world with this trip."

Lindsay's eyes sparkled as she smiled. "Yeah, I have, haven't I?"

Seeing her so pleased with herself made Than's heart skip a beat. *She's a client. She's my friend's sister.* All good reasons to not let his emotions get tangled up with her.

His tablet made a sound, and he looked down to see that some new emails had come in. He glanced back at Lindsay. "Well, if you change your mind about keeping in contact with your family, let me know and I'll set you up."

As if sensing his attention had drifted, Lindsay pulled out a pair of earbuds as she nodded. "Will do."

Out of the corner of his eye, he saw her put the earbuds in and then tap the screen of her tablet. She settled back in her seat, crossing her legs. Soon her foot was moving in time to whatever music she'd put on and her attention was on the screen, her finger swiping every so often.

Taking a deep breath, Than turned his focus to his own tablet and the messages waiting his attention.

After swiping through several pages with no real recollection of what they had contained, Lindsay gave up and turned her attention to the view beyond the oval window beside her. As one of the worship songs she'd downloaded played in her earbuds, she thought about her conversation with Than. Why had she revealed so much? She'd never told anyone what she'd told him.

Well, she'd mentioned some of it to Mark and Mel when they'd met after receiving her application to join the team. When they'd asked her why she wanted to go on the trip, she had shared about wanting to experience life beyond the world she'd known for so long and to help others. She'd played her reasoning over and over in her head since deciding she wanted to be part of the team.

Maybe she'd just wanted to say it out loud to someone else to see if it sounded as crazy as it had started to sound in her own head. From Than's reaction, it didn't appear that he thought she was nuts or anything. Or maybe he was just super good at hiding what he really thought.

Lindsay pressed her thumb against her teeth. And why should it matter what Than thought? It would probably be better if he did think she was crazy. And she needed to rein in her chattiness next time.

She leaned her head back, still watching the white fluffy clouds slide past the airplane. It was mesmerizing, and between that and the soft music, she felt her eyelids grow heavy.

A sudden drop of the plane had Lindsay gasping as her eyes popped open. She pressed a hand to her stomach. The plane's movement made it feel like she'd left her stomach above her while her body had dropped with the plane. She let out a quick breath. This wasn't the first time she'd experienced turbulence while in flight, but being jerked from sleep by it was a bit unnerving.

The plane chose that moment to pitch from side to side. She gripped the arm of her seat in one hand and her tablet in the other. Looking out the window, Lindsay noticed that the clouds that had been white and fluffy earlier now held a gray tinge and moisture streaked across the window. How long had she been asleep?

When the plane seemed to settle, Lindsay loosened her grip on the seat, pulled the earbuds out of her ears and tapped the screen of her tablet. The time popped up, but it meant nothing to her since she hadn't looked at it before she'd fallen asleep.

"You were out for about an hour."

Than's deep voice startled her, drawing her attention to him. He had reclined his seat a bit and his legs were stretched out under the seat in front of him. It couldn't be that comfortable for him, given his height, to have to make a long trip in economy.

The plane pitched again, and she fought the urge to grab the armrests. Than, on the other hand, looked perfectly relaxed. Of course he would. The easygoing man didn't seem to get rattled by anything.

"Is this part of the storm you and Mark were discussing?"

Than shook his head. "We're too far away from that, plus we're coming in from the west and the storm is on the east side of the country. This is just some light turbulence."

When the plane dropped again, Lindsay lifted an eyebrow at him. "*Light* turbulence?"

"The luggage is all still in the overhead compartments. The oxygen masks haven't dropped. Haven't heard anyone throwing up just yet. Yeah, it's just light turbulence."

Lindsay leaned back in her seat and let out a breath. "So is everything still okay back in Minneapolis? BlackThorpe hasn't fallen apart in your absence?"

"Not yet. And yes, everything is just fine. I let Lucas know that things were going smoothly so far."

So far? Lindsay hoped that the whole trip would go smoothly even though she knew that was unlikely. In fact, in the weeks leading up to their departure as she'd done more research on the country and the area where they'd be, a great many scenarios of what could possibly go wrong had gone through her head. Everything from getting malaria or dengue fever to being bitten by a snake.

"How about a Scrabble rematch?"

Lindsay turned to look at Than, recognizing that he was trying to distract her from the turbulence and, most likely, her own thoughts. "Glutton for punishment?"

Than's lips curved into a smile and his brown gaze was warm as he looked at her. "Only when delivered by you."

Though she fought against it, warmth spread through her body. Hoping her cheeks weren't completely red, she said, "Losers go first."

Than chuckled as he bent over the tablet and started the game.

The remainder of the flight was spent playing Scrabble, reading, and sleeping off and on. They were fed two meals. Neither was super great, particularly when Lindsay had an idea of what they were eating in first class, but they succeeded in staving off their hunger in the meantime.

The one thing Lindsay managed to avoid was any more in-depth, revealing conversation. Mark came and checked on them a few more times, and on a couple of her trips to the bathroom, Lindsay had chatted briefly with some of the team members. She'd only met them a few times when they'd gathered together as a team in the weeks leading up to their departure.

It had been hard to lower her guard around them. Too often, people were more interested in being her friend because of her money, but the members of the team seemed to be genuinely interested in her. They hadn't cared about Hamilton Enterprises or anything about her family. To them, she was just Lindsay, mission team member. It gave her a sense of belonging that she hadn't experienced before. And she found that she liked that feeling.

"Ready to go?" Than asked once the plane was on the ground in Tokyo and they were taxiing toward Narita International Airport. "We'll have almost four hours here, so no rush to get to the next gate, but I still recommend we find where the gate is before we do any wandering around."

"Have you been to this airport before?" Lindsay asked as she clutched her purse tightly to her.

Than nodded. "A few times, but not recently. It's nice as far as airports go."

The plane came to a stop with a bump. Almost immediately, people around them surged to their feet and began to pull bags from the overhead compartments. In a repeat of their arrival in Detroit, Than moved into the aisle and got their bags down. He motioned for her to step in front of him. As more people crowded into the aisle in anticipation of the door opening, Lindsay found herself pressed against Than's arm. He had reached out to grab the back of the seat in front of their row once she'd stepped into the aisle with him.

It took everything in her not to look up into his face as she moved a little closer to him in order to not be squished up against a stranger. She felt the warmth and strength of him at her back as she inhaled the subtle scent of his cologne.

When the people ahead of them began to move forward, Lindsay let out a breath she hadn't even known she was holding. As she followed those in front of her, she gave herself yet another lecture on the perils of allowing herself to feel anything—physical or emotional—for Than.

As they exited the jetway and moved to the side to wait for the rest of the group, Lindsay became acutely aware of the fact that she was now the minority. It struck her as kind of funny at that moment that part of wanting this trip was to blend in and just be one of the group, and yet here and in the Philippines, she would stand out more than she ever had in Minneapolis.

This time they stuck with the group when they went in search of the gate. They then decided to split up into smaller groups to get food and look around before it was time for their last flight. When the young married couple seemed at a loss for what to do, Than suggested that they join them. One of the other single women also decided to tag along. Lindsay was grateful to not have to spend the time alone with Than, plus it gave her a chance to get to know a few of the team members a bit better.

By the time they boarded the plane for the last leg of their trip, Lindsay was feeling more relaxed. The time with the other team members had been fun, and she'd also discovered that Barb, the older single woman who had spent time with them, seemed to have no nerves at all about the trip and was, in fact, extremely excited about what lay ahead. The young newlywed woman, however, had expressed her nervousness, but her husband had pulled her into at tight embrace and reassured her that he'd be there for every step of the way.

Lindsay's heart had clenched at the sight. She'd half expected Than to interject something about being there to protect her, but mercifully he'd remained silent.

Once they were settled into their seats—with the extra one again for this flight—Than turned to her and said, "You're allowed to do anything you want but sleep from here to Manila."

Lindsay groaned. She wouldn't have minded a bit more sleep, but she knew that Than was just trying to be helpful when it came to jetlag once they landed in Manila. "Okay. Fine. Are you going to let me beat you at Scrabble again then?"

"Anything you want, sugar."

Sugar. She knew it was an endearment that likely rolled off his tongue for all the women he encountered and for that reason alone, she wished he wouldn't use it with her. But she wasn't going to make a big deal out of it. Protesting too much would just take their conversation in a direction she didn't want to go.

"You haven't won a game yet. Are you even trying?" Lindsay said as she took the tablet he handed her.

After having lost to her for the fourth time in a row, Than wanted to think he was letting her win, but honestly, she just managed to put down better words than him each and every time.

"We need to find a different game," Than said, exasperation finally getting the better of him.

"One you can win, you mean?" Lindsay asked, a smirk on her face.

"One that I have a *chance* of winning, at least. If I'd known you were such a cut-throat player, I wouldn't have suggested even one game of this." Than tossed the tablet down on the seat between them.

"Well, what else have you got on here?"

Before Than could stop her, Lindsay picked it up and pressed the button to go back to the main menu. Smothering a groan, he waited for her to make a comment about the background.

"Isn't that..." She lifted the tablet to look more closely. "Was this on the island for Lucas and Brooke's wedding?"

Lying had never really been his thing so Than said, "Yes. I had taken my camera along. I got some beautiful shots while I was there."

Lindsay scowled at him. "But that's me." She looked down at the tablet again. "Isn't it?"

"Yes, it is. Like I said. I got some beautiful pictures while I was down there. I purposely didn't make it a close-up shot since it was the whole scene—you sitting on that rock with the waves surging up around you—that made it beautiful. Most people wouldn't know it was you."

Than waited for her to rail at him about invading her privacy or something, but instead she just said, "Yeah, but you and I both do."

"I won't tell anyone if you don't."

She shot him a look loaded with exasperation then held out the tablet. "You choose a game. I'm afraid what else I might find on there if I tap the wrong thing."

Than chuckled as he took it from her. There was just that one picture since it had been his favorite of all he'd taken. He'd come across her quite by accident as he'd been walking around the island that afternoon. It had been a particularly blustery gray day, and her hair had been blowing back from her face as she'd sat on the large boulder on the edge of the water, her arms wrapped around her legs. The waves were hitting high on the rock, sending spray up, but not quite reaching her. It had been a stunning shot. Her beauty against the beauty of nature.

He wouldn't tell her that he also had the picture framed in his apartment.

"How about Monopoly?" He gave her a sideways glance. "Unless you're a property whiz as well."

Lindsay laughed. "No. That would be Lucas. You don't want to *ever* play Monopoly against him."

"Monopoly it is." Than got it set up and then handed it to her to start the game.

Given that she'd skunked him so badly in Scrabble, he had no qualms about taking her money over and over again as she landed on his properties. After he'd won the first game, she reluctantly agreed to a second.

Than loved watching her stare at the screen of the tablet each time it was her turn, her thumb pressed between her lips. It was something he'd noticed she did when she was uncertain and thinking hard. Clearly, she didn't like being on the losing end of a game, even just one time.

"Having fun?" Than asked her when she handed it back to him.

She scowled at him for a moment then her features relaxed and she smiled. "Well, I guess I can't win them all."

"Nope. You can't," he agreed as he bought up another property.

Once she had accepted that Monopoly was more his game than hers, Lindsay relaxed. Playing games, Than discovered, was actually something she enjoyed. Though she admitted that she preferred games that challenged her mind like Scrabble did.

"I also like puzzles," Lindsay said as she took the tablet from him for her turn. "I like the sense of accomplishment I feel when I finish one."

"The only times I've worked on puzzles have been during snowstorms."

"I usually have one on the go in my room. I find piecing together a puzzle is a nice way to unwind and give myself a chance to think back on the day. Then I read a bit before falling asleep."

Than wondered if he was actually asleep. And dreaming. The way Lindsay was talking and sharing things with him kind of blew him out of the water. Had she decided he wasn't such a bad guy after all?

"Than?"

"Huh?" He looked over to see her holding out the tablet.

She gave him a curious look. "Your turn."

"Oh, yeah. Thanks."

Not wanting to do anything to shut her down, Than let her take the lead with the conversation they shared. Sometimes they lapsed into silence, focusing on the game they were playing. Other times she'd ask him a question about his family and his life. And every once in a while she'd drop another little tidbit about her own life. Than was quickly coming to realize that Lindsay enjoyed being in charge. Of their conversation. Of their interactions. And clearly, of their dates. Or lack thereof.

Than also liked being in charge. He went after what he wanted. It had never been his thing to just sit back and let someone else lead the way. But he had a feeling that if he wanted to get to know Lindsay—really get to know her—that's just what he was going to have to do. Except, of course, when it came to her safety.

For now and forever, that would always be where he would be in charge.

5

AFTER they had finished their game, Lindsay said she was going to read for a while. It gave Than the chance to check his work email again. He was glad that the teams in Europe would be wrapping up that job in the next two days. Of course, he was pretty sure that they were even more glad than he was. No one liked the glorified babysitting jobs, especially when it came to guarding people who didn't want to be guarded. It was different when the person they were protecting understood and respected why they were there, instead of seeing them as a challenge to outwit.

After dealing with the work emails, Than sent a quick message to Lucas to let him know they were on the final leg of their long trip. He had to admit that he'd be happy to get off the plane when it landed in Manila. These long trips were never his favorite part of travelling, particularly when he had to travel economy. With his height, there was just never enough space to stretch his legs out.

Thankfully, it was just about five hours from Tokyo to Manila, and they were soon making their descent into the city.

"There are a ton of lights," Lindsay said as she pressed her face to the window.

"Yep. Manila and its surroundings are pretty big. Lots of people live there." Than wondered if she was prepared for just *how* many people there were.

Personal space wasn't an idea embraced by the Filipinos for the most part. There was always room for one more no matter how crowded the bus, jeepney or car was. A seat that would have room for two or three in the States would hold five or six Filipinos. Not just because they were smaller than most Americans, but because they had no problem squeezing together in order to fit more.

Something told Than that Lindsay very much liked her personal space. It would be just one more thing she'd need to adjust to in the weeks ahead.

Lindsay could have sworn that someone had just thrown a hot, wet blanket over her when they exited the terminal. The heat and humidity were like a slap in the face, and she began to sweat right away. She tried to take in everything, but there was just...so much...and the darkness of the night, even with lights present, pulsed with the unknown.

People milled around. Vehicles stopped and started, horns blaring. Voices shouted things in a language she didn't understand. And the smells. The good mingled with the not-so-great, and her stomach churned. It was sensory overload.

She'd gotten her first glimpse of how different it would be when they'd disembarked and began the process of getting their luggage and going through customs. It had seemed so chaotic and yet, the customs agents had gotten the job done.

And even though she'd never thought she'd ever feel grateful for Than, Lindsay was very, very thankful he was there. He, Mark and Mel had made sure that they were all together and that their documents were in order. She hadn't realized it until they were dealing with the officials, but both

Mark and Mel also spoke the language. Between the three of them, they'd managed to get the team through all the red tape and out of the terminal.

And into a world of chaos.

Lindsay gripped the handle of her bag and tried to hold her ground against the swell of people around her. They touched her—whether on purpose or not, she didn't know. But skin pressed to her skin. Bodies bumped against her back. She felt as if she were going to be swept along with the wave of humanity around her. Swept away from the group. From Than. Her breath came in short gasps as she tried to see where the group was. Panic began to build inside of her.

What was she doing here? Why had she thought she could do this? How was she going to survive when the first few minutes in a new country she was having a panic attack?

She couldn't do this. She needed to get back into the terminal and get a return ticket to Minneapolis. Or better yet, have Lucas send the plane. She'd just wait in the terminal for it to arrive and whisk her back to the world she knew.

Yes, that's what she would do.

"I've got you."

She heard the words as a strong arm slipped around her back and pulled her against a firm chest. *Than*. She inhaled the scent that she recognized and listened as he spoke to people around them. Sometimes in English. Sometimes in Filipino. She closed her eyes for a moment and just focused on what was familiar and, at that moment, that meant focusing on Than. The panic began to ease away, but she still lifted a hand to grip the front of his shirt in case he lost his hold on her.

"Lindsay."

She opened her eyes and looked up into Than's gaze.

"I'm going to leave you with the ladies of the group while I help the men with the luggage. The bus we're taking to the mission house should be here soon." He paused. "Are you okay?"

Now that she had calmed down, Lindsay felt a little foolish for having panicked like that. She loosened her grip on his shirt, patted out the wrinkles and nodded. "I'm fine."

He lifted an eyebrow at that but didn't comment on it. "Things will settle down once the bus gets here. Just stick with the ladies for now."

Lindsay allowed him to guide her to where the other women from the team stood. She was grateful to see that a couple of them also had rather stunned looks on their faces. At least she wasn't alone in her culture shock.

Mel reached out and drew her into the group. "You okay, sweetie?"

"I think so. A bit overwhelmed, I guess."

She smiled. "That's to be expected. There are a lot of people in Manila. It will be less overwhelming when we get to the mission house and then to the place we'll be for the next couple of weeks. You'll always draw attention, but it will be less of a crowd."

"This is a little nuts," the mother of the teens said then she looked at Lindsay. "Is Than your boyfriend?"

"Uh...no." Lindsay glanced over to see Than standing with the men and their huge pile of luggage. "He's here as my...bodyguard."

"Your bodyguard?" the woman asked, her eyes wide.

Lindsay sighed. It probably would have been a good idea for Than to have attended a couple of the team meetings ahead of time to explain why he was coming. Instead, he'd only met with Mark and Mel and then just showed up at the airport on the morning of departure.

"It was the only way I could come without creating a huge issue with my family. After a close call with one of my brothers last year, my mom was reluctant to let me out of her sight. The only way she'd agree to let me come was if my brother hired someone to keep an eye on me." Lindsay sighed, trying to ignore the bead of sweat she felt slip down her back. "Yeah, I know I'm an adult, but when it comes to my mom..."

"I know how that is," another of the women said. "My mom is kinda the same way. Thankfully, my dad usually talks sense into her so she doesn't give me too much grief when I want to do stuff like this. But I have a feeling that if it weren't for him...well, I'd be stuck at home with only my dog for company."

"Alright, ladies, we can get on the bus," Mark said as he approached them.

Lindsay looked to where he gestured and saw a small bus idling at the curb. Than was helping the men begin to load the luggage in the back. She followed the other women as they walked toward the open door of the bus.

The wash of cool air, as she stepped up into the vehicle behind the other women, was so very welcome. The bus had what looked to be about eight rows of four seats per row with an aisle down the middle. A few of the women sat together, but Lindsay slid into an empty row. As soon as she settled into the seat by the window she knew this was going to be even more uncomfortable for Than than the plane had been. Her knees pressed up against the row in front of her and her butt just barely fit in the curved base of the seat. Didn't people here have hips?

She heard the rumble of male voices and looked up to see that the guys were now climbing onto the bus. She watched as Than's gaze swept over the seats before settling on her. Though he didn't smile or wink at her or anything like that, she felt a flush of warmth that totally negated the air conditioning she'd been enjoying.

He stepped into the row and turned to face the front of the bus but didn't sit down until the other men had all found seats. Once they had, he sat down and stretched his legs into the aisle. Clearly this wasn't his first time riding on a bus like this.

When he leaned back into the seat, his shoulder bumped hers. Lindsay immediately moved closer to the window.

He looked over at her, an eyebrow arched. "I don't have cooties, ya know."

"Sorry. Was just trying to give you a bit more space. It's a little...cramped."

"I'm fine."

She allowed herself to settle back into the seat so that their shoulders were once again pressed against each other. The bus lurched forward amid a chorus of honking horns— some of which were actually musical notes. Very strange.

As the bus pulled away from the airport, Lindsay stared out the large glass window next to her. She was surprised by the amount of people and traffic considering what time it was. By her calculations, it was probably close to midnight and yet the crowds of people and vehicles suggested it was much earlier.

She glanced over at Than whose head was also turned so he could see out the window. His gaze moved to hers.

"What's the time?"

He glanced down at his watch and stared at it for a second. "Eleven fifty."

"So many people."

"This is a city that doesn't really ever sleep. Always lots going on. Plus there are just a lot of people living here."

As the bus picked up speed, Lindsay tried to watch the world slipping past the window but had a hard time seeing much since it was dark. The one thing the darkness didn't hide was the craziness of the traffic. It quickly became apparent that the rules of the road were more like suggestions.

She looked over at Than again. "Is the traffic always like this?"

He grinned. "During the day it's worse."

Lindsay couldn't even imagine. And she was ever so grateful that she wouldn't have to drive at any point during this trip.

They were soon driving on what appeared to be a highway through the city. She could see that there were high rises at certain points because of the height of the lights in the distance. It would have been nice to get a better glimpse of the city, but that would likely have to wait until the next day when they drove out of it in daylight.

It was about forty-five minutes before the bus exited the highway and began to make its way through what looked to be a more residential neighborhood. Soon they pulled up to the gate of a walled compound. The bus honked, and the gates began to swing inside. Lindsay looked down as they passed through them and saw a uniformed man with a rifle of some sort in his hand.

The compound was well-lit, and she could see a large building on the left that looked to be two or three stories high. The bus came to a stop, but before anyone could move, Mark stood up and asked them to stay in their seats for a moment.

"We're going to unload the luggage and ask that you each find your bags. There is someone from the mission house waiting to give us keys to the rooms we'll be staying in tonight. The couples will each have a room. The singles will share rooms according to gender, of course." Mark grinned. "Do try to keep it quiet. Most the other residents here are asleep."

Though there was definitely a drop in the number of people around when they exited the bus, the heat hadn't changed. She sure hoped that the rooms they were going to sleep in had air conditioning or, at the very least, fans.

It took a little bit to sort through the bags, but soon she had hers set to the side along with Than's. Next, the person from the mission house handed out room assignments and keys. She led them into a building and then up a flight of stairs. There was some struggle to get all their bags up to the second floor, but eventually they were shown to their rooms and given the time for breakfast the next morning.

Lindsay had known that she'd be sharing accommodations during the trip, but it was kind of an adjustment to walk into a room and see four single beds. Although, right then, any type of bed would be welcome. She was exhausted.

She let the other two women choose their beds and then took one of the two that were left. Before leaving Minneapolis, she'd tried to pack so she would only have to open one bag for this single overnight. Wearily, she opened the suitcase and found her toiletries.

"I'm going to take a shower," Lindsay said once the other women had made use of the bathroom. "If that's okay. I'll leave the door unlocked if you need in."

"Sure thing, hun," Barb said. "I think I'm going to crank the air conditioner if you ladies don't mind."

"I don't mind at all," Lindsay assured her. "The colder, the better."

Amanda, their other roommate, emphatically nodded her agreement.

Once in the bathroom, Lindsay stripped off her travel clothes and stepped into the shower. The initial blast of cold water shocked Lindsay, and she stepped back. It gradually moved to the lukewarm range as she fiddled with the taps. She took her time washing her hair and then shaved her legs and underarms, well aware that during this trip both those body parts would be exposed more than usual.

The adrenalin she'd been operating on since exiting the terminal began to wane, taking with it her energy level. Though normally she would have blow-dried her hair, Lindsay settled for gathering it on top of her head in a bun. She pulled on a tank top and cotton shorts that would only be used for sleeping during this trip. After brushing her teeth, she gathered up her dirty clothes and left the bathroom.

"Oh, there she is," Barb said.

Lindsay glanced over to see her standing at the door. The open door. She pressed the bundle of clothes she held in her arms closer to her chest.

"Than wanted to talk with you," Barb explained as she moved away from the doorway.

Nodding, Lindsay walked over, knowing she probably looked ridiculous clutching her dirty clothes like that, but for some reason she felt exposed even though she was covered. As far as she knew, Than didn't operate under the same principles as guys like Lucas and Eric. She was pretty sure a woman's body wasn't off limits to him the way it had been to Lucas and Eric before they married.

Because of that, Lindsay appreciated the fact that his gaze didn't drop below her eyes as he said, "Just wanted to check in with you and make sure you're doing okay."

"Yep. Sorry about earlier. It all kind of took me off guard."

He stared at her for a moment then his expression softened. "No need to apologize. I would have warned you, but really, nothing prepares you for dealing with it all at once. You did just fine." He jerked his head to his right. "I'm in room ten. If you need anything just knock. I'm going to send an email to your brother to let him know we've arrived safe and sound."

"Tell him I said hi."

"I will. Sleep well."

"You, too."

He gave her a quick smile before turning and heading down the hallway. Lindsay resisted the urge to watch him until he disappeared into his room. Instead, she shut the door and moved to her bed. The room was quiet, and she glanced over to see Barb and Amanda both watching her.

"He's a handsome one," Barb commented. "And very gentlemanly, too. I noticed that when we were at the airport in Japan."

Lindsay nodded. "I think it's because of his job. He has to hobnob with all kinds of people. He seems to adapt to situations quickly."

"So you know him outside of this bodyguard gig?" Barb asked as she settled down on her bed.

Picking up the bag she'd brought to put her dirty clothes in, Lindsay nodded. "He and my brothers are friends. I think that's why Lucas—my brother—felt confident asking him to take this job."

When Lindsay slipped between the sheets of her twin bed, Amanda asked, "Ready for me to turn out the light?"

"I'm ready," Lindsay said as she curled onto her side, already feeling sleep tugging at her. "Does anyone have an alarm set?"

Barb picked up a small travel clock from beside her bed. "I set it for nine. Is that too late, do you think?"

"I think breakfast is at seven," Amanda said. "But frankly, at this point, I'd take sleep over food."

"Me, too," Lindsay said. "Plus, I have some food in my suitcase that could tide us over until we can get something for lunch."

"Sounds good to me," Amanda said as she switched off the light.

"Mind if I pray before we sleep?" Barb asked once the room had settled into darkness. When neither Lindsay nor Amanda objected, she said, "Heavenly Father, we thank you for the safe journey You granted us as we made the long trip from Minneapolis here. Please give us the rest we need to face what lies ahead tomorrow. I ask that you keep us all from sickness, and I pray that we'll be a blessing to each and every person we come in contact with. Thank you for this opportunity to show Your love to others through our service. In Jesus' name. Amen."

As she settled under the sheet on the bed, Lindsay felt a momentary longing for her comfy queen-size bed with a multitude of pillows and super soft sheets. But as exhaustion pulled her eyelids down, she realized that not even an uncomfortable bed was going to keep her from sleep on this night

Than woke as soon as his alarm went off. He laid in the bed for a bit, glad for the air conditioner that had kept the room at a good temperature for sleeping through the night. He was also glad that Mark had arranged for a room for him by himself. He'd needed to do a little work when they'd first arrived since it had been mid-afternoon in Minneapolis. There had been a few emails he'd needed to answer. And now he had to drag himself out of bed and go meet his aunt and whomever else she brought along.

He'd checked with the people in charge of the mission house via email before leaving Minneapolis to make sure it would be okay for his family to come there for a little visit. While he could have gone to their place, he didn't want to chance getting stuck in traffic or run into something that might keep him from getting back on time. Plus, he needed to still be in Lindsay's vicinity, and he hadn't been sure about taking her to his family's place.

With a grunt, Than pushed up from the mattress and got to his feet. He stretched a bit trying to work out the kinks that had resulted from sleeping on a hard mattress with a flat pillow. Still, it could have been worse. He could have been sleeping on the floor.

Than took a quick shower and then pulled on a pair of black cargo shorts and a black T-shirt. He wasn't out to impress the woman his aunt was bringing to meet him. In fact, if he could have avoided this meeting altogether, he would have. But his uncle was also supposed to be coming and bringing a weapon and some cash for him. He doubted he'd have to use it, but he wasn't about to take a chance.

His aunt had agreed to text him when they were close, so Than sat down at his computer to check his email while he waited. They'd agreed to show up around nine, but with Filipino time that meant it could be anywhere from nine to noon. He hoped it was sooner rather than later because noon would mean a very short visit. Which—when he thought about it—might not be such a bad idea.

He pulled a protein bar from his bag since he'd missed the early morning breakfast the mission house provided. As he ate it, he realized he probably should have given a handful to Lindsay since he highly doubted she'd made it downstairs in time for breakfast either.

His satellite phone chirped and when he checked it, he saw that it was his aunt. He tapped out a quick response then picked up the suitcase containing all the stuff his mom had sent and headed down to the large living room on the main floor.

Figuring the suitcase would be safe enough if he left it there, Than headed out the front door of the building and glanced around to get his bearings. Once he spotted the gate where they'd come in the night before, he began to jog in that direction.

As he reached the gate, he spotted two guards in a shack next to it. He approached them and in Filipino identified himself and explained about his family. Apparently the person in charge had let them know to expect them because the guys nodded.

There was a honk beyond the walls of the compound, and one of the guys stepped through a pedestrian walk-through to talk to the driver before coming back in and opening the main gate. Than watched as the shiny vehicle with darkened windows pulled into the compound. He was pretty sure none of his family drove the luxury car as it was fairly common among the middle and upper class to have drivers in addition to maids and nannies.

The car came to a stop in an empty parking spot near the gate. As Than strode in their direction, the driver got out and opened the back door of the car. His uncle was first out. A well-respected businessman in Manila, Alberto Salazar was actually a very unassuming man in person. He was shorter than Than by at least half a foot and had a slender build.

"*Tito*," Than said as he hugged the man. "*Kumusta na po kayó?*"

His uncle stepped back with a smile. "I'm fine, Than. Thank you."

Next came his aunt, who reminded him an awful lot of his mother.

"Than, darling." Merlina Salazar pressed her cheek to his, bringing with her a cloud of perfume. "It's good to see you again." She stepped back, holding both his hands in hers as she took in his appearance. She reached up and pinched his cheek. "You are so *guwapo* still."

"Thank you, Tita. You are still *maganda* as well." And she was. Like his mother, she had aged well and retained much of the beauty of her youth.

"I have someone for you to meet, *anak*." Though he was not technically her son, she still called him by the affectionate term for one's child. She waved her hand to the driver as he helped the final passenger from the vehicle. "This is Lilibeth Ramos."

A slender beauty exited the car one long leg at a time. Her jet black hair moved like silk as she straightened and held out her hand to him. There was no doubt that she was every bit as beautiful as his mother had promised she would be, but she did absolutely nothing for him.

He took her hand and smiled. "It's nice to meet you, Lilibeth. I'm Than Miller."

"It's a pleasure to meet you, Than." She tilted her head and gave him a smile that might have passed as shy if he hadn't seen the calculating look in her eyes. Yeah, this was no shy girl, no matter how she might present herself to the world.

6

THOUGH they all obviously spoke Tagalog—the national language of the Philippines—and knew that he did as well, Than wasn't surprised that their conversation took place in English. He suspected Lilibeth was doing it to show that she was capable of moving in his world back in the States. Too bad for her, that was never going to happen.

"Why don't we go into the house?" Than suggested. "Mama sent a suitcase full of *pasalubong* for you, *Tita*."

His aunt smiled as she slid her hand into the crook of his elbow. "How is she?"

"As beautiful as ever and keeping my dad on his toes like usual."

She laughed at his reply and pressed her cheek to his arm. "When will they come to visit us again? We miss you all."

"I don't know. Maybe you should come to visit *us* sometime."

His aunt gave him a sly smile. "Perhaps for a wedding?"

Stifling a groan, Than gave her a tolerant smile but didn't rise to the bait.

As they approached the mission house, Than reached out and opened the door. He held it as his guests walked into the house, not missing the smile Lilibeth sent his way as she passed him. Though he smiled in return, he sure hoped this wasn't going to end badly. He'd told his mom to warn his aunt that he was *not* in the market for a Filipino bride, but he wouldn't put it past his mother to have "forgotten" to pass on the message.

"Please, have a seat."

There were several wicker and rattan couches with cushions through the large room which was empty except for them. However, he could hear the sound of muted conversation coming from what he assumed was the kitchen.

Once his aunt, uncle and Lilibeth were seated, he retrieved the suitcase from where he'd left it earlier. "Here are all the things Mama sent for you, *Tita*. You can keep the suitcase as I won't need it to travel home."

"Your mama is so generous," Merlina said with a smile.

They talked for a little while with his aunt doing most of it. She would ask Than questions and then share something about Lilibeth that was no doubt supposed to make him see her as a good potential wife.

"Good morning, Than!"

Looking up, Than saw Barb, the woman who had joined him and Lindsay at the airport in Tokyo. He got to his feet and smiled at her. "Good morning, Barb. Sleep well?"

"Can't complain."

As she stepped to the side, Than saw that Lindsay was a few steps behind her. She wore a pair of jean capris, a gauzy baby blue blouse and a pair of black sandals. Her hair was down in loose waves over her shoulders, and she wore only a little bit of makeup. Now here was a woman that stirred something inside him.

Smiling at her, he reached out with his hand to grasp hers and pull her close. As he wrapped his left arm loosely around her, he bent down and whispered, "Please help me out here."

She pulled back to look up at him, a question on her face. "What?"

Than bent his head and spoke in a low voice. "Just act like you like me. Really like me. I'll explain later and will forever be in your debt."

Her eyes widened briefly before a smile spread across her face. Than wondered for a moment if she meant to toss him to the wolves. Instead, she reached up and cupped his cheek. "Good morning."

"Good morning, sugar." He knew not to push for a kiss or anything like that. But hopefully they could suggest enough that his aunt—and Lilibeth—would get the idea that he wasn't interested or available. "I'd like to introduce you to my family."

Than turned her toward where his aunt and uncle sat. Alberto had a curious expression on his face while Merlina looked like she had just eaten something that tasted unpleasant. He kept his arm around Lindsay's waist as he said, "This is Lindsay Hamilton. Lindsay, this is my aunt, Merlina, and my uncle, Alberto."

As they both got to their feet, Lindsay held out her hand to shake theirs. "It's a pleasure to meet you."

Merlina's lips were pinched shut, but Alberto smiled warmly at her and said, "The pleasure is ours, Lindsay."

"Oh, and this is..." Than let his voice trail off. He knew he was being a bit harsh, but he'd made it clear that he wanted no matchmaking, and they'd ignored his request.

Lilibeth gracefully got to her feet, looking every inch the beauty queen she was. She lifted her chin and said, "I am Lilibeth Ramos." She ignored Lindsay's outstretched hand as her gaze swept over her. "*Siya ay taba.*"

Than saw red at the woman's statement. His hold tightened on Lindsay's waist as he switched over to Filipino and let Lilibeth know exactly what he thought of her calling

Lindsay fat. When her eyes widened, Than wondered if they hadn't let her know that he was as fluent in her language as she was in his.

"*Nataniel!*"

The sound of his full name spoken sharply in an accented voice drew him up short. He turned to his aunt who had a horrified look on her face. He didn't know if it was because of what Lilibeth had said or his response.

Than dipped his head to her even though anger still coursed through him. "I'm sorry, *Tita*." Then he switched back to Filipino. "I told Mama I was not interested in finding a wife the way Stephen did. I prefer to choose my own woman. And even if I were interested in finding a wife from here, it would not be her." Lilibeth gave an outraged gasp. "What she said about Lindsay was rude, and I can't abide that in a woman."

"Than."

He felt a gentle touch on his chest and looked down to see Lindsay's fingertips resting there. When his gaze met hers, her expression was serious. "Why don't we just leave you to finish your visit with your family? Barb and I were in search of something to drink. We can catch up when you're done."

Than took a deep breath and let it out, feeling some of his anger ease away under her touch. She kept her gaze on his until he nodded and then she turned to look at his family. He watched as she smiled and said, "It was a pleasure meeting you."

Albert once again held out his hand and clasped hers between both of his. "It was all ours, Lindsay. Maybe we will meet again someday."

"I would like that," Lindsay replied with a graciousness that stood in stark contrast to Lilibeth's rudeness. However, Than couldn't tell if she was just being polite or if she really was sincere. At any rate, her natural grace and poise drew him in more than any beauty queen ever could.

She turned back to him, once again laying her hand on his cheek. "Behave. See you later."

He pulled her a little more tightly against his side before letting her go. Than watched as Lindsay and Barb walked toward where the kitchen was, waiting until they were out of sight before turning his attention back to his family.

His aunt gave him a resigned smile. "Than, I'm sorry. I think Lilibeth and I will go wait in the car while you finish your business with your uncle."

"The things for Than are in the car," Alberto said. "We'll walk out with you."

Fifteen minutes later, his family was on their way home, and he was in possession of a gun and a significant amount of money. His uncle had taken care of getting pesos for him, and he'd given him US dollars in exchange for it. He hadn't been sure they'd have time to get money changed—especially the amount he wanted to have on hand.

Lilibeth hadn't even said goodbye to him but had stomped her way down to the car and slid in without even looking in his direction. Than should have felt bad, but he didn't. He knew for a fact there were plenty of wonderful women in the Philippines. Surely his aunt could have at least found one that was a little more gracious and friendly. Either Lilibeth had snowed his aunt with her innocent routine or she'd bribed her for an introduction. Regardless, the girl was leaving without the prize.

<hr/>

"Well, that was interesting," Barb said as she approached the kitchen.

That was one word for it, Lindsay imagined. "Than had told me his mom and aunt were matchmaking for him. He wasn't too impressed when we talked about it, and it appeared he was even less so today. She was very beautiful though."

"Ah, but beauty isn't everything, my dear." Barb stopped in the doorway of the kitchen.

Immediately, a young woman approached them. "May I help you, *mum*?"

"We arrived late last night and missed breakfast this morning," Barb explained. "I wonder if you might have some coffee."

The woman smiled brightly. "Yes. We have coffee and also some fresh fruit if you would like."

When Barb glanced over at her, Lindsay nodded enthusiastically. The protein bars had been good, but coffee and fresh fruit sounded even better.

"We would love that. Thank you so much."

"Please just have a seat at the table. We will bring it to you."

Lindsay looked around as she followed Barb to a nearby table. The room they were in was large with huge windows along each wall. The windows were all open, and a breeze drifted through the screens that covered them. The open windows let in more than just the breeze though. In the distance, she could hear the sound of traffic and blaring horns mixed in with dogs barking and music playing.

"Here you go." The woman slid a large tray onto the table and then emptied its contents in front of them. Mugs, sugar and cream for the coffee and a large plate of fruit and two smaller plates with forks. "There are mango and pineapple slices as well as some papaya and, of course, bananas if you want. I'll be right back with the coffee."

"Thank you," Lindsay said as she eyed the fruit hungrily.

After the woman had returned to fill their coffee mugs, Lindsay took a piece of each of the fruits to try. The coffee was stronger than she usually drank it, but a little sugar and some cream helped with that. And she had no doubt she'd be thankful for the caffeine as the day wore on.

She had just taken a bite of the mango when Than sat down on the chair next to hers. "You managed to get some breakfast, eh?"

The woman who had brought them their breakfast reappeared. "Would you like coffee, too, sir?"

He gave her a quick smile. "Yes, please." After she had left, Than looked at Lindsay. "Thanks for earlier. My mom obviously decided not to pass on my request for no matchmaking."

"She was very beautiful," Lindsay said as she stabbed at a piece of pineapple then stuck it in her mouth.

"Yeah, she was, and if she'd been a little more genuine and a little less calculating it might have at least been nice to meet her." He paused to take the mug from the woman when she returned with it along with another plate and fork for him. "*Salamat po.*"

A small smile curved the corners of her mouth and her eyelashes swept down as the woman murmured a reply in Filipino.

Lindsay waited for him to continue chatting with the young woman, but he just picked up the coffee carafe and poured himself a cup. "Did you ladies sleep well?"

Barb nodded. "I was out like a light and slept right through to the alarm this morning."

"Me, too," Lindsay said as she picked up a napkin to wipe the dribble of pineapple juice on her chin. "I wasn't too sure when I saw the bed, but I think I was tired enough that I could have slept on a bed of nails."

"You still might have to," Than said with a grin.

"Well, I'll just have to make sure I work hard enough during the day that it won't matter what the bed's like."

Over the next little while, the rest of the team members began to show up. The kitchen staff had obviously been advised to expect them because as each group joined them, more coffee and fruit were provided. Lindsay drank two cups of coffee and ate a lot of fruit before settling back in her chair. She was glad that whatever panic had overcome her the night before was absent then. Even though Mark had tried to prepare them for what was to come through pictures and descriptions, it was still a big unknown to Lindsay. At least now, with a full night's sleep, she felt a little more equipped to handle it than she had the night before.

Than watched as Lindsay sat back in her chair. She licked the tips of her fingers which were no doubt coated with the juice from the pineapple she'd been eating. At some point, she'd just abandoned the fork and plucked pieces from her plate and popped them into her mouth. He was glad to see her relaxed and apparently enjoying herself.

He had to admit that he'd had a bit of concern the night before at the airport. When he'd turned to say something to her and had seen her expression, his heart had just about jumped out of his chest. The panicked terror on her pale face had taken him off-guard. It was never a look he'd thought he'd see on Lindsay Hamilton's face. But then she'd never been in a situation like that before.

Thankfully, she seemed to have moved past that and would hopefully be able to deal with what was still to come. He was glad to see her interacting with the other women on the team as well. It would have been easier for her to just stick with him since he was a familiar face, but he knew that wasn't the purpose of this trip. Now that she'd made a couple of connections with the ladies, he would step back and give her some space even as he kept an eye on her for his job.

"Can I have your attention, please?"

Than looked over to see Mark standing in the midst of the round tables. The conversation died down as chairs were shifted so people could see him more clearly.

"We need to be packed up and ready to go in an hour. Make sure you have everything from your rooms. We'll be getting a bagged lunch from here, but we'll stop along the way so you can pick up snacks and such. The trip will take about five hours, so we'll arrive at the mission center just before supper." Mark ran a hand over his shortly cropped hair. "A couple of travel points. Remember to keep your valuables such as passport and money close to you. Just like anywhere else, there are those who will be happy to relieve you of your money. Keep your purses or bags in front of you. If you have a backpack, wear it on your front. I know that this is all new to some of you, so if you have any concerns, please let me or Mel know. We want this to be a pleasant experience for everyone."

Mel approached him and Mark bent down to listen as she murmured something to him. When he straightened, he said, "Right. Just one more reminder to not drink the water. And that includes ice. If you want something to drink along the way, get it in a bottle that has been chilled. We do have medication for the stomach troubles and other things you can catch from drinking the water, but it will be much easier if you can avoid it all together."

Once Mark had dismissed them, Lindsay looked over at him. "No turning back."

Than smiled at her. "Sugar, there was never any turning back."

Her brows drew together. "You really shouldn't call me that."

"Call you what?" Than asked.

Her scowl deepened. "Seriously?"

He grinned as he shook his head at her. It was way too easy to yank her chain. "What's wrong with what I call you?"

"It's not my name. And you're supposed to be here in a professional capacity. Calling me that doesn't sound professional."

Than knew she was right even though it was something he did without thinking most the time. He had a feeling it was one of the things about him that rubbed her the wrong way—his tendency to use affectionate nicknames for the women he came in contact with. And he was well aware that his usual approach with women would not fly on this trip.

He sighed. "Okay. Lindsay it is. But you'll have to cut me some slack if I slip up once in a while. I mean, I look at you and all I can think of is how super sweet you are, and sugar just slips out."

Lindsay stared at him, one eyebrow lifted before she started to laugh. "Yeah. I've been described as a lot of things, but sweet isn't usually among them."

Than grinned. She was right about that. He had kind of settled on sugar as a nickname for her because it wasn't overtly romantic, and he figured it would probably rankle her. Clearly, he'd been right.

"Well, I'd better go put my stuff together," Lindsay said. "Don't want to hold anything up."

Than got to his feet when she did and walked with her and Barb upstairs to their room. "Let me know when you're ready to go, and I'll help you guys with your bags."

Once all the luggage was loaded again, Than climbed onto the bus and looked around. He noticed right away that Barb was in the seat next to Lindsay. Instead of making a big deal about it, he made his way to an empty set of seats near the back of the bus. The newlyweds were in the seats across the aisle from him, and Lindsay was in the row in front of them. At least she was still in his line of sight.

Though he would have liked to sit next to her, it was actually more comfortable to be by himself in the two seats. He settled into the one next to the window but sat angled so he could stretch his legs out a bit. Five hours was a long time to feel like he was eating his kneecaps.

Mark said a prayer for their trip and then they were off. Than turned his head toward the window and watched the traffic and buildings slip past. Driving was a start and stop process until they finally made it out onto a major highway. At one point, he found himself watching the newlyweds across the aisle.

They seemed so young. And definitely very much in love. The woman had turned sideways in her seat to lean against her husband while her feet were propped on the edge of the seat under the window. The man's arms were around her and every once in a while she'd turn her head up to look at him, a smile on her face. And more often than not, the man would dip his head to press a lingering kiss to her lips.

They reminded him a lot of his parents and how they were around each other. Even after all the years they'd been together, they still seemed to be totally in love with one another. That could be why his mother was so determined to see them each married. She wanted her children to experience something similar.

And for the first time in...well, for the first time ever...Than was seriously considering it. His gaze went to where Lindsay sat. He could just see the very top of her head, but it was enough. Was there more there than her just being a challenge for him? At the end of the chase, would he really want to keep her? Would they start out like the couple across the aisle but end up fighting? Would the things he liked about her be the things that would drive him nuts later on?

The biggest question for him had always been, how did someone know for sure that a person was their forever? When there were so many women out there, how did a guy know for certain? He'd first asked Lindsay out on a date for the same reason he'd asked any other woman out. He'd thought she was cute, and she seemed like an interesting person. When she'd accepted but then quickly turned the tables on him by dictating where he would take her and what he'd wear, Than had had a moment where he'd wondered what he was doing. But then their date had gone fairly well— or at least *he'd* thought it had—and he'd been interested in going out again a time or two, but she'd had none of it. That's when things had changed a bit for him.

Than Miller was not one to be rejected so strongly, particularly after a date that had gone—as far as he could tell—so well. And it bugged him that it was by a woman he found as intriguing as he had found Lindsay.

At first, Lindsay had had mixed feelings when Barb sat down next to her on the bus. She was so used to having Than beside her when traveling—had appreciated the excuse to have him nearby, if she was honest with herself—that initially, she was a bit put out by Barb's presence. But not for long.

Even as she'd realized that she needed to be interacting more with her teammates and less with her bodyguard, Lindsay discovered that Barb was actually a very interesting person. Her appearance was somewhat deceiving as she came across almost hippy-ish with her graying hair worn long and in a braid. Her style also tended toward a somewhat eclectic, bohemian look.

"Do you have a family?" Lindsay asked after she'd shared a bit about her own.

"I do. I have three kids, in fact. My youngest daughter still lives with me as she finishes up college. My other daughter is a nurse in Chicago, and my son is a professional hockey player."

Lindsay looked at her in surprise—again! "Does he play for a team close by?"

She nodded. "He's actually with the Wild at the moment, but you know that can change at any time."

"Do you go to all his games?"

"You bet." A proud look passed over Barb's face. "He got me season tickets so I'm at every one that I can be."

"And what is your other daughter in college for?"

"She's going into the medical field, too, just like me and her sister."

"What part of the field are you in?" Lindsay hoped Barb didn't mind her questions, but she was quite interested in the woman who had befriended her.

Their interactions were a stark reminder that she usually held herself off from most people she met. She could count on one hand the number of people she might call a good friend, but she wouldn't consider any of them a BFF—though Lucas's wife, Brooke, was coming close. It had been difficult never knowing whether someone was a friend because of her money or because they genuinely liked her. In the end, it had just been easier to not allow anyone to get too near to her. But this trip was forcing closeness and for once, Lindsay didn't mind it.

"I'm an OB/Gyn. I have a focus on high-risk pregnancies."

Lindsay stared at her. "And this is how you choose to spend your vacation?"

Barb smiled, the skin at the corners of her eyes crinkling. "Yes. Sitting on a beach somewhere soaking up the rays doesn't appeal to me overly much. Being able to travel and help out like this is more my thing."

"So you've been here before?"

"Not here. I try to go to different countries, so this is my first time to the Philippines." Barb tilted her head. "What made you decide to come on this trip?"

Lindsay wished she could say it was out of some altruistic motivation or that she'd prayed a lot before joining the team, but she really couldn't. "To be honest, I'm not entirely sure. I was sitting in church when they made the first announcement asking people to consider participating or at least supporting the mission trip through prayer. Something inside me just said I needed to join. Maybe that's not the right way to go about things, but here I am."

Barb smiled. "Sometimes God's promptings can be just like that. The most important thing is that you listened to that little nudge. I think you're right where God wants you."

"I hope so." While she hadn't prayed much about it beforehand, she certainly had since the day they'd accepted her onto the team. "I just hope I can be a help and not a hindrance."

Barb reached out and patted her hand. "Keep an open heart and have willing hands and that will not be a problem."

Lindsay nodded and turned toward the window, watching as the foreign landscape slipped by. There was a heavy cloud over the city, and they'd been told it was pollution. It made her have a real appreciation for the quality air they had in Minnesota.

Her elbow was jostled, and Lindsay looked over to see Barb grinning at her.

"So tell me about Mr. Than and what he is to you."

7

THAN?" Lindsay's stomach clenched just hearing his name. It was hard, but she managed to resist looking back to where he sat. "For the purpose of this trip, he's my bodyguard."

"Oh, come on. You already told me that part. And that he's a friend of your brothers. I'm more interested in what he is to you."

"He's nothing to me. Just an acquaintance."

Lindsay waited for Barb to call her on that, but instead the older woman looked at her intently then said, "Okay. Then what are you to him?"

"A challenge." The words were out of her mouth before she even realized it.

"A challenge?" Barb's eyes widened. "Now that sounds interesting. Do tell."

Lindsay rubbed her fingers on the jean material covering her thigh. She hadn't told anyone much about their date.

When anyone had asked, she'd brushed it aside saying it had been fine but making it seem like she had only ever expected it to be a one-time deal. "Than has a reputation as a ladies' man. He's a consummate flirter and what my sister-in-law calls a serial dater. From what I've heard, he rarely does more than two dates with any given woman."

"And I'm guessing he asked you out?" Barb had drawn one leg up onto the seat and wrapped her arms around it.

"Yep. In front of my whole family, no less. I'm pretty sure he thought I'd say no. After all, I have a bit of a reputation myself. One of being stand-offish, especially where men are concerned. So he was pretty shocked, I think, when I said yes. I told him to wear a suit and take me some place nice."

"And did he?" When Lindsay nodded, Barb said, "Well, so far it sounds good."

"It was a nice evening. The restaurant was really beautiful, and the food was good. We even had a fairly decent conversation. I relaxed with him in a way I hadn't thought possible and was even considering saying yes to a second date if he asked."

"I kinda sense a *but* coming."

"Yeah. A big one. As we were leaving the restaurant, a woman stopped Than and it quickly became apparent he had—at the very least—dated her."

"Sounds like it might be pretty hard to turn around in Minneapolis without running into someone Than had dated," Barb commented.

"Yes, you're right, and I had already anticipated that. And apparently so had he because it seemed totally natural for him to introduce us. There wasn't any awkwardness on his part at all. But I think the final straw for me came when I thanked him for the evening and commented on how nice the restaurant had been. His response made it clear that he'd been there several times before. And I think that's when I realized that there would be no special moments for us. No place where he didn't have a memory of being there with someone else."

"So when he asked you for a second date, you turned him down?"

"Yep. That night and every other time since."

"Did you tell him why?"

Lindsay shot Barb a surprised look. "Why would I have done that?"

Barb shrugged. "Maybe he would have understood and made some effort to make it more special for you on the next date."

She couldn't help the snort of laughter that escaped her. "I knew Than was only looking for a couple of good-time dates. Me mentioning to him what I shared with you would have made it sound like I was looking for something long term. Than doesn't do long term. Plus, I'm at a point in my life where I'm not interested in casual dating anymore, so more than one date with Than would have just been a waste of my time."

"You want someone who makes you feel special. Cherished."

Barb's voice was soft, but Lindsay still heard the words loud and clear. And they resonated strongly with her. Yes, that was exactly what she wanted. She didn't want a man like her father who didn't care about how her mother felt while he was off with his flavor of the month. And she certainly didn't want to be with a man like Than who seemed to think it was his job to make *every* woman feel cherished and special.

"Does your husband make you feel that way?" Lindsay asked, suddenly eager to be done talking about Than. But as soon as she asked the question, she realized that she didn't even know if Barb *had* a husband. She wore a simple gold band on her left hand, but in this day and age, it could mean anything.

Barb's gaze grew distant. "Yes, he did."

He *did*? Oh no… Lindsay laid her hand on Barb's arm. "I'm so sorry."

The older woman's gaze came back into focus and met Lindsay's. "There's no need to be sorry. We had almost twenty years together. It's been ten years since he passed. I miss him. Even more when I see couples like the Rosens and the Armstrongs. That probably would have been us if he'd lived." A gentle smile curved her lips. "But we had good times, and I have three wonderful children who remind me of him every single day. I wish he could have lived to see what they've become. He would have been so proud of each of them."

That was the love Lindsay wanted. That love that Barb had had with her husband. The love Lucas shared with Brooke. And she was pretty sure that she wasn't going to find that kind of love with Than.

"You ladies want some lunch?"

Lindsay looked up to see Mel in the aisle beside their seats. She balanced a cardboard box on her arm and plucked a paper bag from inside it and held it out. Barb took it and passed it to Lindsay and then took the next one Mel handed her. Then she handed them each a water bottle that must have been in a cooler somewhere because it was still cold to the touch.

"Thanks, Mel," she said as she opened the bag.

Lindsay couldn't remember the last time she'd eaten a meal out of a paper bag. She wasn't anticipating anything great but was pleasantly surprised by the obviously homemade bread and chicken salad sandwiches. There was a bag of chips, a boiled egg and a couple of chocolate chip cookies to round out the meal.

Thankfully, their conversation moved away from the previous topic onto more generic things. She hoped that would be the last time they discussed Than.

"I'm going to stretch my legs a bit," Barb said as she stood up and moved into the aisle.

Lindsay leaned back in the seat and turned her head to once again watch the world outside the window. What had she been thinking to reveal all that stuff to Barb? It seemed like spilling her guts was all she was doing on this trip.

Thankfully, the high seats backs and the noise of the bus had kept others from hearing. At least she hoped that was the case. She could hear murmurs of conversation around her but nothing clearly.

"Doing okay?"

Lindsay jumped and jerked around to find Than sliding into the seat where Barb had been, his face inches from hers. He was so close she could see the black flecks in his dark brown eyes. He had eyelashes that any girl would kill for, she thought. Her gaze dropped. And his lips… She jerked back from him, blocking her thoughts from going in that direction.

Than was *not* the man for her.

As she stared at him, a corner of his mouth quirked up as if he knew what was going through her mind. "Everything okay?"

Lindsay swallowed and hoped her voice would sound normal when she said, "Yep. Everything is great."

When Barb had been sitting next to her, there had been plenty of room in the row, but with Than in that seat, it was as if everything had shrunk in size. Without being totally obvious about it, there was no way to sit that at least some part of their bodies didn't touch. Right now, her right knee was pressed up against his. She rested her palms on her thighs with just enough pressure to hopefully dry the moisture that had suddenly dampened them.

"How are you enjoying the trip so far, sugar?"

She lifted her eyebrows at his use of the word, but he looked unapologetic. "It's been fine."

"Even though you decided not to sit with me?"

Lindsay regarded him silently then said, "You need to stop doing that."

"Doing what?"

For a moment, she wondered if he really was unaware of the flirtatiousness of his tone and his words. "Flirting. It seems to be like breathing for you."

"Are you saying you don't think I can stop?"

Lindsay nodded. "That's most definitely what I'm saying."

Than didn't reply to that right away. He just sat there staring at her. Lindsay felt herself begin to flush under his observation, but she didn't look away.

"Well then, how about a bet?"

"A bet? I don't bet."

"Oh, come on. Just a friendly little wager. No money involved."

"Okay. What are the terms?" Lindsay hoped she didn't end up regretting this.

"If I can go the remainder of this trip without flirting, you go out on that second date with me."

Lindsay considered it. "And if I win."

"I'll stop asking you out and leave you alone."

As she thought about it, Lindsay figured it was an easy bet. There was no way that Than could go that long without flirting. This would definitely be an easy way to get him off her back. And really, if he stopped to think about it, it was win-win for him, too. He either got the date he wanted or he got the opportunity to move on from her—maybe sooner than he wanted—but there was no doubt he would have moved on eventually.

"Just one clarification." She held up a finger. "This is flirting with *anyone,* not just with me. After all, it really isn't appropriate for this trip."

A pained look crossed Than's face, but then it disappeared just as quickly, and he nodded. "No flirting with anyone. Deal."

He stuck his hand out. Lindsay stared at it for a moment before sliding hers into his strong, firm grip. She felt his thumb rub a couple of times across the back of her hand before giving it a gentle squeeze and releasing it. Oh, she wanted to say something. To tell him that wasn't allowed either, but the more she objected to things, the more he was likely to realize how it affected her. And that was the last thing she wanted.

"Hello, Than."

Lindsay looked up to see Barb standing in the aisle.

"Hey, Barb," Than said as he pushed to his feet and moved out of the row. "It's all yours."

"You can stay if you want. I can sit in your seat."

Than shook his head. "It's all good."

As Barb reclaimed her seat, she gave Lindsay a curious look. "Everything okay?"

"Yep. We just made a friendly little wager."

The woman's eyebrows rose at that. "A wager? You really think betting against Than is a good idea."

"In this particular instance, I think it is. It's pretty much a guaranteed win for me."

"Really now? What exactly was the wager?"

As Lindsay shared the details, a slow smile spread across Barb's face, and she gave a slight shake of her head. "Oh, honey, I think you better brace yourself for that second date. In fact, I have a feeling that Than is sitting back there right now planning it."

Lindsay frowned as she fought the urge to lift herself up and look back over the seat to where Than sat. "Why would you say that?"

"Because as far as I've seen that boy has flirted with no one but you since we started out on this journey. My guess is that he won't have much trouble keeping that under control for just two weeks if the outcome means he gets his way."

Lindsay let her thoughts drift back over the trip. Aside from helping that one woman with her luggage and then chatting with her—which may or may not qualify as flirting, depending on what they'd talked about—he really *hadn't* flirted with anyone else. Certainly none of the women on the team. And definitely not the woman his aunt had brought along.

Her stomach clenched at the realization that Barb might be right. Had she wagered herself right into that second date?

Thankfully, Barb didn't press on that topic of conversation as the bus continued its journey through small towns and dark green fields. They made a quick bathroom stop midway. If she had thought she'd last until their destination, Lindsay would have turned around and left the bathroom once she'd seen the facilities. But then she'd reminded herself that part of this trip for her was about experiencing something different from her life. And that bathroom had definitely been different. But she'd survived and was rather proud of herself for that. But she resolved to drink less water before embarking on any longer trips.

When they'd gotten back on the bus, Than had handed her a paper bag that felt warm to the touch. Inside she'd found a little bit of heaven. Freshly made circles of bread with white sugar on the top. Than had called them *ensaymada* and said they were a Filipino specialty. After sharing with Barb and eating two of them herself, Lindsay hoped it was a specialty she got to try again soon.

Just around five o'clock, while driving through one of the larger towns they'd come across, the bus turned off the main highway they'd been on since leaving Manila. They drove through a residential area for a little bit and then the houses stopped, replaced by trees. The road narrowed as it wound its way up a hill through the forest.

Soon the bus came to a stop and Lindsay looked out her window to see a barbed wire fence that disappeared into a thick forest of trees. When the bus jolted forward again, Lindsay saw that they were passing through a gate. Another couple of turns and suddenly they were in a large clearing at the top of the hill.

Lindsay pressed her face to the window to get a glimpse of the place she'd be calling home for the next ten days. There were several large buildings around the edge of the clearing as well as one in the center. What she loved most from just the first glance was the abundance of green. In the lushness of the trees. In the grass that covered all but the dirt road where the bus came to a stop.

"Well, folks, welcome to Hope Mission Center," Mark said as he stood up. "We're going to unload the bags and show you all to your rooms, but we'll save the unpacking until after we get some supper."

Lindsay was aware of Than behind her as they moved toward the front of the bus, but she forgot all about him as she stepped out into the wonderfully fresh air. She could smell freshly cut grass in addition to something that made her stomach rumble appreciatively.

A couple of people who Lindsay assumed were missionaries came to welcome them. It took a little while, but soon they had sorted out the luggage and carted it to their rooms. Since school had finished at the end of March, the dormitory on the center was empty. The two story cement brick building was nothing fancy, but it was clean and spacious. They put the single mission team guys and the older couples on the main floor. On the second floor, Than had the room closest the stairs with Mark and Mel across from him. The family of four had the room next to his, and Lindsay, Barb, and Amanda had the room beside theirs. The women's bathroom was at the end of the hallway by their room.

Rolling her bags behind her, Lindsay stepped into a large room and looked around. The three sets of bunk beds dominated the room. At least there wouldn't be a fight over who got the lower bunks. There were large windows along the outside wall with thin curtains over them that drifted with the breeze. The beds were all jutting out from the windowed wall, and it appeared there were closets along the inside wall opposite the windows.

Barb went to the middle set of bunk beds and flopped down on the lower bunk. "Feels pretty good to me. I think I'll claim this one."

Lindsay waited for Amanda to choose her bed before going to the remaining one. Like Barb, she relaxed back on the bed for a couple of minutes. It did feel good. As good as the bed the previous night had been.

Home sweet home for the next ten days.

After dropping his bags in his room, Than took a few minutes to go over what he'd seen in his mind on the final approach to the center. He really didn't believe that Lucas's fears for Lindsay's safety were necessary. Everything he'd read up on the area had indicated that there hadn't been any threats to foreigners at any time in recent history. If they'd gone south from Manila, he might have been more concerned, but they'd gone north to a relatively peaceful area of the country.

Still, he was being paid to do a job, so he would do it. The fence surrounding the center really wouldn't keep out anyone determined to gain access to it. Mark had told him that they did have a guard on duty twenty-four hours a day so that was good. Most likely not for protection from terrorists but from thieves who thought there might be something worth stealing from the place where the Americans lived.

Though he was pretty sure nothing was going to happen, he slipped the weapon his uncle had gotten for him into the holster he wore in the small of his back. He tucked his T-shirt in and then pulled on a loose button shirt that he left open and untucked to hide the gun. Now that he'd seen the property, he'd talk a bit to Lindsay just to clarify a few things. He knew she'd likely balk at even discussing it, but Lucas was counting on him to keep her safe.

He knew that Mark hadn't been too thrilled to have the two of them on the same floor. No doubt the man had picked up a bit on the sparks in their "relationship." Whether Lindsay wanted to acknowledge them or not, they were there. But Than had told him that he needed to be close to her and that a room at the top of the stairs as the first line of defense, if the worst should happen, was necessary. He'd assured him that there would be nothing untoward in their behavior with each other—if for no other reason than he had a bet he needed to win.

He left the door open to his room and listened for Lindsay's voice. Once he heard it, Than stepped out into the hallway and greeted the three women with a smile.

"Ready to go eat?"

Lindsay gave him a skeptical look, but all he did was smile at her just like he did the other two women. Barb slipped her hand into the crook of his arm and said, "Escort me to dinner, young man."

He did just that, hoping that Lindsay wouldn't interpret that as flirting. After all, Barb had initiated it, and his mother had raised him to never be rude.

Once out of the dormitory, they made their way across the grass to the large building in the middle of the center. He reached out and opened the screen door and let the women go in ahead of him. Just as he stepped in, he saw another group making their way over from the dormitory.

The smells that had been just a whiff on the late afternoon air intensified once they stepped inside the building. His stomach rumbled in anticipation of the meal that was to come. Growing up, his mom had made sure they ate as much Filipino food as they did American, so he had no doubt he'd enjoy whatever they served. He just hoped that Lindsay would as well.

Like the mission house they'd stayed at in Manila, this room was filled with round tables. Way more than was needed for their group, but no doubt filled to capacity during the school year. The room had windows on the two longest walls, and it looked like the kitchen was at the far end.

"Hey, guys," Mark greeted them as they walked a little further into the room. "We'll be using the tables closest to the kitchen. Take a seat anywhere at the tables set with plates."

Than went to lay his hand on Lindsay's back to guide her forward but then closed it into a fist and lowered it to his side, not about to give her any ammunition to use against him. He glanced over at Barb and saw a twinkle in her eyes as a smile tugged at her lips. It appeared that Lindsay had shared a bit about their bet with the older woman. He smiled back at her, figuring it couldn't hurt to have an ally in his quest to win his wager.

The tables were set for eight and once they'd sat down, there were still four empty seats. Though he was sure that Lindsay would have preferred it another way, he took a seat next to her with Barb on her other side. The newlywed couple ended up joining them as well as a couple of the single guys.

Once they were all seated, Than realized that, in addition to their group, there were a couple of tables with a mix of missionaries and Filipinos. One of the missionaries got up and introduced himself and then welcomed them all before saying a prayer for the meal. Soon bowls and platters of food were brought from the kitchen to their table.

Than recognized pretty much all of it and knew they would eat well that night. He could tell from the expression on Lindsay's face that she was a bit uncertain about the dishes that now sat on the Lazy Susan in the middle of the table. Probably the only thing she recognized was the big bowl of white rice.

Hoping to ease her concern, Than reached for the bowl that was in front of him. He used the tongs to lift the contents onto his plate then handed it to Lindsay.

Leaning close, he said in a low voice, "It's *pancit*. Rice noodles with chopped up vegetables and chicken."

She shot him a quick glance before she used the tongs to put a helping onto her plate. "Thanks."

Next was the rice which he figured she would know, so he passed it on to her without comment. The next bowl he got, he hoped that they made it the way his mom did as he knew that different types of meat could be used. He would give her that version and keep his fingers crossed.

"*Adobo*. It has pork in a sauce of soy sauce, brown sugar, and other spices. It's not spicy hot." It happened to be one of his favorite dishes, and it smelled almost as good as his mother's did. He noticed that Barb was leaning close as he handed the plates to Lindsay and figured she was curious as well. "These are *lumpia,* the Filipino version of spring or egg rolls. They usually have chopped up vegetables and ground pork. Very good."

When the person seated to his right handed him the basket containing the bread, he smiled. "This is *pan de sal* which is another Filipino specialty bread similar to what you ate earlier only without the sugar. Also very good, especially fresh."

For some reason, Than found himself hoping that Lindsay would like the food. He didn't know why it was important, but it was. Though he didn't often talk about his mixed heritage, he was proud of his Filipino roots and the culture and all it entailed. He knew Lindsay would be able to win his mom over if she knew and enjoyed the food of her native land.

Than sat back as the thought went through his head. Wait. What? *Win his mom over?* That was the first time he'd ever had that thought when it came to a woman. What on earth had even brought that to mind? Introducing a woman to his mother was a sure invitation for his mom to begin to plan a wedding. Than never—ever—brought a woman to meet his family.

"Than?"

8

HEARING Lindsay say his name, Than realized he must have missed something. He looked at her. "Sorry. What did you say?"

Lindsay gestured to the man on the other side of him. "Jeff was asking you about your knowledge of the food."

Than turned to the man. "Sorry about that. My mind wandered there for a minute."

"No problem. Was just wondering why you know the foods so well?"

As they ate, he talked a bit about his background. He knew that the group was becoming aware that his presence there was for Lindsay, but he appreciated that they seemed more than willing to welcome him as part of the team.

As the meal was winding down, the missionary once again got up.

"Welcome again. I just want to go over a few things for your stay here. Breakfast is served at seven, lunch at noon and supper at five thirty. We ask that you please be on time for meals. Starting tomorrow night after supper we will have a time of sharing and prayer. We have two projects we will be working on while you're here. In the morning we will assign you to your project and begin to work." The man looked toward a woman who stood to his left. She murmured something and he nodded before saying, "Oh yes. Just so you know, we have a guard on duty twenty-four hours a day. They are armed, so if you see a man in a blue uniform with a gun, don't be alarmed. We've never had any problems, but it is a precaution we take just to be sure. I know Mark and Mel are your direct contacts, but please don't hesitate to talk with any of us if you have a question or a concern."

Once they were dismissed, Than walked beside Lindsay as they left the building. Night was settling over the center. Because they were closer to the equator, the sun set earlier than it presently did in Minnesota. The length of the days didn't vary to the degree they did in North America.

"Can I talk with you for just a minute?" Than asked as they neared the dorm.

Even though there were lights mounted on the building that cast some light, he couldn't read her expression in response to his request. He took her arm and tried to lead her out of the way of the others.

When she tried to pull away, he said, "It's job related. I just want to cover a couple of things. Okay?"

At that, she relented and followed him. "Job related?"

"Now that I've seen the place, I just want to touch base as bodyguard to client."

"Okay. I've already promised not to try to ditch you."

"I know, and for that I thank you, but there are a couple more things. First," Than reached out and took her hand. She tried to jerk free, but he held firm and placed her hand on the small of his back where his holster was then released it. "I'm armed. I just want you to know that and to know where I'm carrying. I will do my best to keep it concealed, but since protecting you is my job, I must be armed."

"But here? Really?"

"It's just a precaution. I agree with you, it's probably not needed, but if it did become necessary and I wasn't prepared... Well, that's just not going to happen."

"Is that all?"

"No. I realize that this is your mission trip, and I will do my best to not interfere with what you do here, but I will at all times be within your vicinity. If you're planning to go somewhere off the center, I will need to know and will have to accompany you. I don't have to be glued to your side, but I need to be able to see you...well, with obvious exceptions. Which leads me to my next thing. Please wear presentable clothes to sleep in."

"Say what?" Her frosty tone almost made him smile.

"If you have to leave your room in a hurry or if I have to come get you, I don't want to have to stop and wait while you get dressed. Sleep in a T-shirt and shorts at the very least. And I'll do the same, so if you need to come get me for some reason I, too, will be presentable."

"Oh...okay. Mel had already sort of suggested that for sleeping."

"I didn't realize that. I just know that there are different standards on this particular job being that it involves another culture and a more conservative environment."

"Is that it?"

Than sighed. "No. One more thing and it's the most important. If things go south—and I really don't anticipate that happening—but if they do, you must do *exactly* what I say. Please, Lindsay, this is important. I know we have had our issues, but when push comes to shove, I *will* protect you with all that I have. Don't second guess what I'm telling you to do, just do it. Promise me."

Silence stretched between them for a long moment before she said, "I promise."

"Thank you." He paused for a moment, fighting the desire to pull her into a hug. "Is everything else going okay?"

"Yes, so far. The food was great at supper. Thank you for telling me what it was. I might have been a little more leery to eat it if you hadn't explained."

"I figured that might be the case. If you have any questions about cultural or food stuff, let me know. Or if you need someone to translate something."

"You should be charging Lucas double for your skills as a bodyguard and a cultural expert."

Than touched her arm to indicate they should move toward the dorm and then fell into step beside her. "I might just do that. You'll have to give him a rave review first though."

"Well, we've still got a few days to go..." Lindsay said, a trace of humor in her voice.

Than chuckled as he reached out to open the door leading into the building. Thankfully, the stairs were wide enough they could walk side by side to the second floor. As they reached her door, Lindsay turned to him. "I think I'm going to call it an early night. I'm still feeling a little out of whack and want to make sure I'm up for breakfast in the morning."

"Sounds good. Hope you sleep well."

"Thanks. You, too."

After she had disappeared into the room she shared with the two other women, Than turned and went to his own room. He spent a little time unpacking in the rather sparse space. He eyed the bunk beds, pretty sure that his feet were going to be hanging off the end for the next two weeks. He couldn't really complain though. He'd slept on a lot worse over the years. That didn't mean he wasn't going to be excited to get back to the California king size bed in his apartment.

After unpacking, he hooked his laptop up to the internet provided by the center. He didn't anticipate it would be the fastest, but at least it would let him stay in contact with BlackThorpe stateside. It didn't take long to get hooked up and to check his email. The team who'd been in charge of the kid and her friends spending spring break in Europe had delivered all their charges safely back to their parents and had returned to base.

The team members had each sent in a report with most of them offering Than everything from an all-expense paid trip to the destination of his choice to their first born if he'd keep them off all future rich kid babysitting jobs.

He answered them as a group to thank them for finishing out the job without any casualties. They would each have a week at home before they would be given new assignments. Eric would be in charge of assigning those later in the week.

After reading through all the emails that had been waiting for him and dealing with the important ones, he took the time to type out a quick email to Lucas. He followed that up with one to his mother giving a few details about his visit with Merlina and Alberto. He also told her in no uncertain terms, never to try matchmaking for him again. Who knew if she'd listen this time, but he had a feeling she'd be getting an earful from her sister after the debacle earlier that day.

He took a minute to check the course of the storm that was headed for the country. It looked like it was still on a trajectory that would take it south of where they were, and it still hadn't been upgraded from a tropical storm. That was a good sign. That meant it would mainly just be rain and not the damaging winds that came with a typhoon.

He decided to take a quick shower and then call it a night because he was starting to feel the same tiredness Lindsay had mentioned earlier. He gathered up a towel, his shaving kit, and fresh clothes before heading to the men's bathroom on the main floor. Apparently when the school was in session, the male students were on the first floor while the women had the second one to themselves.

Than gave his head a shake when he thought of how he'd probably would have tried to circumvent the division of genders back when he was that age. Since starting work at BlackThorpe three years earlier, he'd been confronted with men whose moral code had definitely been higher than his. At first he'd kind of looked askance at the choices they made when it came to things like dating and their language.

As far as Than knew, Marcus Black and Alex Thorpe didn't have much of a social life or if they did, they definitely kept it off the company radar. Eric McKinley had been dating, but it became clear pretty quickly that his dates didn't end the way Than's usually had. Trent Hause was the same. It didn't escape Than's observation that both those guys attended the same church. And then there was Justin. Who knew about Justin's social life? All Than knew was that none of the guys had been interested in conversations about the weekend's highlights on Monday mornings.

At first he'd pegged them as fuddy-duddies even though they weren't that much older than him, but gradually he'd begun to see that perhaps there was something to the way they lived their lives. And now Eric and Trent had both settled down with women whom they cherished and who, by all accounts, cherished them. The same could be said for Lucas Hamilton.

That was why almost a year into his employment at BlackThorpe, Than had begun to change his outlook on his social life. He had actually started to do his serial dating as a way to keep from getting involved with one woman enough to give in to the physical side of things while still being able to have a social life. After all, he did enjoy spending time with women, but he was trying to hold himself to a higher standard. No one expected anything after just one date, but more than three or four and women began to hint at things, and he started to feel tempted. So he'd go on a date or two and then move on. He hadn't met a woman who had tempted him to go beyond that...until he'd met Lindsay.

The first time she'd flicked her gray gaze over him and dismissed him, he'd been a goner. He was so used to women responding to his friendly flirting that it had been a bit disconcerting when Lindsay hadn't just not responded but had made it clear she had no interest in him at all. He still wasn't sure what it would take to be the man that *would* interest Lindsay, but he was trying to figure it out. The first step, apparently, was to stop flirting. It was his go-to behavior around women but had become less so in the months since he'd met Lindsay. In fact, he'd realized that he'd begun to reserve the flirting for women who wouldn't read anything into it—like Barb.

"Hi, Than."

Than looked up from where he stood in front of the sink shaving. "Hey, Mark. How's it going?"

The man dropped a shaving kit onto the counter that ran between the four sinks. "Not too bad. Checked the storm out again."

"Yep. Me, too. Looks like we're still in the clear. Even if it does upgrade, its trajectory still seems to be toward the south of us."

"We'll just keep praying it stays that way."

"Do you pray about everything?" Than asked before he'd really thought about it, and he hoped the man didn't take offense to his question. The thought of praying was something of a foreign concept to him. He relied on his own skills and abilities to get him out of sticky or difficult situations.

Mark bent and splashed water on his face. "Sure do. The Bible says to pray without ceasing. I find that I just keep up a running conversation with God throughout my day."

"Always asking for stuff? Like about the storm?" Than asked as he wiped the last of shaving cream from his face.

"Nah. It's not always asking. When Mel comes up to me and gives me a kiss, I thank God for blessing me with her as my wife. Every morning when I swing my legs over the bed and get to my feet, I thank Him for my health and ability to face another day. And when I *am* sick, I thank Him for doctors and the medicines that will make me better. So no, it's not a running request line."

Than zipped up his kit and then leaned a hip against the counter. "And how do you handle it when you pray for something and it doesn't happen?"

"Well, I've always approached my prayer requests with the understanding that God knows so much more about what's best for us. Yes, I ask for what *I* think is best, but in the end, it's His will that I want for my life. Sometimes that means doors shut for me."

"So if you're praying that storm stays tropical and to the south, what does it mean if it kicks up to a category five and heads right for us?"

Mark straightened and met his gaze. "I don't know, man. In cases like that, I just have to trust that God sees the bigger picture, more than what I see with my own narrow vision. Bad things happen and not just to bad people. Typhoons have ripped through this country before leaving devastation and death in their wake. This one might be no different, but I'm still going to pray that it is. And if it's not, we'll deal with that as well."

As Than made his way back to his room, he thought over Mark's words. That was probably the one thing he balked at the most—having someone else take control of his life. He hated it when his mother tried to do it with her matchmaking, and he wasn't altogether sure how comfortable he was with it coming from an unseen being.

But that didn't stop him from saying a quick *please, God, let the storm miss us.* And then, just for good measure, he added, a*nd please let Lindsay agree to go out with me again.*

In the darkness of his room, Than gave a sheepish grin. He really had nothing to lose by asking for a little help with Lindsay. He wasn't doing such a hot job of it on his own.

Lindsay woke to the sound of incessant beeping the next morning. She heard Barb mumble something before the noise stopped. Knowing that this wasn't a morning to linger in bed, she kicked the sheet off her legs and pushed herself to a sitting position. A lock of hair that had escaped her braid slid in front of her face. Lindsay shoved it behind her ear and sat for a moment trying to get her brain to kick in. She had never been a morning person and now combined with jetlag and feeling like someone had left the heat on high, she was dragging, and her day had barely started.

She wondered if she had time for another shower even though she'd taken one the night before. If nothing else, it would wake her up and cool her down—hopefully.

Making up her mind, she said, "I'm gonna go take a quick shower."

"Me, too," Barb said as she stood up and stretched. "I hope they don't have a limit to how many showers a day we can take. I have a feeling one a day just won't cut it."

Lindsay agreed as she grabbed her toiletries from the closet she'd put her things in the night before. It was actually not just a closet. Half of it had space to hang clothes but the other side had drawers halfway up and then open shelves above that. She'd managed to get all her things into just one closet, but at the rate she was going through clothes, she was a bit worried that she was going to run out soon. Hopefully, they had laundry facilities she could make use of.

After a super quick shower, Lindsay pulled on another pair of capris and a green T-shirt. She worked her hair into a single French braid and then smoothed a tinted moisturizer with high SPF on her skin. She didn't add anything else but a little waterproof mascara and some lip balm—also with SPF. Her mother had lectured her about protecting her skin from the sun. Though she normally faced the world with much more makeup than she'd applied that morning, Lindsay knew that it would just melt away anyway, so it wasn't worth the time or effort.

"You ready to go?" Barb asked when she got back to the room.

Lindsay slipped her feet into a pair of slip-on canvas shoes—the most practical and plain shoes she'd ever owned until this trip. Now she also owned a pair of expensive, sturdy hiking boots. "Yep."

She, Barb and Amanda walked down the hallway and as they neared Than's room, he stepped out and greeted them, as if he'd been waiting for them—which undoubtedly, he had been. She remembered his words from the night before about always being within her vicinity. Even though she knew it should rankle her, Lindsay found a strange comfort in it. If she felt overwhelmed or lonely or homesick, she'd just have to look for Than. He was her *piece of home* in a way. Not that she'd ever in a million years admit that to him, but he was just the same.

He wore a pair of black cargo shorts and an untucked light blue T-shirt. If she hadn't known why it was untucked, she would have thought it odd. Anytime she'd seen him, he'd always had his shirts tucked in with a belt around his waist.

"Morning, ladies. Sleep well?" Than asked as he fell into step beside Lindsay.

"Yep," Barb said. "Though I can't believe it's this hot already. And it's going to get hotter, isn't it?"

"Most likely," Than replied. "But hopefully we'll get a nice breeze, and if you stay in the shade it shouldn't be too bad."

As they stepped out of the building, a breeze stirred the air, and Lindsay hoped it would be a strong wind by the time they had to do any work. The upside to this heat and the physical work they'd be doing was that she'd probably be able to lose a few of the pounds that had been plaguing her for years.

She enjoyed the breakfast provided. It had included lots of fresh fruit, toast, eggs, and some sort of sausage that she had to be honest and admit she hadn't really enjoyed. In fact, after one bite, she'd known she wouldn't be able to eat more. It was just a bit too sweet for her taste. The others at the table didn't seem to have a problem with it, especially Than, so after making sure no one was looking, she'd slipped the remainder of her sausage onto his plate. She hadn't wanted anyone to think she was rude by not finishing what she'd taken.

When Than turned his attention back to his food from the conversation he'd been having with the guy next to him, he paused then looked at her. A corner of his mouth tipped up when their gazes met. She lifted her eyebrows and dared him to say something. Instead, he used his fork to cut off a chunk of the sausage and popped it into his mouth. Lindsay couldn't help but smile as she finished the last piece of pineapple on her plate.

9

ONCE breakfast was finished, the missionary—Lindsay thought his name was Elliot—got up to speak to them. Over the next half hour, he led them in a time of prayer before going on to explain a little about the mission and what they did. And then it was time to hear the details about what they were going to do.

"The two main areas we want to work on are the school and the clinic. We'll be painting the inside and outside of both buildings over the next couple of weeks as well as doing some minor repairs to each. Also, we'd love it if some of you would volunteer to help in the orphanage for a little while each day. Usually, the students help out but with them gone for the summer, the cuddles the little ones are used to have dropped considerably."

Lindsay felt something spring to life in her. Cuddling little ones? At one time, she would have brushed that aside and stuck with the painting, but ever since Danny had come into her life, she'd changed her perspective on children.

Maybe this would give her a chance to be around some younger ones to see what they were like and if she could handle them. She and Danny got along great, but maybe that didn't translate to smaller children. But right then she sure hoped that it would.

After they had been divided into their groups, they set off to their respective jobs. She hoped that after lunch she could volunteer to go to the orphanage. But for now she was going to be wielding a paintbrush.

By the time lunch rolled around, all Lindsay wanted was another shower and a nap. Not only was it hot, she was out of shape. Badly. Exercise had never been her favorite thing, but she'd figured that painting wasn't exactly the most physically demanding thing on the planet. Her arms and shoulders, however, were telling her something different.

Lindsay wished she could skip lunch except she was hungry on top of being tired and sore. Even as she felt like she was wilting away, Than looked like he'd spent the morning on some leisurely stroll. It made her want to throw the *pan de sal* she'd plucked from the basket at him. Luckily, manners and the fact that she *loved* the bread kept it in her hand.

"You doing okay?" Than asked as they passed food around the table.

"I'm fine. How are you?"

He stared at her for a moment as if judging her response. "I'm fine, too. I just hope the paint dries quickly. I think we're going to get rain tonight."

"Really? Is that storm getting closer?"

"Yep."

"I like storms." Lindsay took a bite of the fried rice she'd scooped onto her plate.

"Yeah, I do as well as long as they're not damaging."

Lindsay paused with another forkful halfway to her mouth. "Is it possible this one will be?"

Than shrugged. "If not here, somewhere, likely."

She lowered her fork and stared at Than. "Is there a chance we'll get part of the storm?"

"Definitely a chance," he said as he ripped apart a *pan de sal* and put a piece in his mouth.

Lindsay glanced around the table to see if others were paying attention to their conversation, but none of them were. She leaned closer to him, trying to ignore the very male scent of soap and sweat. "Is this something we should be worried about?"

Than turned toward her, his brown eyes just inches from hers. "Right now, no. If that changes, just trust me that I'll make sure you're safe."

She frowned at him. "But it's not just me, Than. What about the rest of the group? The kids in the orphanage? Everyone who works here?"

He regarded her seriously, his dark gaze hard, before saying in a low voice, "I'm paid to make sure *you* are safe. For the duration of this trip, you will always be my first concern. Only when I know for certain that you are safe—and will stay safe—will I be able to help others."

Lindsay knew what he was saying to her. If he left her somewhere safe and she didn't stay put, he would be forced to stop helping others to come make sure she was safe again. She nodded that she understood and moved back from him. When she glanced around the table again, she saw that this time they did have the attention of a few people. Unfortunately, from the way they smiled at her, they must have assumed that she and Than were sharing an intimate moment.

If only they knew!

Once lunch was over, Than anticipated a return to the painting they'd been doing that morning but instead, Lindsay went to talk to Mark and the next thing he knew they were off to spend some time at the orphanage. He found it rather surprising since Lindsay had never struck him as a baby-oriented person. He'd seen her enjoy time with her nephew, Danny, but hadn't seen her with younger children before. Personally, he had no objection to children and usually spent time each week with his nieces and nephew. The time at the orphanage would be a piece of cake.

An older Filipino woman met them at the door and held it open for them. Mel, who had brought them over, greeted the woman warmly. "Hello, Fina. *Kumusta ka na?*"

"*Mabuti namán akó. At kayó po?*"

"I'm fine, too," Mel said with a smile. She gestured to Than, Lindsay, and Barb, who had decided to join them at the last minute. "They've come to help with the children for a little while. This is Lindsay, Barb, and Than."

"Welcome," Fina said with a smile and a nod of her head. "Please come this way."

Than followed the women into a large open area. It had big windows that allowed a breeze to float through the room. There were also a couple of oscillating fans as well as one on the ceiling that turned lazily. The room held several rocking chairs in addition to a bunch of toys spread across a large carpet in the middle of the room. There were two other Filipino women who looked up at their entrance. Than did a quick count and figured there were at least five children in the room.

Mel greeted the women and then turned to Lindsay and Barb. "There are currently six children in total here. Usually, we have more, but a few children have left recently."

"Were they adopted?" Lindsay asked.

Mel shook her head. "In these cases, there were family members who stepped up to take them. And really, orphanage is a bit of a misnomer. Many of the children are here because their parents—often it's just the mother—are unable to care for them. We try our best to place the children with family members or work with the mothers to reunite them, but when that doesn't work, they are then available for adoption."

Than turned at the distant sound of a wail. One of the women stood up and moved down a hallway. She returned very quickly with a baby in her arms. He couldn't tell if it was a boy or a girl, but it had a headful of black hair and big brown eyes that regarded the group standing there with curiosity. Even as the woman laid the baby down to do a diaper change, the dark gaze stayed on them.

"So do we just play with them?" Barb asked as she bent to run her fingers through the hair of a toddler who had come up to her.

Mel nodded. "If it were closer to a mealtime, you could help feed them as well, but I think that's over now."

"Come." One of the women motioned to Lindsay. She glanced at Than before going to where the woman stood.

"Here, you can sit and feed this one. She is due for her nap and likes a bottle first. Her name is Maya."

Lindsay settled into the chair, her expression a little apprehensive. Than shoved his hands into his pockets as he watched the woman place a baby in her arms, then show her how to hold the bottle. When the woman stepped back, giving him a clear view of Lindsay, his heart clenched. Her head was bent close to the baby's as she held her in the crook of her arm and slowly rocked.

"Here. One for you, too." The woman who had greeted them at the door led him to a chair near Lindsay's and motioned for him to sit. She handed him the baby who had just woken up from a nap and was now freshly changed.

"Boy or girl?" he asked the woman.

"Boy. His name is Benjie."

Than looked down at the kid in his lap and smiled. "How ya doing, little man?"

The baby stared at him for a moment and then smiled. A big toothy grin that reached out and grabbed ahold of his heart. Ah, this wasn't good. He had not anticipated that he might run into a situation that would require him to leave pieces of his heart in this country.

He put his hands under the arms of the baby and stood him on his thighs. The little guy seemed to really like that. He stomped his feet a couple times and then bounced up and down, gnawing on his chubby hand.

Such innocence, Than thought as he watched Benjie pull his fist from his mouth, a string of saliva still attached. The baby had no idea that he wasn't being raised by his parents. Had no idea the uncertainty that lay ahead of him if he wasn't adopted or returned to his family. Than couldn't help pulling the little guy close to press a kiss to his forehead.

He thought of his brother's kids and how fortunate they were to have been born where they were. In his years of traveling with BlackThorpe, he'd seen situations where conditions were less than ideal for the children in them, but it had just been in passing. This particular assignment was more like a humanitarian mission, and he was being pulled right into the middle of it in a way he hadn't anticipated. For someone who'd always taken his job seriously, but not much else, Than was discovering that maybe it was time he took that approach to a few more areas of his life.

He looked over at Lindsay and found she was watching him. Or rather, she was watching the little guy he held. She lifted her gaze and met his. There was something there, but he couldn't put a name on it. When she looked back down at the tiny girl in her arms, he figured that she'd found the sight of him holding a little one as peculiar as he'd found the sight of her cradling a baby close.

Peculiar and something else...something Than wasn't all too keen to dwell on right then.

As soon as the woman had placed the baby in her arms, Lindsay had felt as if an emptiness she hadn't even known about had been filled. The weight of the soft, warm body cuddled against her was like nothing she'd ever experienced before. She'd long told her mother to never expect grandchildren from her. But had that been more because she hadn't met a man she could imagine having in her life in that way?

She hadn't been able to imagine trusting a man enough to be there for her and any children they might have. Oh, her father had been there for them in the way he thought was most important. As long as he had provided them with the lifestyle he'd chosen for them, he thought he'd done his part. Lindsay was fairly certain that he'd never taken the time with his sons that Lucas had taken with Danny.

And never in a million years could she picture him sitting in a rocking chair with a baby on his lap. She glanced over in time to see Benjie grab at Than's cheeks and press his open mouth to Than's chin. Lindsay waited to see if Than would recoil from it, but instead he lifted the baby and rubbed his face against his plump tummy. Benjie gurgled with babyish delight that made Lindsay smile.

When the baby in her arms stirred, Lindsay looked back down in time to see Maya eject the bottle's nipple from her mouth.

"Time to burp her." Fina laid a cloth on her shoulder and showed Lindsay how to position her. "Pat like this."

After seeing what Fina did, Lindsay followed her example and not too long after, little baby Maya let out a loud burp that seemed too big for her tiny body. Lindsay shot a look at Than and saw that he had a wide smile on his face.

"Well, that's the way it should be done," he said.

Lindsay smiled back and kept rubbing Maya's back. She rested her cheek against the thick black curls on the baby's head and rocked back and forth. Her eyes shut and her world narrowed to the little one in her arms and she found herself praying for her.

God, please let her grow up to know the love of a family. Let her know joy and happiness. Please keep her safe.

How could a mother hold a baby like this and then abandon her? But then her thoughts went to some of the neighborhoods they'd driven through. Mark had also shared some stories in the meetings leading up to the trip about the abject poverty in parts of the Philippines, particularly in Manila. Maybe it was a mother's love to know that handing their baby over to a place like this meant the baby would get the food and shelter she might not be able to provide otherwise.

Knowing that any child she had wouldn't face that should have brought comfort to Lindsay but instead it brought grief.

She had so much—so *very* much—and yet there were women around the world who didn't know where their child's next meal would come from. Though she knew that she couldn't solve all the world's problems, Lindsay knew that things would be different when she returned from this trip.

When they stepped out of the orphanage a little while later, Lindsay stared at the dark clouds gathering to the east of them. She looked up at Than and saw that his gaze was fixed on them as well.

She grasped his forearm and waited for him to look at her. "Is it coming this way?"

Her previous thoughts of the storm hadn't been really fearful, but after having sat with a helpless baby in her arms, the damage a powerful storm could wreak filled her with dread.

"I'm going to go get my laptop and then check in with Mark. You stick with Barb and Mel."

Remembering his instructions from the previous night, Lindsay nodded. While Than strode off, the women returned to the building where they had been painting earlier in the day.

Elliot, the missionary in charge of the center, was speaking as they approached. "We might be changing what we're doing. It looks like we have a bit of a storm headed our way. We will need to start boarding up some windows just to be safe."

Just to be safe? Recalling the expression on Than's face, Lindsay had a feeling that these preparations were not just in case the storm hit but were necessary because the storm was headed in their direction.

"Roberto will help you wrap up things here and put the paint and supplies away for the time being. After that, we'll meet in the dining room to update on the storm."

Lindsay stayed with Barb and the group as Than had instructed. His words from earlier still echoed in her mind. *I'm paid to make sure* you *are safe. For the duration of this trip, you will always be my first concern.* On one hand, it kinda sucked to be reminded that his concern for her was tightly tied to his job, but it also was very reassuring.

Than bent over the table in the dining room to stare at the image on his screen. He frowned as the radar confirmed his suspicions. That storm had veered to the north and was rapidly climbing the classification scale. It had reached severe typhoon status already which meant it was sustaining winds of almost one hundred miles an hour. That was so not good. Even though they were located inland and there was every possibility it might weaken once it hit land, there was also every possibility that it wouldn't.

Than wanted to kick himself for not having checked on the storm earlier. When he'd looked over the weather data that morning, it had gained strength but even though its trajectory had shifted slightly north, it had still been on track to hit closer to Manila than to where they were. Clearly it had continued to gain strength even as it had shifted further north through the day.

It should have been safe. The majority of typhoons occurred during June to November. Being that it was just April, one of this size shouldn't have been likely. But he knew that when dealing with Mother Nature there were never any guarantees. It was time to switch his mindset. No longer was he hoping—praying—the storm would miss them or wondering why it was happening right then, he had to focus on what he needed to do to make sure Lindsay was safe. And Barb. And Benjie. Everyone....

"Looks like God's decided to let us endure this storm."

Than straightened and looked at Mark as he approached him. "Yes, it does appear that way. Do they have some sort of emergency preparedness plan in place?"

Mark shook his head. "Not really. Although all the buildings are fitted with storm shutters."

Though this wasn't exactly his forte, Than's training allowed him to consider each building and evaluate its weaknesses and strengths. None of them was one hundred percent safe. Too many windows. Too many trees.

"How much time do you figure we have?" Mark asked.

Than shook his head. "I'm not sure, but it looks like it will be making land within the hour. And then we're probably only about seventy or eighty miles from the coast. I'm most worried about the wind speeds and the fact that we're up on a hill surrounded by lots of trees."

"I suppose the upside to that is that we won't have to worry about flooding."

Than nodded. "That is probably a very big upside." He glanced around the dining room as he noticed the rest of the team was beginning to file in. "Here are my pros and cons about the structures. The buildings on the outer edge are most likely to sustain damage from the trees if the wind blows them over. This place will be safer from that sort of damage but has no real protection from the wind which makes its roof more vulnerable."

Mark held his gaze for a long moment without saying anything then asked, "Where would you put Lindsay?"

"Preferably a room with no windows, but I'm not sure there is such a place that would fit everyone."

Elliot joined them then along with a couple of the other men who worked at the mission. "We have people working to close all the storm shutters on the buildings, but we need to choose the safest one to ride out the storm. We've never faced a storm of this magnitude headed directly for us."

Than thought through everything he'd seen earlier. "I've been looking over the buildings and the surroundings, and I personally feel that the dorm would be the best place for us to be. My reasoning is this—the trees immediately behind the structure aren't that much taller than the building. And given the denseness of the forest, I doubt that the wind will blow those trees over. In fact, the trees will give some protection. The roof will be the most vulnerable, but if we confine everyone to the main floor, I think that will be the best place."

He saw Elliot and Mark exchange looks. Than hoped he wasn't stepping on toes, but he had a job to do here that went beyond holding babies and painting walls. When both men nodded, he let out a sigh of relief.

"We need people to help move the babies and their supplies. We'll need to get food and water." Elliot rubbed his forehead. "And I suppose we need to allow people a few minutes to gather things for themselves. If the power from town goes out, we do have a generator, but in the meantime, I'll have them bring the lanterns we've used during power outages before."

When the three of them had all agreed, Elliot called for the attention of everyone there and explained the process. "We'll have a group head over to the orphanage to organize what we need for the children. Mel and my wife will lead that group. We will have others here packing up food and taking it over to the dorm. We also need to get some supplies from the clinic. Once that's all set up, those of you who live elsewhere on the center will have a few minutes to gather any items you want to have with you. We probably have less than an hour before the rain and winds really hit us, but they can start at any time now."

Mark addressed the mission team and directed them where to go. Than and Lindsay were assigned to the orphanage group along with Barb and a few of the other women and their husbands.

"I'm going to run my laptop back to the dorm then I'll meet you at the orphanage. Do not leave until I'm there." Lindsay's eyes were wide, and he could see the fear on her face. Reaching out, he took her hand and squeezed it. "It's going to be fine. I'll see you there."

Within five minutes, he walked into the orphanage and found things in a state of organized chaos as supplies were gathered for the impending storm.

"We need to take the playpens. The babies will be able to sleep in them since we can't move the cribs," Mel said. "So guys, you take care of that and get them set up, if you can. Just pick one of the larger empty rooms on the main floor.

Ladies, we need to gather up diapers, clothes, formula, and bottles. Fina and the other ladies will help you get that together. We need to move quickly, but we don't want to forget anything. We'll take the babies over as soon as we have the playpens put up."

Than and the other guys collapsed the playpens with quick, efficient movements and then set them up again once they got to the dormitory. Next to Lindsay, keeping the babies safe was Than's greatest concern.

When they got back to the orphanage, the women were just leaving, their arms filled with baby supplies. He spotted Lindsay and nodded to her as he went back inside to see what else needed to go.

"Here are more diapers and some clothes," Mel said as she shoved a large bag into his arms.

As Than stepped out of the building, rain drops splashed down, cooling his heated skin. It looked like the edge of the storm was just about at their doorstep. He jogged toward the dorm and handed off the bag to one of the ladies in the room. He glanced around for Lindsay and motioned her to come with him. They needed to get the babies over before the rain got any worse.

Once they left the dorm, Than reached for her hand and together they sprinted through the rain to the orphanage once again. Mel and the other women were standing in the large living room now empty of playpens with the babies ready to go.

"It's raining," Than told them as he let go of Lindsay's hand. "Do you have something to cover them? Like a blanket or a towel?"

Fina nodded and gestured to a pile on a nearby chair. She handed him baby Benjie and then draped a blanket over the little boy. Next she gave Maya to Lindsay and covered her as well. The door opened as they were getting ready to head back out and Barb and one of the other women walked in.

"It looks like we have enough to carry the babies now," Mel said. "I'll have Roberto come back and shut everything down and lock it up."

As they approached the door, Than looked at Lindsay. "Ready?"

At her nod, he pushed open the screen door and led the way back to the dorm, mindful of the baby he pressed tight to his chest. The rain pelted at them, and he hoped the blanket covering the baby would be sufficient. Someone was watching for them because as they approached the building, the door swung open.

Than dashed into the dorm with Lindsay right on his heels. Once inside, he peeled back the blanket and gazed down at the baby. Benjie looked at him, his brown eyes wide in his pudgy face. Then he gave him a toothless grin like he'd given him earlier.

"Hey there, buddy. Ready for an adventure?"

10

THAN and Lindsay walked side by side down the hallway to the room where the babies would stay. It wasn't long before the other women were there with the rest of the children. Though Than would have liked to hang around and hold Benjie, there were other things that needed his attention.

The babies were put into the playpens for the time being and left in the care of the three Filipino women and the teenage daughter of the one mission team family.

"Lindsay, if there are things you want from your room, you should go get them now. I need to get a few things from my room as well. Don't take too long. Just what's necessary." When Lindsay gave a jerky nod and walked away, Than realized that there was a storm brewing inside her as surely as there was one outside.

After he'd finished in his room, he left his bag at the top of the stairs and went to find Lindsay. He found her with one knee pressed into the mattress of the lower bunk, jerking on the tab of the zipper of her suitcase.

"Ready to go?" he asked.

She nodded but didn't say anything. The zipper seemed to be giving her trouble, so he reached out to help her and as soon as he touched her hand, Than could feel her shaking. He gripped her arm and turned her to face him. She kept her head down, so he slipped his fingers along her jawline, tilting it up.

His heart clenched as he glimpsed a vulnerability there he'd never seen before. Her eyes looked like molten silver with unshed tears. Well aware it could lose him the bet, he gathered her into his arms, tucking her head under his chin. "Hey. It's going to be okay. We've taken every precaution, and one of the worst things about storms like these is the flooding, but we're high enough that won't be a problem."

He felt her grasp his shirt and take a deep shuddering breath. "I'm sorry. I've just never been through a storm of this size before."

As he rubbed a hand up and down her back to soothe her, Than said, "No need to be sorry. I know it can be scary when you haven't faced something like this. We're going to be okay." He reached down and tilted her face up to his again. Oh, how he would have liked to press a kiss to her lips right then, but instead he just said, "And so will the babies."

She nodded and lifted a hand to swipe at the tears on her cheeks. And when she loosened her grip on his shirt, he relaxed his arms and allowed her to step away from him.

"I managed to get all my stuff packed again. I hope that's okay."

"That's fine. So did I." He quickly finished zipping up her suitcase and then hefted it off the bed.

Back downstairs, Mark was trying to assign beds to everyone. Than wasn't sure there would be a whole lot of sleeping going on, but he supposed it was best to make sure everyone had a place to lie down if they needed to. He really wanted to be near Lindsay and yet understood that Mark would likely separate them for morality purposes. He was surprised then when Mark assigned him to a room with the three single ladies and the newlywed couple.

After all of that was done and their bags were at their beds, Than went to Mark. "Thanks for keeping me close to Lindsay. She's a little concerned about the storm."

"I figured as much. I also figured that there isn't much likelihood of impropriety occurring with everything going on."

Than nodded his understanding. He wasn't sure if his hug with Lindsay would have been considered improper, but at that moment he didn't really care. She had needed comforting, so he'd offered it. Anyway, he doubted that it would be happening again anytime soon.

Never in a million years would Lindsay ever admit to anyone how thankful she was that Mark had put Than in the room with her and the other mission team members. Up until the past day, she'd really only seen the joking, easygoing Than. Now it seemed that every time she looked at him, he had an intense, serious look on his face. Definitely all business as he'd dealt with the news of the storm.

The wind had begun to kick up outside and the sound of the rain on the tin roof of the building, even a floor below it, was at times both soothing and terrifying. Needing something to distract her, she went to where they had the children and was immediately handed the baby she'd held earlier in the day.

They hadn't brought the rocking chairs over so she just walked around the room, bouncing the baby to settle her. It seemed that the little ones were as anxious as the adults were. Several of the mission team women had gathered in the room as well.

It felt a bit like being in the ark. They had scrambled to get prepared for the storm and to bring the supplies they needed, but now that they were inside and hopefully secure, all they could do was wait.

She caught the scent of food just as Mel appeared in the doorway of the room.

"We've got supper ready. It was basically done by the time we had them move everything here, so if you're hungry, head into the last room on the right."

Lindsay glanced down at the baby in her arms. She looked like she'd finally settled as her eyelids drooped sleepily. Though some of the women in the room followed Mel, Lindsay walked another couple laps, pausing every once in a while to bounce the baby. Pretty soon her eyes stayed shut, her dark lashes fanned out across her light brown skin.

"You can lay her in the crib there, *mum*," one of the workers said as she gestured to one of the playpens.

Though reluctant to give up the comforting weight of the baby in her arms, Lindsay carefully bent over the playpen and laid her down. She stood watching the little girl sleep and said a prayer asking God to keep her and the other babies safe from harm in the midst of the storm.

She turned toward the door and looked up to find Than there, leaning against the doorjamb, watching her. A flush of warmth crept into her cheeks, but Lindsay didn't look away as she approached him. His expression was unreadable, and her thoughts went back to the embrace they'd shared earlier. He was no doubt seeing a side to her he wasn't aware existed. Just like the side she'd seen of him earlier.

Half expecting some sort of joking comment, she was a bit surprised when all he said was, "Are you hungry?"

"Actually, I am. The food smells good."

Than nodded. "Let's go grab something before it gets cold."

They walked in silence to the room where people had gathered to eat. It was still one of the bedrooms, but the bunk beds had been pushed flush against the outside wall and tables had been set up in the space that created.

Than once again bent down and spoke in a low voice to tell her what the different foods were. She put a scoop of each type of food on her plate and then grabbed a couple of the *pan de sal*. After Than had finished getting his food, she followed him to two empty chairs.

As they ate, the storm seemed to rage even harder around the building. Part of her wondered what it looked like outside. She hadn't been kidding when she'd told Than she liked storms. She particularly liked the storms that would roll through when they were at their cabin on the island. Sitting outside on the porch while the storm made its way across the lake had always been an enjoyable experience. She liked to hear the rain and watch the waves on the lake. She'd never experienced a storm that had been damaging like this one had the potential to be, though. There had been a few hailstorms that had damaged cars and some property, but it was all covered by insurance. Something told her that the people in the path of this particular storm didn't have insurance that would help to repair the damage they would be left with once it was all over.

She had just finished her food when the whole building seemed to shake and the lights flickered. Lindsay edged closer to Than and held her breath, waiting to see what would happen. The lights came back to full strength, but suddenly there was a flurry of activity as lanterns were set up on the tables. Lindsay took Than's plate with hers and went to where they were stacking the dirty dishes.

"Do you need help washing?" she asked.

The women who worked in the kitchen of the mission center shook their heads. Though Lindsay usually didn't think twice about people cooking and cleaning for her, it was a bit harder for her to accept in this type of situation for some reason. But she didn't want to push, so she turned to head back to her seat.

She'd barely taken a step when the lights flickered again. This time, they went out completely, plunging the room into complete darkness. Lindsay froze, her hands going out in front of her. "Than?"

Immediately, flashlights began to come on. Though holding hands wasn't something they'd done much of, she recognized the hand that gripped her as Than's and held on. He shone a flashlight in front of them and took her back to where they'd been sitting. Barb was there now too, and Lindsay sat down on a chair next to her.

"Well, this is a bit more than we signed on for, isn't it?" Barb commented as she patted Lindsay's knee. "Are you doing okay, hun?"

Before she could reply, Than leaned close and said, "I'm going to check with Mark. Stay here with Barb."

Once he'd left her, Lindsay said, "It's had a few overwhelming moments." She paused, swallowed, and then continued, "I'm really out of my depth here."

An arm slipped around her shoulders and Barb gave her a quick hug. "I think you're not the only one. I'd hazard a guess that none of us here have gone through something of this nature."

As if to reinforce her words, the building began to shake again. Lindsay held her breath, waiting for it to stop like it had last time. Only this time it didn't. The shaking continued as Lindsay reached for Barb's hand. As they huddled close together, she heard the murmured words of the older woman.

"Heavenly Father, we pray now for Your hand of protection upon us and all those in the path of this storm. Give us peace, Father, and help us to remember that You are still in control in the midst of all of this."

When her words ceased without the traditional end to the prayer, Lindsay knew that this would be an ongoing prayer for Barb. Just as it would be for her. Her thoughts went to her mom and Lucas and she hoped that they weren't too worried, but if this storm was as bad as it seemed, they had to be aware of what was going on. While she knew that Lucas would likely keep a calm head, she wasn't so sure about her mom. Even with the knowledge that Than was with her, this was something they hadn't anticipated.

As the ferocity of the wind and rain grew, the storm shutters rattled and the building shook. Lindsay stared at the darkened windows, wondering if the shutters would hold, or would they give way and allow the fierceness of the storm to reach them?

Lanterns cast flickering light through the room and out into the hallway. Suddenly, there was a crash and the building shuddered. There were shouts of alarm from people around her, but Lindsay couldn't get any sound past the tightness in her throat. Her heart pounded as she waited to see what would happen next.

Lindsay heard a male voice yell, "Was that the roof?"

The roof? She heard shouts back and forth out in the hallway. If the roof was gone, what next?

As she and Barb huddled together, Lindsay heard crying and looked to the bunk bed closest to them. The teenage girl was there, her head buried against her mother. She could only imagine how this experience must be for her. No doubt she was as out of her depth as Lindsay felt.

Lindsay closed her eyes, trying to figure out how to keep the fear at bay. It clawed at her in a way she'd never experienced before. She was used to being in control. Of not fearing anything that would come her way. This storm, however, was totally out of her control and that knowledge was doing a number on her. She tried to take steady breaths, but it was hard when she wanted to take huge gulps of air and cry at the same time.

What was happening to her? She rarely cried and when she did, it was never in front of anyone else. Even when she'd learned the news of Lincoln's death, she'd been able to control her emotions to be strong for her mom. She didn't recognize this version of herself...this weaker, more vulnerable version of Lindsay Hamilton. And she wasn't sure she liked it, particularly because Than was around to see it. But fear had gripped her in its clutches, and she couldn't seem to shake free from it long enough to get her defenses back into place.

She recognized the scent of his cologne before he even spoke her name, and Lindsay opened her eyes to see Than standing in front of her. Her gaze dropped to the bundle in his arms even as she reached out.

"I think she could use some attention." Than bent to place Maya in her arms. He cupped her chin once the baby was settled and said, "Everything is going to be okay. We're going to be safe."

Lindsay took another deep breath and let it out, trying to absorb the strength and confidence that Than had. She felt his thumb move across her jawline before releasing her.

Somehow Than's words along with the baby in her arms gave her the strength to gather herself together again, but those defenses she wanted...the hard shell she kept around herself remained elusive. Barb slipped an arm around her as she began to sing and soon the others in the room began to join in.

Amazing grace! How sweet the sound
That saved a wretch like me!
I once was lost, but now am found;
Was blind, but now I see.

'Twas grace that taught my heart to fear,
And grace my fears relieved;
How precious did that grace appear
The hour I first believed.

Through many dangers, toils, and snares,
I have already come;
'Tis grace hath brought me safe thus far,
And grace will lead me home.

When we've been there ten thousand years,
Bright shining as the sun,
We've no less days to sing God's praise
Than when we'd first begun.

It was a hymn that Lindsay knew so she was able to sing along. As the group moved on to other songs she didn't recognize, she just kept rocking the baby as the words soothed her. And in the midst of it all was the prayer.

Please, God, keep us safe. Protect all of us.

It was on a continual loop through her head because she was at a loss as to what else to pray for. It seemed as if she'd been stripped of everything in that moment, and she was left with nothing but the knowledge that only God could give her the peace and the strength to get through the hours and days ahead.

Than fought the urge to stay right at Lindsay's side, but he was trying to help the men as well as do a couple of other things that he'd set in motion before the storm had hit.

After a discussion with Mark and Elliot, he'd been given a list of contact information for all the missionaries who lived on the center, as well as the mission team. He'd forwarded that information on to his assistant as soon as he'd realized the direction of the storm with instructions to keep it with her even when she went home. Though he had the phone his uncle had given him, he knew it would be useless soon if not already. Knowing it was likely that the cell service would go down as soon as the typhoon hit, Than had made sure to charge the satellite phone he'd brought with him. Satellite phones were standard procedure for out-of-country jobs, so he'd brought one with him in case local service went down or if service wasn't available in the area they were in.

He, Mark and Elliot had decided to keep the presence of the satellite phone to themselves. The plan was for Than to phone BlackThorpe to give reports and then his assistant and others who were helping her would phone the contacts on the list to keep them updated. If they let one person speak to their family, they'd have to let everyone, and for now, it was more important that they be able to get through to give regular general updates until after the storm had passed through.

However, since Lucas was paying him, Than did take the time to call him directly with an update. He knew that Lindsay's mom was also very worried about her daughter since the storm was on the news back home. The current plan was to phone in a report every couple of hours unless it was deemed necessary to report sooner.

After giving his latest update, Than returned to the room where he'd left Lindsay with the baby. He hoped that his plan to give her the baby to hold and something to focus on besides the storm had worked. It seemed the crashes they'd heard had come from tree branches falling, but a quick check of the upper floor with Elliot had shown that the roof was still intact.

Two lanterns were strategically placed around the room, casting enough light for him to see where Lindsay sat. He stood watching as she bent over the baby in her arms. The initial attraction he'd felt for her was changing into something else. Something deeper. An admiration of the way she was adapting to their situation even though it was a struggle, and at the same time also allowing her vulnerabilities to show in a way he suspected she'd never allowed them to be seen before.

Slowly, he walked to where Lindsay and Barb sat and sank down beside them. Lindsay glanced up at him.

"Is everything okay?"

Though there were a million things going through his mind—most of them scenarios where things went bad—he simply said, "Yes."

He decided not to tell her that Lucas was pressuring him to get her out of there as soon as the storm ended. The Lindsay he'd known before this trip would likely have agreed with her brother, but over the course of the past three days, he'd begun to see some changes in her. Heck, he'd seen changes in *himself* over the past few days. Something told him that getting her away from here any sooner than she was ready to go would be more difficult than Lucas might have anticipated.

Than knew they were worried about her, but they needed to trust him. He wasn't going to let anything happen to her. Though he'd always known that he might be required to sacrifice life or limb in the course of a job, it was only with Lindsay that he could say that he'd gladly do that for her.

As he looked at Lindsay sitting beside him, Maya tucked up against her, Than found himself thinking about the future in ways he hadn't before. His mother had been pressuring him to settle down and give her more grandbabies for years, but Than had happily brushed aside her attempts—like the latest beauty queen—and kept himself focused firmly on the present.

Another crash drew Than's attention. He hoped that he hadn't been wrong in saying that this was the safest building for them. Using what he knew from analyzing situations for safety, he was still confident that it was the safest place, but storms like this one could be unpredictable. These weren't straight line winds coming in with the typhoon. The circular swirling of these winds could bring debris to them from any direction. Though he felt fairly confident that the cement structures would stand firm, he didn't hold as much hope for the roofs.

"How long do you think this will last?" Lindsay asked.

"It's hard to tell. Could be hours. It depends on how quickly the storm is moving. Now that it's hit land it might slow some, and it also might weaken."

"My arms are starting to shake," she said. "I didn't realize how heavy a small baby could get."

"Do you want to take her back to the others?"

"Yeah. She's sleeping so I think I could put her down." She slowly got to her feet.

"I'll come with you." Than stood and flicked on the flashlight he held.

Keeping it trained on the floor in front of them, he guided her to the room where they were keeping the other babies. There were no sounds of crying or fussing, so apparently Maya wasn't the only sleeping baby. One of the women showed Lindsay where she could lay her, and after placing Maya in the playpen, she shook out her arms.

"Boy, moms must get some serious muscles if they have to carry babies like that all the time," Lindsay commented as they left the room.

"My sister-in-law used a sling a lot of the time with hers. Just strapped them to her body and then her arms were still free to do other things."

"Well, that's pretty ingenious. I'll have to remember that."

And just like that, Than had an image in his mind that started with Lindsay pregnant and slid into one of her holding a baby—one with dark hair and eyes. It was startling, scary and attractive all at once. He rubbed at his chest as he tried to take a deep breath.

"Hey, Than, it sounds like it's dying down."

Than felt the band around his heart loosen as he spotted Elliot in the darkened hall. He paused to listen and realized that the man was right. The beating the elements had been giving the building seemed to be easing.

"Are you going to take a look outside?" Than asked him.

"I'd like to check what kind of damage is out there. Not that we can see a whole lot in the darkness."

"I'd like to see, too," Lindsay said.

Than's first instinct was to say no, but then he figured that as long as it had truly died down, it would be okay if she stayed close. "Okay. Just stick with me."

Mark joined them as they made their way to the main entrance of the building. It seemed that the storm was dying down as quickly as it had kicked up, but Than knew that this wasn't the end of it. If his guess was right, they were just in the eye of the storm and the back end of things was still to come.

Elliot opened the inside wooden door and peered out into the stormy night. When there wasn't an immediate gust of wind through the screen door, Elliot pushed that open as well. Soon the three beams from their flashlights were casting fingers of light in the pitch black night.

Than reached for Lindsay's hand as he stepped out of the building and onto the wet grass. "Stay close. I don't know what might be lying around."

Her hand momentarily tightened on his. "I will."

He swept his flashlight beam back and forth across the grass. There was still some wind and the lightest spray of rain, but definitely nothing like it had been. They quickly came upon large tree branches that had been ripped from their trunks. And it wasn't long before Elliot called out that he'd found some tin sheeting. One of the buildings had lost part of its roof, but, given the darkness, it was hard to know which one it was.

"More over here," Mark shouted.

Than pulled Lindsay closer to his side. "Watch for any more of that stuff. It could do nasty things to your legs."

While Mark and Elliot wandered further away from the dorm, Than edged along the front of it and around the corner to get a look at the back.

"Did any trees fall on the building?" Lindsay asked as she pressed against his arm.

"It doesn't look like it, but definitely some branches broke off and hit it."

"Is that what the crashes were?"

"Possibly. Given that the wind was going in circles essentially, they could also have been those sheets of tin hitting the dorm." He continued to wave the flashlight up and down the back of the building to see if there was any damage. Suddenly he felt Lindsay tense. "What's wrong?"

"What's that noise?"

Than listened and heard what had alarmed her. It sounded like a freight train was headed their way.

Her grip on his hand tightened almost painfully. "The wind is picking up again, too."

Than stepped back from the building and realized she was right. Round two was on its way. They'd barely cleared the corner of the building when the wind and rain started to lash out again. Than wrapped his arm around Lindsay's shoulders and together they ran for the front door. Elliot and Mark were right on their heels.

"Guess that was the eye of the storm," Mark remarked as Elliot secured the heavy wooden door behind them. "I will be very glad when this is finally over."

"That makes a few—or most likely, all—of us," Elliot said as he ran a hand through his damp hair.

"I'm going to get dried off," Lindsay said. "That was an unexpected shower."

When she moved out from under his arm, Than tried not to think of how good she'd felt there. He looked at his watch and did a little calculating. "I guess I'll send another update to let them know we're still doing okay."

As he turned from the men, Than felt a hand on his arm. When he glanced back, he saw it was Mark. He angled toward him to see what he wanted.

"I just want to thank you, Than, for all you've done on this trip so far. When Lucas came to talk to me about needing to have you come with Lindsay, I had my doubts. But you've been an answer to a prayer we didn't even know we should be praying. I know that you're here to protect Lindsay first and foremost, but I appreciate that you've extended that care to all of us with what you've done."

Than swallowed hard. He'd never been told he was an answer to prayer before. It took him off guard and left him at a loss for words...momentarily. "I'm glad I've been able to help out and have had the resources to do what I can." He cleared his throat. "I'll just go upstairs to make the call to my assistant."

As he climbed the stairs to the second floor, Than gave his head a shake. He was being bombarded by emotions he had never felt before. At that moment, he just wanted everything to stop so he could process it all. He needed a quiet room to allow him to work through the things he was feeling for Lindsay, and the new awareness he had of God and the faith of these missionaries and workers at the center.

11

INSTEAD, Than went into the room that had been his before they'd all moved downstairs. He ran the flashlight over the outside wall and the windows to make sure it was still secure before sitting down on the bed and pulling the satellite phone from one of the pockets of his shorts.

It wasn't long before the connection was made and his assistant picked up. He figured it was around noon there, so he was glad he'd caught her before she left for lunch.

"It's Than," he said when she answered.

"Than! Is everything okay there? We're hearing reports that it's pretty bad where it came on land. The storm surge has done significant damage. Are you in that area?"

"No. We're inland so we won't have to worry about the storm surge, plus the center where we're staying is up on a hill. I don't doubt that there will be flooding in the surrounding towns just by virtue of how much rain we're getting."

"That's good that you're safe. Is that the report you want me to pass on?"

Than rubbed his forehead. "Not the part about the flooding in surrounding areas. Basically, we've just had the eye pass over us so we're on the back edge of the storm. The power has gone out, but we've had lanterns for light. We have plenty of food and water and will likely try the generator once the storm has finally passed."

"Okay, I've made note and will begin to call." He heard a muffled sound and then she said, "Eric wants to talk with you. I'll transfer you."

Than waited for Eric to come on the line.

"You doing okay, man?"

"It's certainly turned into a more eventful job than I had originally anticipated."

"How are you faring with the storm? Brooke said Sylvia is going a bit nuts about all of this."

"Lindsay is doing just fine. She's a real trooper and has been taking it all in stride. We're in a safe building with plenty of water and food. There is some damage to the buildings around us, but the one we're in is very sturdy." Than paused. "One thing maybe you can help me with. Lucas is making noises about getting Lindsay out of here as soon as possible. If that's what Lindsay wants, I'll do that, but I'm not entirely sure that it is. It would be helpful if you could sort of prepare Lucas for that."

"Seriously? You think she wants to stick around after all of this?"

Than thought back to seeing Lindsay with Maya cuddled close. "Yes, I think she actually might. She's changed a bit since we've gotten here. We both have, actually."

There was silence on Eric's end, making Than wonder if they'd lost their connection.

"It sounds like a conversation is in order once you get home," Eric finally said. "Lucas was just saying earlier today that he could definitely see God's hand in how you ended up being over there with Lindsay. We're all praying for you. Let me know if there's anything more we can do on this end."

Than pondered the second reference to God being involved in his being there. "I will. I'd better get back downstairs. The storm is kicking up again. It almost sounds worse than earlier. We've probably got a couple of hours to go yet."

"Take care, bro. Look forward to seeing you both back on this side of the pond."

Than ended the call and sat for a moment with the phone in his hands, his head bent. At that moment, he felt an incredible weight on his shoulders. Not just the weight to keep Lindsay safe, but to somehow fulfill some mission that people seemed to feel God had sent him for. Never had the fear of failure weighed so heavily on him.

He'd set out on this trip with just two goals. To bring Lindsay Hamilton safely home. And to get her to see him as more than just a flirting ladies' man. Now he had the responsibility for the forty or so people on the center and was feeling like he just couldn't do it on his own.

Please, God. If You did, in fact, send me here for this, help me. Don't let me miss anything that might make someone get hurt. I don't know if I can do this.

It was almost like he'd stepped outside of his body and someone else had taken it over. He had never been one to feel overwhelmed by a job. He'd never questioned his ability to do what needed to be done. And he'd certainly never felt the need to call out to God for help. He'd had the best training, as had all BlackThorpe employees. He should be taking all of this in stride, but instead he was worried because, for the first time, he was responsible for the safety of someone who had found their way past his defenses into his heart.

He just knew he would never be able to live with himself if something happened to Lindsay.

When Lindsay had gone to the room where her bag was, she'd found that Barb and Amanda were both there lying down. She was exhausted, too. It had been a long day, but she wasn't sure she'd be able to sleep until the storm had calmed. Still, she grabbed her toiletries and a towel and some clothes and went to the bathroom which was illuminated by a single lantern. It was the men's bathroom, but they were all using it. She went into one of the stalls and closed and latched the door before quickly changing out of her clothes into a pair of capris leggings and a loose T-shirt.

Once done with the toilet, she cleaned up at the sink and pulled her damp hair back into a ponytail. She scrubbed her face and brushed her teeth using some of the water from the bottle she'd brought with her. As she made her way back to the room, she met Than in the hallway.

"Are you going to lie down?" he asked.

"Yes. Though not sure I'm going to sleep. That storm is raging pretty good." She looked at him. "Are you going to?"

He shook his head. "I won't be sleeping until things have calmed down. Why don't you lie down with your headphones and see if you can get some sleep? If something comes up, I will make sure to wake you."

"Are you sure?"

"That's what I'm here for, sweetheart."

Sweetheart? That was a new one.

As silence stretched between them, Lindsay felt warmth engulf her. Afraid that the silence was giving more significance to something that was undoubtedly a slip of the tongue on his part, Lindsay swallowed and said, "Okay. I think I will see if I can sleep for a bit."

Without waiting for him to respond, she walked into the room and over to the bunk bed where their things were. Since he wasn't going to rest, she decided she'd take the lower bunk and hopefully by the time he decided to sleep, they'd be back in their rooms on the second floor. She fished her iPhone out of her purse and found the earbuds in the outside pocket of the bag.

Though she had no cell service or internet, she still had her playlists and a full charge so she slipped the earbuds in, found the songs she wanted and curled up on the mattress. Surprisingly, she found herself relaxing. She supposed part of that was because she had seen with her own eyes that the building had survived the first half of the storm. It had helped to reassure her that they were in a relatively safe place.

But if she was totally honest with herself, the main reason she felt secure enough to relax was because she trusted Than. He'd said he'd wake her if she was in danger and she believed him. Four days ago she might not have, but right then, in the midst of the worst storm she'd ever encountered, she did.

In the early morning hours, the storm finally began to calm. Than had spent some of the time on a chair in the hallway outside where Lindsay slept. He'd called in two additional updates and after the storm had died down enough for him to go outside with Mark and Elliot for another walk around, he called in his final one for the storm.

"Everyone has been telling my assistant to assure you of their prayers for our safety," Than said after that last call.

"I think we've definitely felt them," Elliot said as he rubbed a hand over his face. "And I know Mark has thanked you already but let me thank you as well for everything you've done to help us out."

"I will say that this job is not going to be one I forget anytime soon," Than said with a weary laugh. And not just because of the storm.

"Yes, this has been one of the more exciting mission trips we've been on," Mark agreed. "Well, I think we should try to grab a few hours of sleep before we tackle what's out there tomorrow."

"Good idea," Elliot said. "I will be taking a group into town in the morning. We have some people we need to check up on. I'm not sure what we'll find, but if anyone on the team wants to come with us, I'm sure there will be plenty of work to do."

Than hoped that Lindsay wouldn't want to be one of those people, but something told him she probably would. In the meantime, he had to get a little sleep so he had the energy to do what needed doing in the days ahead.

Moving quietly into the room, he removed the holster from his waist and slid it under the pillow of the top bunk. Now that the storm had passed them, the adrenalin that had been feeding him slowly ebbed away. Lindsay was safe. As were the rest of the people in the building. It was time for him to get some rest to replenish his energy.

He could see the shape of Lindsay as she lay on her side. The sheet that covered her was just up to her waist and he could see that she had done what he planned to do—sleep with his clothes on. Hopefully, they'd be able to move back to their rooms the next night, but for now, Than figured he was so tired he could sleep pretty much anywhere.

Moving slowly so as not to jostle the bed, he climbed to the top bunk and crawled onto the mattress. He preferred to lie on his stomach to sleep, but this upper bed had some rails around it that made it kind of difficult. Instead, he had to lie on his side and bend his legs at the knees in order to fit.

Just before he drifted off, Than found himself whispering a prayer of thanks that they'd made it through the storm with no injuries.

Lindsay shifted on the mattress and slowly opened her eyes. The room was shadowed and stuffy because the windows were still covered, and it took her minute to orientate herself. She pulled the earbuds out of her ears—a bit surprised they were still there—and pushed herself up into a sitting position, swinging her feet over the edge of the bed. She lifted one shoulder and then the other, trying to stretch out the kinks in her torso. It seemed that she hadn't moved the whole time she'd slept, and her body was not happy about it.

She noticed that the beds across from her were all empty, so the others were obviously up already. It made her feel a bit like a slug that they were all up and about, and she'd been sleeping like she had nothing better to do. Although she wasn't altogether sure what she would be doing. The storm had certainly changed the immediate plans of the group. Something told her that new paint was now the least of the missionaries' concerns. She had no doubt that in the cold light of day, the damage revealed would be so much worse than what they'd seen briefly when they'd ventured out in the eye of the storm.

Knowing that hanging around her bed wouldn't accomplish anything, Lindsay stood up and ran her hands over her hair. She pulled out the scrunchy and gathered the loose ends that had escaped while she slept and secured it all into a ponytail once again. She turned to gather up her iPod and earbuds but stilled when she noticed a figure lying on the top bunk. Though she couldn't see clearly in the dimly lit room, Lindsay was sure it was Than. His bag had been next to hers on the floor when they'd had to move rooms.

Certain that he hadn't gotten as much sleep as she had, Lindsay decided not to try to riffle through her suitcase for clothes to wear. Instead, she quietly wheeled her bag out of the room and down the hall to the bathroom. She poked her head inside to see if any men were there, but it was only the mother and daughter from the mission team. Lindsay was glad to see a smile on the girl's face this morning after hearing her crying the night before.

They'd already opened the storm shutters in that room as it was flooded with natural light. The abundance of light seemed to indicate that the storm had passed.

"Good morning, Lindsay," the woman said with a smile. "Did you get some sleep?"

"Yes. Although I'm not sure how much. I'm still a bit out of whack with the time here."

"I hear you. I'm constantly asking my husband the time."

"Speaking of which, do you happen to know what time it is?"

"I think it's close to six."

"Thanks," Lindsay said as she lifted her suitcase up on the counter to look through it for clothes. "Have you been outside yet?"

The woman shook her head. "I'm a little scared to see what's out there, to be honest. I've never been in the midst of a storm that packed such a punch. I can't imagine the damage it's done."

Lindsay nodded, pulling out a pair of black cotton capris and a hot pink T-shirt. "Neither have I. And to be perfectly frank, I hope I never am again."

"Me, too," the teenager agreed.

"There's some breakfast in the room we ate in last night. Now that that's all over, I think I have an appetite once again," the woman said as she zipped up her toiletries bag and tucked it under her arm. "See you in a few."

Lindsay went into one of the stalls and quickly changed out of the clothes she'd slept in. When she stepped to the sink to wash her hands, she caught a glimpse of herself in the large mirror on the wall. She definitely looked the worse for wear and didn't have her full kit of makeup to rectify the situation.

At that thought, she scowled. Where on earth was her mind? And how screwed up were her priorities? A storm had just ripped through a country where poverty was a way of life for so many. There were no doubt people wondering how to feed their children this morning, and she was worried about makeup?

As she stared at her reflection, Lindsay knew that this was one more important shift that needed to happen in her life. For too long she'd worn her clothes and makeup as a shield. She portrayed to the world what she wanted them to see. The person she was when it was just those she loved and trusted was the one she kept hidden from the world. It wasn't that she thought they wouldn't accept her, but it was more about her sharing that person with people who—in her mind—hadn't earned the right to come into that part of her life. She compartmentalized her life quite well when it came to business and even church versus her family and close friends. Too well.

Her thoughts went to Than. He'd had glimpses of that side of her life already, even though it wasn't because she'd wanted him to. Today though, she would make that conscious choice. And even though she'd only brought along a little bit of makeup, Lindsay made the decision to let even that go.

Before she could change her mind, she switched on the tap and splashed cold water on her face. Using her towel, she patted it dry and then put on the moisturizer with SPF in it just in case they were going to be outside later. She might be forgoing the makeup, but she didn't need the agony of a sunburn on her face to distract her either.

After running a quick brush through her hair, she pulled it back once again and then began to return her things to her suitcase. As she headed back to the room, Lindsay was surprised she didn't feel more tired after the events of the past night. She was thankful that she'd managed to get some sleep and hoped that her energy levels would stay up as they dealt with the aftermath.

As she stepped into the room, Lindsay immediately noticed that it was no longer shadowed by the storm shutters. Her gaze went in the direction of the bunk bed where Than had been sleeping earlier, but it was empty. She spotted him bent over his suitcase that was open on the bed she'd slept on. As she approached, he straightened. His expression was indecipherable as his gaze went from the top of her head to her feet and then met hers.

"Did you get enough sleep?" he asked, his voice gravelly. The five o'clock shadow he usually sported looked a bit heavier than usual, almost heading in the direction of a full beard.

Lindsay nodded. "More than you got, I'm sure."

"I'm fine. This isn't the first job where I haven't gotten my eight hours of beauty sleep."

She tilted her head as she took in the dark smudges beneath his eyes. "I'm sorry you got dragged into this. It was supposed to have been an easy gig for you."

Than's eyes narrowed briefly. "Why are you apologizing? None of this was your fault. I doubt even a Hamilton can control the weather."

Lindsay shrugged. "That's true. But still."

"But nothing. I've now been told by three people that they think God brought me here, so who am I to argue with that?"

As she took in his words, Lindsay realized that she felt the same way. She may have balked at having him come along initially, but once things began to unfold the way they had, she had been very grateful that he'd been there. "No, it's not a good idea to argue with God."

A smile lifted the corner of Than's mouth. "Listen, let me get cleaned up and then we'll see what's on the agenda for today. I'm pretty sure it will have very little to do with painting. I also need to talk to you about a couple other things that have come up."

Lindsay nodded. "Okay. Someone said there's breakfast, so I'm going to go see if I can find some coffee." She gestured to her suitcase. "Should I just leave this here? Or are we able to go back to our rooms upstairs?"

Than ran a hand through his hair making it stand out in all directions. "I'm not sure. I think they'll want to make sure there's no damage to the roof before they allow people back up there."

"I'll just leave it here then." She pulled it to the end of the bed and snapped the handle down. As she straightened, she found Than's gaze on her face. "What?"

"You look different."

And just like that, her resolve to go on without her mask began to slip away. She grasped onto it and squared her shoulders. Looking him straight in the eye, Lindsay said, "No makeup."

A full on smile spread across Than's face. "I like it."

Lindsay was pretty sure her eyebrows shot up nearly into her hairline, but then she remembered that Than was all about making women feel good. Of course, he'd tell her he liked it. Anything else would have made her feel bad. Telling herself that it really didn't matter, she just gave him a quick smile. "I'm going to find that breakfast. Or at least some coffee."

"Save some for me." Than's voice followed her out of the room.

Once in the hall, Lindsay stopped and looked back at the doorway. Had any of that exchange violated the *no flirting* wager? Probably. But then she realized that she didn't really care about that anymore.

Not wanting to be caught loitering, Lindsay continued in search of caffeine and sustenance of some sort. When the aroma of coffee greeted her, she knew her caffeine search would be successful. Hopefully, there would be food of some nature, too. If not, she would eat some of the protein bars she'd brought.

As she stepped into the room, she spotted Barb sitting at a table with a mug in her hands. The woman smiled as she joined her.

"Is that coffee?" Lindsay asked.

"You bet." Barb gestured with her head to the other end of the room. "And they've got some fruit and bread, too."

Lindsay greeted the others who were at the table. One of the kitchen workers handed her a cup of coffee and then gestured to where the sugar and powdered creamer sat. Though she usually didn't use anything but liquid cream in her coffee, she wasn't going to be fussy about it this time around. There was an assortment of fruit on a large plate and a basket held more of the buns she liked.

Grateful for anything to stave off the hunger pangs in her stomach, Lindsay placed a banana and some pineapple on the plate they handed her and then took one of the *pan de sal*. After she had settled down in the seat next to Barb, Lindsay lifted the cup of coffee and closed her eyes as the first hot sip slid down her throat.

For just that moment, she could imagine she was sitting at the desk in her office having her second cup of coffee of the day. She always had her first cup while getting ready for work. She even had a Keurig machine in her suite of rooms at the mansion.

Her eyes popped open at the memory. She hadn't really thought it was a luxury when she'd bought it, but suddenly it seemed like a huge extravagance.

Setting the cup down on the table, Lindsay picked up the banana and peeled it but then paused to say a prayer of thanks for the food and for safety through the night. That first bite of the banana was near to perfection for her. And her stomach growled in appreciation as well.

Lindsay glanced over at Barb. "Did you eat already?"

She nodded. "And I'm on my second cup of coffee. I have a feeling I'm going to need the jolt today."

"Have you been outside?"

"Yes. But I just stood on the porch. Didn't venture out too far."

Lindsay lowered the banana to her plate. "How bad is it?"

"No doubt better than it could have been if the buildings hadn't been as sturdy and the windows hadn't been covered by those shutters. Lots of branches all around."

"I wonder how bad the town we came through is."

Barb shrugged. "I imagine that it's in worse shape. We didn't get flooding, but they may have with the amount of rain that came down."

Than appeared in the doorway, and Lindsay watched him as he walked to the table where the breakfast food waited. He'd changed into a pair of jeans and a white T-shirt. She realized he was armed when she spotted the noticeable bulge in the small of his back.

"I've heard nothing but praise for your young man," Barb said.

Lindsay glanced over at her. "You know he's not my young man."

Barb just smiled as she lifted her cup to her lips.

Without looking in Than's direction again, Lindsay picked up the banana and finished it in two bites. As she moved onto the pineapple, she let her gaze take in the rest of the people in the room. It looked like all the team members were there and a couple of the missionaries as well. She was sure that they were wondering about what lay ahead for them like she was.

She remembered that Than had said he'd needed to talk to her about a couple of things, and Lindsay had a funny feeling she knew what at least one of them was. And if he thought she was going to pack it in and head for home, he had another thing coming. She suspected he already knew that—he wasn't a stranger to her sticking to her guns on something—but she was pretty sure he had to at least present her with the opportunity.

"Morning, Barb."

12

LINDSAY looked up to see Than take a seat across from them. Her eyes widened briefly as she took in his appearance. She tried to remember if she'd ever seen Than with a completely bare face. It seemed that he had cultivated the ultimate five o'clock shadow because he'd always had a bit of scruff on his face whenever she'd seen him.

Obviously reading her reaction correctly, Than rubbed a hand across his chin. "It was either this or tracking down a weed whacker by tonight."

Barb chuckled. "You remind me of my husband with that. If he went more than a couple of days without shaving, it was already looking like a full-fledged beard."

Than nodded as he peeled a banana. "And with the heat that's likely to come, it would be more of a nuisance."

Barb continued to chat with Than as he ate, but before he had finished, Mark joined them.

"Did you manage to get some rest?" Mark asked as he swung a chair around and sat down, leaning his arms on the back of it.

Than nodded. "You?"

"More than I thought I would, but now the harsh reality is kinda setting in."

Again Than nodded. "What's on the schedule for today?"

Mark looked at Barb. "Actually, I'm hoping that you'll do us a favor, Barb."

The older woman's brows drew together. "What's that?"

"Elliot is going to take a group down into the town to check on some people and see what happened there overnight. I know you have medical training, and I wonder if you'd be willing to go with him in case there are situations where help is needed."

Barb nodded. "I can do that. Would I be able to look over the supplies you have in the clinic before we go?"

"I'll have Mel take you over there now if you'd like. There is usually a doctor who comes in a couple days a week and a nurse who is at the clinic full time. With school out, however, the doctor doesn't come around as much, but the nurse is here and she's coming, too."

As Barb stood, she laid a hand on Lindsay's shoulder. "See you later."

Lindsay watched her friend walk away and then met Than's gaze. "What are we going to do?"

"Well, first of all, before you commit to doing anything, you need to know that your brother is adamant about you returning home as soon as it's possible to get you out of here. He's almost to the point where he's prepared to round up a helicopter himself to fly in here and get you."

Lindsay scowled. "That's not what I want. I need to stay here. I am here for a reason—just like you are. I'm not going anywhere. Besides, how do you know he wants to do this?"

"I have a satellite phone that I've been using to keep in contact with the office and your family during the storm."

"Really? Why didn't you say anything?"

"We decided to keep the presence of the phone a secret because we couldn't have everyone trying to call their families." Than went on to explain about a list of contact information and how he'd called his assistant with updates. "But I think you're going to need to be the one to tell Lucas you do not want to go along with his plan. He might think I have an ulterior motive for trying to get you to stay here."

Lindsay arched a brow but then nodded. "I can do that. And I also want to go down into the town with Barb."

Than stared at her, his gaze serious. "Are you sure? We have no idea what we'll find down there."

"I'm sure. I came here to help, and I think that means I need to be where help is needed most. And I don't think that's up here."

"First, you call and talk to your brother. I'll chat with Mark about us going with Elliot. But if we do go, you need to change into jeans and shoes with a good sole on them. I don't want you getting your legs or feet cut up by debris that might be down there." Than took one last swallow from his cup. "Let's go back to the room, and I'll let you make the call from there while I talk to Mark."

But before they could get to their feet, Elliot walked into the room and greeted those there.

"I want to update you all on how things stand this morning." He pulled off the ball cap he wore and ran a hand through his hair before replacing it. "First of all, it could have been so much worse, so for that, I'm very grateful. However, the reality is that we did sustain damage and some of it is significant. There is a portion of roof blown off two buildings. The second level of the school has quite a bit of damage to the floor and the furniture that were on that end of the building where the roof is gone. The same is true for the dining room. Thankfully, the kitchen is basically still intact.

"The power went out so we've fired up the generator we have. At the moment, it is just powering the appliances in the kitchen. We need to check the lines to see if we can go ahead and power up the rest of the center. The branches that were blown down may have done damage to those lines.

"For now it is safe to go back upstairs to your originally assigned rooms. You should be able to take showers though they may be with cold water for the time being. Also, don't drink water from any of the taps. We will provide bottled water as long as we can, but eventually we will have to move to boiled water. Food-wise, the meals will be a bit simpler from here on out. We may not have much in the way of fresh fruit until we can see what's happened to the town below." Elliot looked over to where Lindsay and Than sat. "One final thing. I know several of you have asked about making contact with your families back in the U.S. At the moment, cell service seems to be unavailable, most likely due to a lot of people trying to use the network. However, we have had access to a satellite phone during the storm. Than Miller, who works for BlackThorpe Security, forwarded a list of all of your contact information to his assistant before the storm hit, just in case. Throughout the duration of the storm, he phoned his assistant and gave her updates. She in turn passed those updates on to everyone on that contact list. Your families are all aware that the storm has passed, and we are all safe."

There was a round of applause through the room, and Lindsay glanced at Than in time to see him dip his head but otherwise give no acknowledgment for the appreciation of what he'd done.

"I realize that some of you might want to utilize the phone, but I am asking that unless it's a dire emergency, you hold off for now. We appreciate all that Than has done for us already, so for now we're asking that you allow us to keep the phone free for emergencies. He will continue to phone in an update at least once a day unless more is warranted."

"We will be putting you to work helping to get the center cleaned up instead of the painting and repair we'd originally planned on. There will be a group going into town to check out the situation there. Lunch will be ready around noon, and we'll re-evaluate the situation then."

Once Elliot had finished his update, people began to get up and return their dishes to the table. Lindsay watched as a few headed in their direction and braced herself for them to plead their case with Than about how it was an emergency that he let them contact their families.

She was pleasantly surprised when each of them just expressed their thanks at having passed on the updates to their family. Once they'd gone, Than got to his feet and gathered up his mug and plate. Lindsay followed him to take their dirty dishes to the table.

Back in the room where they'd slept, he dialed Lucas's number and handed her the phone. "I'm going to take our bags back up to our rooms."

Left alone to deal with her big brother, Lindsay sank down on the bed with the phone pressed to her ear.

"Than?"

She wished. Lindsay sighed and then said, "No, Luc, it's me."

"Lindsay! It's so good to hear your voice. How are you doing?"

"I'm doing really well and probably better than a whole lot of people who went through the storm last night."

There was a pause on the other end, and Lindsay figured Lucas was gearing up for his demand. "Listen, Linds, I think it would be best if you came home as soon as possible."

"Why's that?"

"It can't be safe there now, Lindsay. This is a completely different ball game than what you signed up for."

"First of all, it's not safe for a lot of people here, Lucas, and the majority of them have nowhere to go. Why should I skip out early because of that? Than is here and is taking care of me and yes, I'm listening to what he tells me to do and not arguing with him."

"Is he saying you should come home?"

"He didn't express an opinion on that either way, but it wouldn't matter if he did. I'm staying. If he wants to leave, he's more than welcome to."

"Lindsay, please, this isn't what you were supposed to be involved in when you agreed to go."

"Are you saying God didn't know what was going to happen? I felt at peace about coming here, and if God gave me that peace, I can only believe that this is where He wants me to be, regardless of the storm that just ripped through."

She heard Lucas sigh and could almost picture him with his head bent, running his hand through his hair. He'd assumed that position more than once over the years when he'd been frustrated by her determination to buck what he wanted her to do. "Mom is really worried."

"I'm sure that's true. If need be, I'll speak with her, but I'm not—repeat *not*—coming home yet. I'm staying with the team. However, if the decision is made as a group to leave early, I will do that, but I'm not leaving them just because circumstances have changed a bit."

"A *bit*, Lindsay? You're definitely the master of understatement these days." Lucas sighed. "Fine. I'll plead your case with Mom, but if at any time Than feels your safety is compromised by being there, you're out. I don't care if he has to knock you out and carry you over his shoulder, you will be extricated."

"I already told you that I'm being a good girl and doing what Than tells me when it comes to safety. Ask him. I haven't rebelled against anything he's told me to do."

"I just hope Than remembers who's paying him, and he doesn't get swayed by wanting to please you."

Lindsay laughed. "No worries about that. I'm pretty sure he takes his job very seriously, and if it comes down to pleasing me or keeping me safe, I think safety will trump everything else."

"Well, I'm glad to hear that."

"Listen, I don't want to tie this up. We're getting ready to tackle some of the damage around here. I'm sure Than will call you later to keep you updated."

"Okay. Stay safe. I swear you're giving me more gray hair..."

Lindsay grinned. "Love you, Lucas. Give Mom a hug and kiss from me."

After the call had ended, Lindsay went looking for Than and her suitcase so she could change into jeans. When they joined the others at the vehicle they would be taking into the town, Lindsay noticed that everyone else was dressed similarly.

"Here." Than handed her a gray ball cap with a BlackThorpe Security logo on the front. "It will help to keep the heat off your head."

Though she normally hated hats, Lindsay took it and threaded her ponytail through the opening at the back and settled it on her head. He was wearing a similar one, she noticed.

"Let's load up," Elliot said.

In addition to her, Than and Barb, two of the single guys from the mission team had joined them. There was also a young Filipino woman and two Filipino men. The vehicle they climbed into wasn't like anything she'd seen before. The front was just a bench seat for the driver and two passengers. In the back, there were two long seats facing each other. Though there was a roof over the back, there were no windows, just wide open space.

She climbed up into the back and slid onto the seat. Once everyone was loaded, she found herself sandwiched between Barb and Than. The two Filipino men hung on the back of the vehicle instead of coming inside with the rest of them though there was room.

"Hold onto that," Than said, gesturing to a metal pole that was suspended horizontally from the ceiling.

The vehicle jerked forward, and Lindsay quickly realized she needed to be holding onto it so she didn't slide all over the place or end up on the floor. As it was, when the vehicle gained some speed, she slid across the smooth vinyl seat right into Than. He'd stretched his arm across the back of the seat behind her and Barb so she found herself pressed against his side.

"Sorry," Lindsay said with a glance over her shoulder at him as she used her grip on the pole to put some distance between them once again.

He was wearing sunglasses so she couldn't see his eyes, but he only nodded and then looked back out the side of the vehicle. As they swerved and lurched, bounced and jolted along, Lindsay realized that Elliot was trying to avoid the larger branches that lay on the road while having to drive over some of the smaller one. She figured that by the time they got down the mountain, her arm was going to have cramped from trying to keep from sliding all over the place.

After what seemed like the hundredth time she'd slid into Than and then tried to move away from him, she felt his hand on her shoulder as he said, "Lindsay. Relax. I'm not reading anything into this, okay? And I won't bite or take advantage of the situation. Just relax."

At her nod, his hand left her shoulder and the next time she slid into him, she just stayed there. He might not bite or plan to take advantage of the situation, but in reality, the distance had been for her sake, not his. She found herself relying on—and, to be honest, appreciating—his strength a little too much these days.

Suddenly, the vehicle came to an abrupt halt. This time she slid into Barb with Than right behind her.

"Sorry about that, Barb," Lindsay said as she tried to move back from the woman.

Barb smiled. "No harm done."

She heard Elliot and the Filipino men talking loudly in their language. Than left his seat and got out, and even though she was tempted to follow him, Lindsay decided to stay put. After her conversation with Lucas earlier, Lindsay realized that in a sense, her chance to remain with the team hinged largely on Than. If she put herself in danger or did something stupid, he could pull the plug on this and it would all be over.

While she didn't like to be told what to do, Lindsay also knew that on this trip, in particular, ignoring common sense just to spite Than and Lucas would definitely not be in her best interest. Thankfully, Than obviously knew she would be dying to know what was going on and as he walked from the back of the vehicle toward the front, he paused and said, "There's a tree down on the road. We're going to see if we can cut it up and move it. Stay put."

She bristled at the sharp command but didn't go against it. The sudden roar of a motor prevented any conversation. She realized quickly that Elliot must have anticipated coming across fallen trees since it sounded like they were using a chainsaw to cut the tree up. Shifting on her seat, she looked through the opening between the back and front seat and through the windshield to see the guys moving around a large tree that lay in front of the vehicle.

With the six men working, it didn't seem to take too long to get it cleared off the road enough so they could get through. She wondered how many more fallen trees they'd run into on the trip down the hill.

Than followed the two team guys back into the vehicle and slid onto the seat beside her. She noticed a sheen of sweat on his upper lip and a drop ran down his cheek. He pulled his ball cap off and lifted his arm to rub his upper arm against his forehead, using the T-shirt sleeve to absorb the sweat there.

After making another stop for another downed tree a little further along the road, Lindsay realized that Than was pulling a lot more than just bodyguard duty on this trip. He'd stepped up time and again without complaint and did what needed to be done. Up until this trip, she'd only seen him in suits or lounging around with her brother. He hadn't struck her as being a particularly hard worker before, but each day on this trip he was showing her differently.

Than watched out the front window as the vehicle made the final turns before reaching the road that led straight into town. His gut twisted at the thought of what was to come. Though he'd never experienced the aftermath of a typhoon of this size personally, he'd closely followed past storms that had ravaged the Philippines. The family connection to the country meant that he had a vested interest in what happened here.

He'd watched countless hours of footage after the last big typhoon had ripped through the Philippines south of Manila. Every time he'd stopped by his parents' place they'd had the television on the Asian channel they got through some cable package they had. He couldn't have avoided it even if he'd wanted to. The only thing that made this current situation a bit better was that this particular town hadn't had to deal with a storm surge. That seemed to be one of the more dangerous aspects of most typhoons. He hadn't been able to find out yet if something similar had happened when this typhoon had made landfall.

For now he was focused on what he could do here to help. And to keep Lindsay safe. He glanced down at her as she sat closer to him than he figured she was comfortable with, but she'd given up trying to fight the slip and slide the vehicle kept making them do as it jerked and bounced on the road.

He had thought about making her stay at the center, but then he would have had to stick with her since that was his job. However, he really wanted—needed—to see how the town had fared and to help where he could. And he figured maybe it would be something Lindsay needed to see as well. She'd come on this trip for an experience and so far she was getting one. Than just hoped she was up for what lay ahead. He wasn't sure *he* was, even though he had a pretty good idea of what they'd find when they got there.

As they neared the edge of town, Than could already see some of the destruction with more downed trees and branches strewn across the street ahead. Elliot pulled the vehicle off to the side of the road and stopped. After turning off the engine, he swung around in his seat to face them through the window between the front seat and the back. He rested an arm on the opening.

"I'd like to say a word of prayer before we head in there." There was a murmuring of agreement, and Than pulled the hat from his head just as Elliot began to pray. "Heavenly Father, we are so thankful that we can be here today. That You brought us safely through the storm. We pray that You will go before us as we head into town to see how we can help those who were more deeply affected by the storm. Guide us, we pray. And we pray for continued safety as we help those here. In Jesus' name."

All those around Than joined in with an *Amen*.

"We'll start out together," Elliot explained, "but may have to split up at some point. We'll meet back here around noon to see how things are going. That's about four hours from now. Should give us enough time to evaluate the situation."

As they piled out of the back, Than grasped Lindsay's arm. "Please stick close by. Don't go wandering off because we just don't know what the situation will be like."

Lindsay's gaze went to the town and then back to him. "I'll stick close by."

As a group, they followed Elliot back out onto the road and headed toward the edge of town. He hadn't parked far from it so within five minutes they'd reached the first of the residential houses. Right away Than could see that the buildings that were made from the cinder blocks seemed to have sustained little to no damage—just like the ones on the mission center. However, the ones made with wood had definitely been impacted by the strong winds and rain.

Elliot and the two Filipino men approached first one house and then another to enquire about the well-being of the inhabitants. Than was beginning to feel more hopeful as each house revealed families who were safe and though without power were doing okay. It was so very different from the pictures he'd seen after the other typhoon.

Lindsay stuck close as he'd requested, but she seemed to fall into step more with Barb than with him. He had a hard time reading her thoughts this morning. The openness she'd had with him the past couple of days wasn't present anymore. She kept a stoic expression on her face as they moved from house to house. Something told him she was storing everything up inside to process later. He understood that. His job required him to push forward and leave his reactions and emotions to be dealt with later. And he was glad she had forged a friendship with Barb. Hopefully if those emotions got the better of her, she'd have someone to turn to, because he was pretty sure she wouldn't be turning to him.

13

LINDSAY watched as an elderly woman came to the door of the house Elliot had just approached, calling out a greeting. The man lifted the woman's hand to his forehead and then proceeded to speak with her in her language. Lindsay looked around as she had at each house they'd stopped at so far.

Even without significant storm damage, she had a hard time taking in the living conditions. So far most the houses could have fit into her suite of rooms at the mansion with room to spare. They were simple houses—some cinder block, some wooden structures—with small yards that had been pounded through the night. Such a simple way of living and yet none of the people they'd met so far seemed to be depressed or angry about their circumstances. In fact, the opposite seemed to be true. The houses' occupants greeted them with wide friendly smiles.

At the last place they'd stopped, the woman had brought out a tin of cookies and had offered some to them. Lindsay had wanted to decline, but Than had whispered that the woman would be hurt if she refused her generosity. They had so little and yet what they had, they still offered to share.

"She said that she thinks part of the tree fell on the back of their house," Elliot said as he turned from the woman. "Let's go check it out and see if we can help move it."

As the men went around the side of the small building, Lindsay heard a child's voice and turned to see a young boy scampering in their direction. He was talking but, of course, she couldn't understand a word he said. Thankfully, the nurse with them did, and she dropped to her knees in front of him and listened as he talked, large tears falling down his cheeks.

Lindsay's heart clenched, wondering what could be causing this boy so much distress. She didn't have to wait long to find out because the nurse quickly straightened and said, "He said he thinks his mother is having a baby. They are alone because his father went to Manila to work."

"We'll go check her out," Barb said without hesitation. She looked at Lindsay. "Tell Than to come with us."

Lindsay ran around the corner of the house and immediately spotted Than lifting a large branch off to the side of the small yard. The chainsaw had started up and was deafening. She cupped her hands around her mouth and yelled for him.

He glanced up and dropped the branch to jog toward her when she motioned to him. She took him by the arm to the front of the house so they could talk over the roar of the chainsaw.

"What's wrong?" Than asked as he lifted the hem of his shirt to wipe his face.

"A little boy said that his mom was in labor. Barb and the nurse have gone to check on her. Barb said you should come, too."

His gaze went past her, his brow furrowed. "Let me tell Elliot."

Lindsay didn't know if she should wait for him or head over. In the end, she walked slowly toward where the young boy had led the nurse and Barb. When Than caught up with her, they moved more quickly and could hear Barb's voice as they got closer to a small house—even smaller than the ones they'd stopped at already.

They slipped through the open doorway, and Lindsay had to blink to adjust to the dark room. Barb was bending over a woman on a bed against the wall. She glanced at them as they walked in.

"I need some light, Than. Can you help Imee find some? Lindsay, can you get on the bed and sit with her?"

As she moved near the bed, Lindsay hoped she'd be able to do what Barb needed her to. She'd never been around a woman giving birth before. She shucked off her shoes and climbed up onto the bed, getting her first glimpse of the young woman. Even in the dimly lit room she could see the sweat dripping down the woman's face. Her long black hair hung in damp strands, sticking to her cheeks.

Reaching out, Lindsay brushed the hair back and then took the woman's hand in hers. "It's going to be okay."

When light flooded where they were gathered, Lindsay realized that Than must have found a lamp. He set it on the table near the bed which gave light for Barb as she examined the woman. Lindsay noticed that Than kept his gaze averted as he walked behind Barb to the other side of the bed near her.

"She's already nine centimeters dilated," Barb said. She stood between the woman's legs and ran her gloved hands over her bulging abdomen.

For the next ten minutes, Barb and the nurse spoke back and forth using terms that were completely foreign to Lindsay. Knowing there was nothing she could do to help with that side of things, she focused instead on the woman.

"What is your name?" she asked, hoping she'd understand English.

"Marissa." The name was spoken softly, and Lindsay could hear the woman's exhaustion in her voice.

"My name is Lindsay. We're going to take care of you and your baby, okay?"

Marissa nodded, her eyes wide. "Thank you."

"Barb, I'm just going to let Elliot know where we are, and I'll be right back," Than said.

Lindsay heard him say something in Tagalog and the little boy responded. She glanced over to see him take the boy by the hand and lead him from the house. It hurt her heart to think the little guy had been all alone with his laboring mother throughout the storm. He looked to be even younger than Danny.

Dear God, please let this have a happy outcome.

The woman gave a guttural moan, and Lindsay turned back to her. "What's happening, Barb?"

"She's bearing down. Her body has decided it's time to push this baby out." Barb spoke to the nurse again then said, "Lindsay, can you move in behind her and support her back?"

Feeling completely out of her element, Lindsay did as Barb requested. Moving as quickly as she could without jarring Marissa, she slid behind the woman.

"Marissa, on this contraction I want you to hold the back of your knees and push to the count of ten. Can you do that?" The woman nodded and reached for her knees. "Here we go. Take a deep breath. One. Two."

Lindsay felt the strain in the woman's body as she curved forward and pushed. The ten count seemed to take an eternity and when it was over, the woman slumped back against her. The nurse pressed a damp cloth into Lindsay's hand, and she used it to wipe the woman's forehead as she rested with her eyes closed.

Before too long though, the woman was reaching again for her legs. With another deep moan, her body tightened, and Barb began to count. Lindsay felt equal measures of helplessness and awe as she watched the woman in front of her struggle to bring her child into the world. She lost count of how many ten counts they'd done—it felt like hundreds—

but she was sure that no matter how many it seemed like to her, it felt like way more for Marissa. As another contraction gripped her, Lindsay found herself willing her strength into the young mother.

"You're doing great, Marissa," Barb said, her voice gentle and soothing. "I can see the top of the baby's head. You're almost there."

Lindsay was grateful that Marissa understood English. It would be much harder if their words of encouragement meant nothing to her. "You can do it, Marissa."

She heard Than's voice outside the house, once again speaking in Tagalog, but he didn't come back inside. No doubt he was trying to entertain the little boy while his mother labored.

"Here we go," Barb said, excitement edging her voice. "Push. Push. Push, Marissa!"

There were no more counts now as Barb encouraged Marissa to continue to push. The woman's body tensed back against her as if trying to escape from the pain, and Marissa gave a low growl. Then it was over. Marissa's body slumped back against her, all the rigidity suddenly gone.

"It's a girl, Marissa," Barb said. "A beautiful girl."

When a cry suddenly filled the air, Lindsay felt tears slip from her eyes. She pressed her cheek to Marissa's damp hair. "You did it. You did it."

Barb lifted the baby and laid her across Marissa's chest. From her vantage point, Lindsay could see straight into the baby girl's face. Though scrunched up and swollen, she'd never seen a more beautiful sight in her life. She lifted her hand to gently touch the baby's head. "She's beautiful, Marissa."

There was still more to come, but she was so focused on the baby and the young mother, it slipped past her. Soon Barb told her she could move away so they could help Marissa shift position. They cleaned her up and helped her to get the baby nursing. As the intensity drained away, Lindsay was left feeling weary. She couldn't imagine what it must be like for Marissa.

Her emotions were on overload. First holding little Maya in her arms and now watching a new baby come into the world. She could hardly take it all in. Pregnancy and childbirth were something she hadn't given much thought to. Even in her circle of friends—acquaintances—there was no talk of having children. Women like Adrianne and Melanie Thorpe were as focused on their careers as Lindsay was.

As she had been.

Lindsay didn't think she could go back to her day to day life without giving all of this some thought. As she watched Marissa bend over her new baby, Lindsay realized that she wanted it all. The love, the marriage, the pregnancy and the baby.

She had a sudden image in her head of a little boy with dark hair, dark eyes and a mischievous grin. Lindsay shot a look toward the doorway just as Than reappeared with the little boy's hand in his.

No.

Than barely qualified as dating material. She was pretty sure marriage and parenthood weren't in his immediate—or even distant—plans. Her gaze went back to Marissa as her son scrambled up on the bed beside her. He pressed a kiss to his mother's cheek and then the top of his sister's head. Though the father was currently absent from the scene in front of her, the love was clearly evident as Marissa wrapped her arm around the little boy and pulled him close.

Lindsay swallowed hard as tears pricked her eyes. She wanted a love like Lucas and Brooke had as a couple and the love they shared with Danny as his parents. As the ache in her heart grew, Lindsay crossed her arms and took a deep breath.

She sensed his presence behind her even before she felt the light touch on her back as Than said, "You doing okay?"

Not willing to trust her voice to be free of emotion, Lindsay just nodded and kept her gaze on Marissa and her children. She wanted to lean against him, feel his strength. And she wanted to share this moment with him, but that wasn't how their relationship worked.

"Elliot's gone to get the jeepney. Given that Marissa is on her own here, he thinks she'll be better off up at the center. She can stay at the orphanage since they are equipped to handle babies there."

This time she did look at him. "I think that's a great idea."

Than nodded. "One of the workers with Elliot knows the family. The husband went to Manila last week to deliver something and apparently didn't get back before the typhoon."

"Why would he leave her so close to her due date? Didn't he think she might have the baby while he was away?" Lindsay could hear the indignation in her voice even though she spoke softly, but she really didn't understand.

"It's the way their life is. This job would bring in money for the family. If he passed it up, they might not have had money for food or rent. He can't turn down jobs to stay at his wife's side. And the typhoon complicated the situation. No doubt it delayed his returned and isolated her from those who might have helped her. But she's okay. The baby is okay. That's all that matters now."

"Is that what you'd do?" Lindsay asked, pulling her arms closer to her chest. She sensed his gaze on her.

"What I'd do?"

"If your wife was nearing her due date and you got a job that took you away from home. Would you leave her?" Lindsay didn't look at him...couldn't look at him.

"Completely different world, Lindsay. I have vacation pay. I can take time off without losing my income. I have people who could cover for me. But to answer your question, no, I wouldn't leave her. But you know, even back home there would be guys who would have to take jobs away from home and their wives, even if they were ready to deliver. People do what they have to do to survive. You and I are fortunate to live and work in places where we won't face choices like that."

This trip had opened Lindsay's eyes to the truth of Than's statement. The privileged life she lived was so far removed from what she saw here it seemed to be on a different planet.

She stared at the sight before her, trying hard to commit this moment—these feelings—to memory. When she was tempted to grumble or whine about something in her life, she wanted to remember this. She had nothing to complain about. Absolutely nothing.

Than could feel the emotions rolling off Lindsay as she stood watching the young woman and her children. The stoic expression she'd had earlier was gone now. He wondered if she was aware that regardless of how tightly she tried to keep a rein on them, there were times her emotions still spilled over. The experience she'd just gone through was likely something she'd never encountered before. And for some reason, Than wished she'd share what she was feeling with him.

To watch a baby come into the world—even if it wasn't hers—had to be an amazing experience. Though he'd been outside with the little guy, he'd heard everything that had gone on as the young woman had labored to give birth to her second child. He felt a little chagrined by the fact that he hadn't been interested in hanging around the hospital to wait for the births of his own nieces and nephew, but it had seemed important to stay for this one. And not just to help the little boy. He'd wanted to be there to share that experience with Lindsay.

Only she wasn't interested in sharing it with him. Sooner or later he'd learn not to look for that from her. But for some reason, he kept hoping.

Before he could say anything more to Lindsay, Elliot came into the house. After greeting the woman, he spoke to her in Tagalog and explained that they were going to take her back to the mission until her husband returned.

"*Salamat po.*"

Than could hear the relief in the woman's voice as she thanked Elliot. And as he watched Barb gather up the supplies she'd used for her care of the woman, he realized that just like people had said that he was an answer to prayer on this trip, so was she. He knew her background and though it appeared nothing had gone amiss with the delivery, if anything had, she would have been the best one to care for the woman in their current circumstances.

Over the next few minutes, they all worked together to get Marissa and her children loaded into the vehicle. Because the trip would be uncomfortable for Marissa to make so soon after childbirth, they brought the thin mattress from her bed and laid it on the floor between the two bench seats in the back of the vehicle.

They helped Marissa lie down on the mattress and then Barb settled the baby in the crook of her arm. The two male team members crowded up front with Elliot while the Filipino guys hung off the back. Barb and the nurse sat on one side while Lindsay sat with him and the little boy on the other. Than was thankful that they'd taken the time to clear the road of the larger branches, but the ride back up the hill was still jarring.

With the little boy between them, he could see Lindsay working hard once again to stay in one place on the seat. The ride was made in relative quiet. Than didn't miss the fact that Lindsay's gaze stayed on the woman and baby in front of her. Not so long ago, if someone had said that Lindsay Hamilton would have been interested in babies, he would have laughed. And something told him that she would have as well. It wasn't that she didn't like children. In fact, he knew the opposite was true because she absolutely adored her nephew, but he was ten years old and able to communicate with her.

The thing with babies was different though. Babies tended to put thoughts into women's head in a way that older children didn't. He'd been around a few women who had commented about the ticking of their biological clocks. Than had always made sure to steer clear of those women. They hadn't even gotten one date out of him if he had any advanced warning of where their heads were at when it came to babies.

Strangely enough, even though he could now see those same thoughts gaining ground with Lindsay, Than still wanted that second date. And more.

Lindsay leaned her head against the back of the rocking chair as she cradled the baby she'd help deliver. They'd been at the mission center for a few days now as they waited for word on Marissa's husband. The little girl still had no name, but her own mother and the other workers in the orphanage had taken to calling her Girlie. Apparently the delay in naming wasn't that unusual. Nor was it unusual for a nickname like that to stick even after they were given a proper name apparently. She figured that explained the men she'd met named Boy.

As she rocked, Lindsay breathed a sigh of relief. This was her favorite, most relaxing time of the day. Each morning they'd been up in time to eat breakfast by seven and then they headed down the hill. She'd discovered that even though they helped anyone who needed it, Elliot had been specifically looking for members of their church. They had helped remove fallen tree branches, fix roofs and windows and any other damage that had been done by the storm. She, Barb and the nurse had tended to any injuries they came across. Though they hadn't run into any more laboring women, there had been plenty of heartbreaking stories of families who'd suffered damage or injury during the storm.

But from everything they'd heard so far, this town had been fortunate. The town on the coast, where the typhoon had made landfall, had been struck with a storm surge that hadn't just destroyed property but had taken lives. Lindsay had had a hard enough time with the emotions that had come with the devastation she'd seen that had just been caused by the wind and rain. She couldn't imagine how much worse it was when combined with a sudden storm surge.

Most afternoons after they'd had some lunch, they'd tackled some of the projects on the center and then Lindsay would escape for a bit to hold the babies in the orphanage. It was definitely the highlight of her day. Than was usually there as well. He seemed as taken with little Benjie as she was with Maya and Girlie.

Her gaze went to where he sat on the floor, his back against the cement brick wall, legs stretched out, holding the little boy's hands as Benjie attempted to stand on his own. Lindsay figured this was probably one of the more bizarre assignments he'd ever had. But at least it didn't involve getting shot at, so that was probably a good thing.

Knowing that he was doing a lot more than what would normally have been expected of him on a job, Lindsay had tried not to make any waves herself. She didn't argue with him when he gave her direction. In fact, she'd tried to keep their conversation to the bare minimum.

The rush of emotions she'd had during the storm had not gone away. It scared her to feel what she did for someone like Than. He'd stayed true to their wager, but realistically, he'd had it easy. The atmosphere didn't lend itself to flirtatious conversation, plus there just weren't a lot of women around to flirt with. The true test would be when they got back on familiar ground. But by then, their bet would be over.

Would he go back to his old ways? Lindsay wasn't sure she could take the chance of finding out. He was attentive and courteous when they were together, but that was his job. It wouldn't have reflected well on BlackThorpe if he'd been anything but. For all she knew, this trip had opened his eyes to the "real" her, and he wasn't interested in that second date anymore.

Lindsay sighed and gazed down at the baby in her arms. Too many confusing thoughts and emotions. She liked everything to fall into place perfectly. She didn't like having to try to figure out subtleties or vague innuendos. There had been times over the past few days when she'd felt like she didn't know who she really was any more. These days, Lindsay felt words like "vulnerable" and "emotional" were more accurate than the words that had been used in the past to describe her. Words like "reserved", "cold", "aloof." Her self from just a year ago would have scoffed at the way she was now.

The truth was...these parts of her weren't really new. At least not to her. She didn't know why her emotional reactions were so much more visible than they usually were. Was it just the circumstances? Finding herself more vulnerable than she'd ever been before in her life? If that was the case, could she get her defenses back in place once she was back on familiar ground? Would she want that?

The sound of a man's yell jerked Lindsay from her thoughts before she could formulate any answers to her questions. Her grip on the baby tightened as she tried to make out what he was saying. She glanced at Than and saw him get to his feet and hand Benjie to one of the workers, concern on his face. Marissa, however, was smiling as she pushed herself up from the rocking chair she'd been sitting in.

"Rissa? *Mahal?*"

The door of the orphanage opened, and a man burst in. His gaze swept the room and then landed on Marissa as she moved toward him. Lindsay's heart clenched as she watched the man gather Marissa into his arms and hold her close.

Lindsay couldn't understand what they were saying, but she didn't need to. The love they had for each other was evident in the way he took her face in his hands and pressed a kiss to her lips. He moved back and murmured something to her before kissing her again. When that kiss ended, Marissa pointed to Lindsay.

The man's gaze met Lindsay's for a moment, and she could see the wealth of emotion within him. He took Marissa's hand and headed toward where Lindsay sat. As they neared, Lindsay held Girlie out. With gentle movements, the man took the baby and cradled her to his chest. The little boy had joined them and was hugging his dad around the hips.

As she watched the small family, Lindsay felt her chest tighten. She had all the money she could ever want, but this...she didn't have anything close to this. As she recalled her anger toward this man who had left his wife for work, Lindsay knew she'd been oh, so very wrong. He hadn't gone for the sake of the money, he had gone to do what he could to provide for this family he loved. There was no doubt that he loved and cherished his wife and children.

Elliot had followed the man into the house and now spoke with him and Marissa. The ache in Lindsay's chest was making it difficult to take a deep breath. Tears threatened to spill over, but she refused to let them. This young woman who had a home that was small and without any luxury had something that counted for so much more.

Love.

14

THAN watched the reunion between Marissa and her husband with a smile. They'd had no news from him since bringing Marissa to the center. Elliot had left a note in the family's home with information on where Marissa and the children were, but they'd had no idea how long it would be before he showed up.

When the man moved to take his daughter from Lindsay, it was her face he focused on instead of the continuing reunion. Her lips were drawn tight as she watched Marissa with her family. When he saw her swallow and blink rapidly, Than knew she was fighting hard to keep her emotions in check. That seemed such a strange idea when it came to Lindsay Hamilton.

From the moment he'd first met her, she'd struck him as being self-assured and in control. This trip had torn layers off her and left her with emotions that bubbled so much closer to the surface than they likely ever had for her. He wondered what Lucas was going to say about the changes in his sister.

For himself, Than felt privileged to have been able to witness this change in Lindsay. Or maybe not really a change so much as a deepening awareness of who she really was. He'd always known she was a caring person—he had seen that with her family—but what she'd experienced on the trip seemed to have widened and deepened what she felt. And he knew that was true for him as well.

As he listened to Elliot speak to the couple, he realized that they were asking to be taken back to their home. He walked over to where Lindsay sat and dropped down on his haunches.

"They're telling him they'd like to go home," Than said, his voice low.

Lindsay's head whipped around. "They want to go back there?"

"Of course. It's their home. Elliot made sure that any damage from the storm was taken care of. Their house is safe for them."

"But what about the baby?"

Than looked into her gray eyes and, seeing the worry there, wished he could gather her into his arms and assure her everything would be okay. Instead, he just said, "She'll be fine. Babies are born every day in this country—some in worse conditions than this—and they survive. They love her. They'll make sure she's okay."

Lindsay's brows drew together as she looked at him. It was almost as if she was searching his gaze to make sure he was telling her the truth. "You can't guarantee that."

"You're right. I can't. But I do know they love her as much as they loved their son who was born in similar conditions and look at him. He's a happy, well-loved child." Than motioned toward the family. Lindsay looked over, and he knew she saw what he did. Marissa now held the baby while her son was in his father's arms. "They may not have what you and I do, but they do the best they can with what they have, Lindsay."

"I know. It just seems...wrong."

"It seems to me they have something more precious than wealth."

Than was surprised when Lindsay nodded and then softly said, "Yeah. That love they have for each other."

Was that longing he heard in her voice? Did she want a love like that for herself?

Before he could respond, she spoke again, her voice so low Than almost didn't hear her words. "I guess when you have basically nothing, you know the person truly loves you for who you are, not for what you have."

Than sat back on his heels at her comment. A shaft of pain went through him at the emotion he heard in her words. Than had never considered that there might have been a man in her life who had used her like that. It would certainly explain the distance she tended to keep from most people— particularly men. He never considered her money when he thought of her. That was something she had, not who she was. It was how he viewed his friendship with Lincoln as well. He had no expectations of them when it came to their wealth. He had his own money and paid his own way.

He was still searching for a response when Marissa walked over to them, a smile on her face.

"We have decided on a name for the baby," she said in her accented English.

Lindsay smiled up at her. "Really? What is it?"

"We are so thankful for what you and *mum* Barb did for us that I wanted to name her Lindsay Barbara. My husband has agreed. We will call her Elbee."

"The initials LB?" Lindsay asked.

Than looked at Marissa. "I think she means E-L-B-E-E."

Marissa nodded. "Elbee. In thanks for what you have done for us."

Lindsay leaned forward and pressed a kiss to the baby in Marissa's arms. "Nice to meet you, Elbee."

Marissa then bent over and hugged Lindsay. "*Salamat po*. Thank you."

"You're welcome."

As Marissa turned from them to her husband, Lindsay's shoulders slumped. Than touched her hand, wanting to comfort her in some way. "We'll see them again before we go."

Lindsay nodded but didn't look at him. "How did you know about the name?"

The sudden change of subject surprised Than, but he assumed she was searching for something that didn't take such an emotional toll on her. "It's not uncommon for Filipinos to combine names and initials for names. I'm sure you've already figured out that a lot of them have nicknames."

She glanced at him. "Did you have a nickname?"

Than grinned. "Yeah. Everyone called my older brother Jun because he was a junior. Steven Miller Jr. Then when I came along and looked a whole lot like him people said I was a junior of Jun. Everyone started calling me Junjun."

Lindsay's eyebrows rose. "Junjun? Seriously?"

"You bet. Thankfully, by the time I turned ten, I'd managed to convince people to stop using it."

"How did you manage to do that?"

Than shrugged. "I simply didn't respond when they called me Junjun. My mom was the lone hold-out, but even she got tired of having me ignore her."

A small smile played around the corners of Lindsay's mouth, and Than felt the tightness in his chest ease. He was glad to see that she'd been able to pull back from the emotional cliff she'd seemed to be standing on.

"So your mom calls you Than now, too?"

He shook his head. "Nope. She calls me Nathaniel. After I managed to get them to stop calling me Junjun, my brother followed my tactic—even though he's several years older than me—and got them to stop calling him Jun. No one would think twice about those nicknames here, but man, Jun for a boy just didn't go over well in Minneapolis."

"I imagine not," Lindsay said, a quick smile lifting the corners of her mouth. "Kind of like a boy named Sue."

"Johnny Cash fan?"

"My mom is. I heard a lot of his music growing up." Lindsay's gaze left his. "Looks like maybe our work here is done for today."

Reluctantly, Than looked away from Lindsay and saw that she was right. The babies were either napping or playing quietly on the big carpet that covered the middle of the floor.

As he got to his feet, Than said, "I think Elliot said that the rest of the afternoon was downtime. And tomorrow there's nothing on the schedule except church."

Than had been inside a lot of places—even churches—for a lot of different reasons over the years, but he couldn't recall ever having been in church for an actual worship service since becoming an adult. Weddings and funerals, sure, but a worship service? Just one more unique thing about this job.

A breeze greeted them as they left the orphanage, and there was a quietness in the air that allowed him to hear the rustle of the leaves on the trees around them. There were no sounds of work like there had been most other afternoons.

"I think I'm just going to get a drink and then lie down for a nap," Lindsay said as she moved in the direction of the dining room.

The roof of the building had been repaired, and the tables that had been damaged by the water were being refinished. Though the main power was still off, the lines around the center had been checked and the generator now powered all the buildings. Thankfully, they'd been okay for food due in large part to the planning of the missionaries to have a fully stocked pantry and two large freezers. Even though the power had been off for a few hours, the frozen food had still been fine when they'd fired up the generator the next morning.

As they got to the building, Than reached out and grabbed the handle of the door to open it for Lindsay. He caught the whiff of her shampoo as she walked past him and he knew that he would forever associate that light musk scent with her.

"Hey, you guys," Barb called out as they walked into the room. "They've made us an afternoon snack. Banana lumpia. You need to try them, Lindsay."

Lindsay had been a trooper with most of the food they been served, so Than wasn't too surprised when she made her way over to the counter that separated the dining room and kitchen. One of the kitchen staff met her there and explained what it was.

"If you decide you don't like it, just pass it my way," Than said as he peered over her shoulder.

Lindsay glanced at him, a glint of humor in her eyes. He knew that she'd snuck food onto his plate on more than one occasion. Though they had had a few nights of more American type food—fried chicken and lasagna—for the most part, the food had been Filipino. Even his sisters didn't like everything their mom served, so Than hadn't expected Lindsay to enjoy it all, but she'd surprised him with how much of it she'd eaten without passing it on to him.

She would be well prepared food-wise when she met his family.

The thought stopped him in his tracks. It was the second time something like that had shot through his mind. There was really no denying that at some point in the past week that desire for a second date had morphed into something much more serious.

After taking the plate the woman behind the counter handed him, Than followed Lindsay to the table where Barb sat with Amanda and a couple of the other team members. Once seated, he watched as Lindsay took a tentative bite of the banana treat. When her eyes widened slightly and she went back for another bite, Than sighed. He wouldn't be getting any extras from her plate this time around. Too bad. He really liked banana lumpia.

He finished his more quickly than Lindsay and was taking a long swallow of cold water when Amanda said, "Um...Than, could I talk to you for a minute?"

"Sure thing." He leaned back in his chair. "What's up?"

He saw her gaze shoot to Lindsay and then back to him. "Alone? Please?"

Though Lindsay didn't appear to look at Amanda, he saw her body stiffen. Why did this have to happen now? "Okay. Shall we step outside?"

Amanda nodded and left her half-eaten banana lumpia to join him as he led the way out of the building. He didn't go far from the door and positioned himself so Lindsay could observe them through the window and see that nothing untoward was going on.

Than put his hands on his hips and looked down at the petite blonde. "How can I help you?"

She ducked her head and seemed to be intent on staring at her hands where her fingers were clenched together. "I need to ask a...um...favor. You can say no...I just thought maybe... I mean, I'll understand if you don't want to."

"Amanda." Than said her name firmly, waiting for her to look up. When she did, he continued, "Just spit it out. What do you want? I can't say yes or no without knowing what you need."

He saw her take a deep breath. "Can I use your phone?"

Than stared at her for a moment. "My phone?"

Amanda nodded. "Your satellite phone. You see, it's my boyfriend's birthday today, and I really miss him." Her blue eyes suddenly went liquid, and it took her a few seconds to compose herself. "I just wanted to call and talk to him for just a couple of minutes. I know it costs money. I'll pay you."

Than bent his head toward her. "Let me get this straight. You want to use my sat phone to call your boyfriend and wish him a happy birthday?"

Tears again filled Amanda's eyes. "It's okay to say no. Mark said you might, but I just had to ask."

"You talked to Mark about this?"

She nodded again. "He said not to ask you in front of anyone so you didn't get a whole lot of people asking to use it since this wasn't an emergency." Her shoulders slumped a little as her head dipped. "It's okay to say no. I'll understand. He's not expecting me to call anyway."

Than reached out and tapped her lightly under the chin. When she looked up, he said, "Far be it from me to interfere with love."

Her eyes lit up as she clasped her hands under her chin. "Really? You'll let me?"

"Sure."

Before he could say anything more, she threw her arms around him. "Thank you. Oh, thank you."

Than returned the hug quickly and then stepped back. He had a feeling the damage had already been done though, and even if he tried to explain, Lindsay would likely just brush it aside.

Trying to keep his frustration from showing, Than said, "You do realize that with the time difference it's like two in the morning back home, right?"

"Yes, but I thought maybe I could use the phone around eight or nine tonight? Then I could be the first to wish him happy birthday."

"Okay. Come find me around eight thirty. And it would be best if you could keep it to yourself."

She laid her hand on his arm and looked up at him. "Thanks, Than. I really mean it. You don't know how much better I feel now."

As he looked down at her, Than realized that in the past, even though he knew she had a boyfriend, he'd probably have flirted with her a little and spent some extra time chatting with her. He didn't feel that urge now—and not just because of the wager—but because Lindsay was the only woman he wanted to coax a smile from. She was the only woman he wanted to make feel good about herself.

She was the only woman who mattered.

Slightly stunned at the path his thoughts had taken, Than managed to say, "Uh, you're welcome. Glad I could help."

Amanda spun away from him and practically skipped back into the dining room. Knowing that Lindsay would be safe with Barb there, Than turned toward the dirt road that led down the hill. He didn't plan to be gone too long, but he just needed a little space right then.

It was like all these little thoughts had been hanging at the edges of his mind, flitting around like little puffs of smoke. Then suddenly, *bam*, they solidified in his heart, and he couldn't ignore or deny them anymore.

If he didn't feel that his current relationship with Lindsay was tenuous at best, he would embrace the feelings. But their presence in his heart and mind only served to remind him that he might just be facing his first heartbreak as an adult. And, unfortunately, it was by a woman he wouldn't able to avoid. Seeing as he was friends with Lincoln and Lucas, Lindsay was destined to be in his world for years to come, even if it was just on the fringes. It would be close enough to hear about any men she dated and eventually married.

That thought twisted his gut, and Than kicked at a pile of dirt on the road as he made his way down to the gate. Yeah, he definitely needed a little space to get his head back on straight.

Lindsay watched as Amanda returned to her seat, a big smile on her face. When she looked toward the door for Than, she realized he hadn't followed Amanda back inside. Her gaze went to the window and she spotted him heading away from the building, his head bent.

What on earth had gone on between the two of them that had caused Amanda to return with a smile on her face—after hugging Than—but had sent Than walking away?

"Everything okay, Amanda?" Barb asked.

"Everything is perfect," Amanda assured her, her face alight with joy. "Than is such a great guy."

Lindsay turned her attention back to her snack and finished off the last piece, suddenly not enjoying it as much as she had earlier. She felt Barb's gaze on her but refused to meet it.

"Yes, he is. We're fortunate that he came with Lindsay," Barb replied. "You want to share why *you* think he's such a good guy?"

Lindsay glanced over in time to see a small frown cross Amanda's face. "Oh well, you know. He's helped a lot. And he was great making sure our families knew we were okay. Stuff like that."

And so much more.

Lindsay didn't want to dwell on that thought and quickly pushed it aside. Technically, she probably had a case for saying the bet was over and he'd lost, but for now she was going to hold her tongue. And try to push the image of Amanda in Than's arms from her mind.

Sitting forward, she reached for the plate Than had abandoned earlier and slid it under her own. She pushed away from the table and gathered up their dishes.

"I'm going to go take a bit of a nap, I think, since we're having a free afternoon." She looked at Barb. "Can you let Than know if he asks where I am?"

"Sure thing, hun." Barb smiled at her, but Lindsay didn't miss the spark of concern there as well. Sometimes she forgot that Barb had two daughters and was likely to read her emotions better than most.

After leaving the dishes on the counter, Lindsay wandered out into the warm afternoon air and slowly made her way to the dorm. She grabbed a tank top and a pair of shorts and went to the bathroom to change. The room was warm, so she left the door propped open in hopes of getting a good cross breeze.

She slipped her earbuds in and found the playlist she wanted before lying down on the bed, curled up on her side. After what had just transpired, Lindsay wasn't sure she'd actually be able to fall asleep, but the heightened level of physical activity of the past week plus early mornings dragged her slowly into slumber.

When Than returned from his walk, he had no answer to how to bring about the result he wanted with Lindsay, but at least he felt he was back in control of his emotions. He returned to the dining room and found Barb there talking with some of the team members. Amanda was there as well, but Lindsay wasn't. His heart sank.

"Lindsay went to take a nap," Barb said before he could even form the question.

Recalling that she'd mentioned wanting a nap earlier made him feel a bit better. He still didn't know if he should tell her what Amanda had wanted or just let it go. What he needed from her was trust. If she ever did feel something for him, if it wasn't coupled with trust, they wouldn't stand a chance. He was trying to show her that he'd changed, but he couldn't completely cut himself off from women. They were everywhere in his life, and he was just naturally a friendly person. He wanted Lindsay to accept that and to know that if—*when*—their relationship became more serious, she would always be the only woman in his heart. That he would be true to her.

Something told him that trust was the biggest issue for Lindsay. She hadn't trusted her father after finding out about the women he'd had while married to her mother. Then she *had* trusted a man only to have that trust shattered when she found out he was only using her to get to her money. He would be patient with her, and hopefully she'd see that there was something worth trusting between them. Because in spite of what she may have said, Than really didn't feel that it was all one sided.

Since there was no reason to return to the dorm—he certainly couldn't go to Lindsay's room to check on her, propriety and all that—Than settled into a chair next to Barb. The older woman gave him a quick smile. Inasmuch as she'd taken Lindsay under her wing, she'd also extended that maternal care to him. And it appeared she'd picked up on the situation between him and Lindsay, and had become something of a silent cheerleader for them. He appreciated that about her—among the many other things she'd brought to the team.

He'd no sooner sat down than she turned to him and said, "I know you just went for a walk, but would you care to go for another?"

Than lifted a brow at her request but only gave a nod and stood back up. Once outside the dining hall, he offered her his elbow. She slipped her hand into the crook of his arm and together they began to walk along the dirt road he'd taken earlier.

"Are you going to tell Lindsay what Amanda wanted of you?" Barb asked once they were a distance from the building they'd just left.

Than glanced down at her, but she was looking straight ahead at the road. "I shouldn't have to."

Barb nodded. "You're right. You shouldn't have to, but she's going through a lot on this trip. What she's always believed is being challenged on several levels. Her faith, her understanding of God, her own views of the world and herself. Also mixed in there is you."

"I'm going through a lot on this trip, too," Than said, a little unsure why he'd revealed that to her.

"I can see that. I know that your purpose on this trip has been eclipsed by a lot of things, not the least of which was that storm. I'm not ashamed to say that your presence here has made me feel more secure, and if I feel that way, I'm pretty sure Lindsay does as well. God definitely knew we needed you."

And there it was again. "I find it hard to believe that God would use someone like me."

Barb's hand tightened on his arm. "Someone like you? What do you mean by that?"

Than chuckled. "Well, let's just say that tomorrow when I walk into that church, it will be the first time in my adult life that I've gone to church for anything other than a wedding or funeral. Not sure why God would use someone like me, someone who hasn't made time for Him in my life."

"Well, maybe this is His way of bringing that to your attention."

"The fact that I haven't made time for Him?"

Barb nodded. "I'm sure you've heard that God works in mysterious ways. Whether or not you had an interest in Him, He had a purpose for you in being here. I don't presume to know God's purpose for you, but I do know that His desire is that all people come to know Him in a real and personal way. That's why the missionaries are here. That's why I came on this mission trip. We've had the chance to share about God every time we've come in contact with people. This storm opened doors to us that might not have been open otherwise."

Than didn't reply right away. He still had a hard time wrapping his mind around the fact that there might have been a higher purpose to his accepting the job to protect Lindsay. He'd thought that Barb had wanted to talk to him about Lindsay on this walk, but he saw now that it was something different that she had her heart set on.

"I know you want a relationship with Lindsay, but her faith is becoming more and more important to her and that will be something you won't have in common if you choose to reject God. I'm not saying you should accept Him just because of Lindsay, but I will say that having a shared faith in a relationship helps to smooth out some of the difficulties that might otherwise overwhelm a couple."

"Is that how it was with you and your husband?"

"Very much so. Knowing that we both wanted God's will for our lives and our marriage helped strengthen us as individuals and as a couple. Nothing strengthens a couple's relationship like being connected on all levels—physical, emotional and spiritual."

Than pondered her words. Did he think the spiritual connection was necessary in a relationship? He thought of his parents' marriage. They shared that connection that Barb had mentioned. The physical, emotional and spiritual. Was that why they were still so in love after all these years? Why they were so strong together?

Barb gave a slight tug on his arm. "But having said all that, the most important thing is that personal relationship with God. Before you can even consider sharing that faith with Lindsay, you need to find it for yourself first." She came to a stop and Than turned to look down at her. The expression in her green eyes tugged at his heart. "I know it sounds really odd, but I've come to think of you as a son, Than, and I hope you know that I say all this from a place of love."

Though he knew his own mother loved him to the depths of her heart, she'd never showed such concern for the state of his soul. He suspected that she worried if she pressed him about it, he'd just stop spending time with them. Her approach had been more subtle. Than covered Barb's hand with his own. "I have spent plenty of time thinking through everything I've learned while on this trip. Believe me, I haven't dismissed any of it. It's just all very new to me. I'm trying to sort through a lot of stuff."

Barb nodded. "I understand." A smile spread across her face. "Enough about that for now. Tell me about your family."

15

THE next morning, Lindsay decided to take a few extra minutes with her appearance for church. She'd only brought one dress along, a simple light blue sundress with wide straps, a fitted bodice and a flared skirt. It didn't take long to apply a light layer of the makeup she'd avoided all week. After seeing the teenage girl with her curling iron, Lindsay had asked to borrow it to coax a little life into her hair. It was one of the things she'd left out of her suitcase when she'd packed.

She put on a dab of her favorite perfume and slid simple hoops into her ears. The necklace that hung around her neck was one Lucas had given her on her sixteenth birthday. It was a simple chain with a locket. It was silver with no expensive stones so it held little monetary value, but it had meant the world to her when he'd presented it to her. And today it made her feel a little bit closer to him even though they were separated by an ocean and half a world.

Amanda came into the bathroom just as Lindsay was putting the last of her things into her bag.

"You look pretty," she said with a wide smile, her blue eyes sparkling.

Lindsay thanked her and tried not to think about what had made the other woman so happy. She'd disappeared around eight thirty the night before and reappeared about a half hour later. Lindsay tried not to speculate, tried to not think about it, but it was hard. Especially when there was a part of her that didn't think for a minute that anything was really going on between Amanda and Than. Because every time she reminded herself of that, the little voice of doubt would interject.

But this situation with Amanda was just a blatant reminder of why she knew it wasn't in her best interests to get involved with Than—even in the short term. When she already had trouble trusting men, in general, why would she choose to get involved with a man who would challenge her to trust him on a daily basis? That even if she wanted to trust him, there would always be that little voice in the back of her head. No relationship would ever survive a stress like that. And maybe that's why Than was strictly a short-term relationship type of guy. He had yet to find a woman who could deal with the way he interacted with other women.

Leaving Amanda to her own church preparations, Lindsay returned to the room and put her bag in the closet with the rest of her things. It was kind of hard to think that in just a week she'd be back to her old life. Though she'd only been away seven days, it felt like forever since she'd first boarded that plane to Detroit. She knew that this trip had been a turning point in her life. She remembered Mark's words during one of their pre-trip meetings.

Each of you is likely here to take advantage of an opportunity to help others. You want to touch the lives of others and share God's love. And that's what I hope will happen, but for a few—maybe all—of you, this trip will impact your life in a way you might never have thought it would. Your life will be touched as much as those you've gone to help.

Little had she known.

She heard a knock and turned to see Than standing in the open doorway. Her breath caught in her lungs at the sight of him. He wore a light blue button up shirt that was tucked into a pair of tailored slacks. The color of the shirt served to contrast the dark of his hair and eyes and the tan of his skin that seemed to have deepened in the time they'd been there. And that scruff was back on his face. She liked it.

"Ready to go?" he asked, his expression unreadable.

Since his talk with Amanda, he'd been different. Through dinner and the short team meeting afterward, he'd seemed...distant.

"Morning, Than!"

He stepped back out of the doorway to let Amanda into the room and gave her a quick smile. "Morning, Amanda."

His gaze came back to Lindsay and again he asked, "You ready?"

Pushing aside the yucky feeling that Amanda's appearance had brought on, she gathered up her purse and Bible. "Yep."

As she joined him in the hall, he said, "Mark told me they need to take two trips to the church so I thought we should go on the early one."

"Sure. That sounds fine. I think Barb will likely go on that one, too."

They walked in silence down the hallway and the stairs. Than pushed open the door and waited for her to walk past him out into the bright Sunday morning. She felt him touch her back lightly as he pointed to the van where several people had gathered.

"Looks like they're almost ready to go."

Barb gave her a quick hug when they joined the group. "You look beautiful, my dear."

"Thank you," Lindsay said.

"And you're one handsome man," Barb said as she slipped her arm around Than's waist for a quick squeeze.

"Well, I can take no credit for it," he said with a grin. "But I'll pass the compliment on to my mom and dad. And might I say you're looking lovely this morning as well. The green in your blouse makes your eyes especially stunning."

Lindsay stared at Than and then looked over at her friend. Barb's cheeks were pink and her eyes—yes, those incredible green eyes—sparkled with joy. This was what Than did. He made women feel special. All women. And maybe for someone like Barb, who didn't have a man in her life, it was a simple compliment that brought her joy.

So how was it even possible for one woman to feel that she was special to him? Because more than anything, Lindsay had always hoped that the man she fell in love with would make her feel special in a way no one else had. Not her father and certainly not her ex-fiancé.

Noticing that others were climbing into the vehicle, Lindsay followed them, hoping that Than's manners would make him allow Barb to go in next so that she would sit between them. Keeping her gaze toward the front of the vehicle, Lindsay bit her lower lip. Okay, so maybe part of her reaction to all this was that while he'd complimented Barb on how she looked, Than hadn't said one word about her.

Lindsay looked down and smoothed a hand over the skirt of her dress. At that moment, she'd never felt more un-special in her life. She hated that a man could make her feel this way. It stung to know she'd given a man the power to hurt her like this. It shouldn't matter that he hadn't said anything to her that didn't fall in line with his job so far that morning. It shouldn't matter that the only smiles she'd seen on his face had been when he'd looked at Amanda and Barb.

It shouldn't matter...but it did.

How was she going to survive this? Her heart going in one direction, her thoughts going in another? Sometimes she thought she was going to lose her mind. She knew all the reasons she should run very far and very fast from Than, but her heart—her traitorous heart—wanted to run toward him instead. Her mind knew it was foolishness to indulge her heart when pain was sure to follow...but her heart kept trying to convince her it was worth the risk. Because maybe...just maybe...he would come to feel about her the way she did about him.

But was she stupid enough to think that she could be *that woman*? The one that would change his mind and make him commit to just her?

Surely she was smarter than that...

Than shifted on the pew which had clearly not been made for men of his height with long legs. He felt like his butt was barely on the seat...the very unpadded seat. Lindsay sat on one side of him, her legs crossed, her back straight as if she sat in pews like this every day of the week. Her hands were folded over the Bible in her lap, and she stared straight ahead.

With a frown, Than rubbed a hand over his chest. He figured any minute now he was going to get hit with a lightning bolt since the only thing going through his mind was that he would pay good money to be anywhere but on that pew in that church. He hadn't slept well at all the night before, and he still felt like a battle was raging inside of him.

Barb's words about a relationship with God and how it would make a relationship with Lindsay better—if they should ever get to that point—had gone round and round in his head all night. Did he really need that personal relationship with God she talked about? He was a good guy. He didn't steal or cheat. He did his best to be nice to everyone he met and make them feel better about themselves—especially the women. He helped people out who were in need. He loved his family and treated them well. How could God's presence in his life make *that* big a difference?

Would he really be denied heaven because he didn't have that type of relationship with God? Though he didn't spend a lot of time thinking about it, he always believed there was a God and a heaven, and he'd always believed that if he lived a good life, he'd go there when he died. Now Barb had him questioning it all. Just when her comments would begin to make sense to him, a little voice would pop up reminding him that he'd gotten by just fine without church and God all these years.

And it had been no different when his thoughts had turned to Lindsay. There was a voice that kept asking him why he was so hung up on her. It reminded him there were any number of women who would happily go out with him. He'd been frustrated by her reaction to his conversation with Amanda. Oh, she hadn't said anything and she hadn't even given him a suspicious look when they'd met up for supper. There had just been...nothing. He'd gotten used to seeing more emotion on her face over the past week. She'd let down her guard and her emotional reaction to everything had been much more evident.

Even to him.

She probably would have denied it, but he'd seen it in her eyes. That spark of interest when she'd looked at him. The flush that would creep up her cheeks when their gazes met. It had been a softer side of Lindsay that he'd only ever seen when she was around her family—especially Danny. But she'd let him see that side of her more recently, had even shown it when it was the result of their interactions. But now...nothing.

Than knew he could have explained what had happened with Amanda and put her mind at ease, but he shouldn't *have* to. She should be able to trust him. He would have even accepted her asking him about it. But she hadn't. He'd been tried and found guilty without even being given the benefit of the doubt. And that ticked him off. He knew she had trust issues, but seriously?

However, as soon as he'd convinced himself to just write off any future relationship with her, he'd remembered all the things that had drawn him to her in the first place. He wasn't ashamed to admit that the first thing that had attracted him to her had been her looks. The gray eyes framed by long dark lashes that could move from quicksilver to diamond hard in a flash. And yes, he'd noticed all the curves she had in all the right places. He'd heard her comment a time or two about needing to lose weight, but as far as he could see, she was just fine the way she was. Very fine.

Seeing her in the context of her family had endeared her to him further. He also felt his family was important and he liked that she valued hers, too. And he'd never forget that night out at the Hamilton cabin when she'd unleashed more emotion than he'd ever seen from her before when she'd thought Lucas was stepping aside to let Lincoln have a shot at making things work with Brooke. That was when he'd realized that she believed strongly in love and would fight for it if she felt it was worth it.

He wanted her to turn that passion toward what was between them. But maybe she didn't feel as strongly about it...yet.

Than sighed and shifted on the pew, his arm rubbing against Lindsay's. She didn't look his way, and all the turmoil swirled to life again. He was beginning to wish they'd taken the second trip so they hadn't had to sit waiting for the service to start. It was giving him too much time to think, and after having spent a night doing that already, he really didn't want to do it anymore.

Instead, he tried to focus on their surroundings. The church was a fair size building that had managed to withstand the storm for the most part. The cement brick walls had been strong enough, but he could see that some windows were missing. There were fans around the room, though none moved due to the lack of electricity. Thankfully, it wasn't a super hot morning and there was a breeze that came through the windows.

Finally, a piano began to play and Than watched as people who had been standing in clusters began to find their way to pews. A few minutes later, a man climbed onto the platform and greeted the congregation.

In a mixture of Tagalog and English, the man expressed how thankful he was for each of them and that God had protected them through the storm. Then he requested they bow their heads for prayer.

Than listened to the man as he prayed, and people around the room murmured or called out *amen* along with him. He was thankful he had a grasp of the language or it might have had no impact on him at all. But as he listened to the man thank God for hearing their prayers and sparing them from the storm, Than could hear the emotion in his voice.

When the prayer was over, a man with a guitar and a couple of women joined the leader on the stage. Than stood with the rest of the congregation when they began to sing. It didn't escape his notice that he stood a good head taller than most around him. And it made him even more self-conscious when he didn't know the songs they sang. Rather than allow the embarrassment over that pull him down, Than tried to focus instead on the words of the songs.

Still, he was relieved when they were invited to sit once again. He anticipated a sermon next, but instead the leader invited people to share how God had protected them during the storm.

An elderly woman stood and began to talk. Thankfully, she was near them so Than could hear her even without a mic. Realizing that Lindsay wouldn't know what she was saying, Than leaned down and spoke in a low voice.

"She's saying that during the storm, the roof was blown off part of her home. Her husband is old so he couldn't repair it, but then their neighbor came and fixed it for them. Praise the Lord."

Lindsay glanced at him when he said that.

He shrugged. "That's what she said."

He interpreted a few more of the stories that were shared, keeping his voice low. Then he saw Marissa and her husband stand. She held the baby, and the little boy was in his father's arms.

He listened for a minute before he began to interpret. Lindsay looked at him as if wondering if he'd forgotten her. "Marissa is saying that her pains started when the storm first died down. Her son was finally asleep, and she couldn't leave him to get help. Then the storm started up again and she knew she was alone. She says that all night long she prayed that God would send someone to help her." He paused again to listen. "She said in the morning when her son woke, she sent him out to see if he could find help since she was having trouble walking. Then, the next she knew, two beautiful white women walked into her home and answered her prayers."

Than glanced at Lindsay and saw a sweep of pink in her cheeks. "She said that she had stopped going to church after her mother died because she was angry at God for not saving her. Now she knows that she was wrong to do that because God still listened to her when she cried out to Him. She understands that it was her mother's time to go, and God didn't take her to punish her. She is very thankful for Lindsay, Barb and Imee for helping her bring her baby into the world. And for the generosity of the missionaries who cared for her until her husband came back."

The congregation applauded, and Than heard many saying *praise the Lord*. Marissa had settled back down on her seat, but her husband remained standing. He set the boy down and gripped the back of the pew in front of him.

Slowly he started to talk, and once again Than began to translate the words. "He says that he hadn't known about the storm before he left for Manila. And when he heard it had hit their town, he had no way to get back. And no way to find out if his family was okay. The roads were closed in some places because of the possibility of landslides from the rain. He felt so helpless not being there for his family and for the first time he prayed to God asking Him to protect them. He knew he could do nothing more than trust God to protect his family. And then when he got back to their home and found it empty, he thought he'd lost everything." Than paused as the man's voice broke and he bent forward. He found that he had to swallow to ease the tightness in his own throat before he could continue. "Even though his house still stood, without his family, he had nothing. He said he cried out to God again, asking Him to please take him too. That he didn't want to live if his family was gone. Then he saw the note the missionary had left, and he ran the whole way to the mission center to find his family. And they were safe."

The man lifted his hand into the air. "*Salamat sa Diyos. Salamat sa Diyos.*"

"Thank you, God. Thank you, God."

Lindsay's head dipped forward, and he saw her brush her fingers over her cheeks. Than shifted again and laid his arm along the back of the pew behind Lindsay. As more people got up to share their stories, he continued to interpret for her. She kept her head bent and periodically brushed at her cheeks. As he heard story after story of how grateful people were—some even after having lost everything—Than realized that here was the personal relationship Barb had talked about.

These people believed in God and His presence in their lives. The trust and faith they had in Him was something he'd never witnessed to this degree before. Than knew that Eric McKinley often said how grateful he was that God had given him a second chance—not just with his wife, Staci, but also as a Christian. Lucas was also quick to thank God for how things had worked out with his wife Brooke and the return of his twin brother, Lincoln. Having a personal relationship with God didn't seem to stifle these men. In fact, they seemed super content and joyful in their lives.

Than wished right then that he could sit down with Lucas and Eric and talk to them about all of this. He could understand Lucas and Eric's joy in their lives. They had nice homes, money, women who loved them, children and family. But here were people who had next to nothing, still rejoicing and praising God as if they had everything in the world. Didn't they know what they were missing? Or was their joy really complete in God, and everything else was secondary to that?

At one point, Lindsay straightened and leaned back in the pew. Than's fingers brushed against her bare upper arm, and he waited for her to shoot him a look or to move away, but she didn't. It seemed that when her emotions were most near the surface, she was more likely to accept his nearness. It was when her brain got involved that things tensed up between them.

It seemed that her heart and mind were as much at odds as his were.

Lindsay might have been able to keep her emotions locked down during the service if Than hadn't been there to translate for her. But each story, each praise, touched her in a way she hadn't expected, given her mindset when she'd first sat down on the hard pew.

Once the service was over, people gathered around to talk to them. Than had turned to talk with people in the pew behind them. Standing between Than and Barb, Lindsay was a bit taken aback when a young man sidled down the row in front of them and asked if she was married, and if not, would she marry him. Uncertain how to extricate herself without offending the man, Lindsay looked around for help.

She must have looked like a deer in headlights because Barb spoke up and said, "Her heart is already spoken for."

Though she wasn't quite ready to embrace the truth of that statement, Lindsay shot Barb a look of thanks. The man gave a shake of his head and murmured something she didn't understand.

"He said that's too bad because you're very beautiful."

Lindsay jerked when she heard Than's voice next to her ear at the same time as his hand landed lightly on her lower back. She glanced at him and then back at the man. "Uh...thank you?"

Than said something in Tagalog to the young man. The man looked Than up and down and replied. They went back and forth for a couple of minutes before the man held his hand out to Than. He moved his hand from her back in order to shake the offered hand. The man gave her a wide smile before moving away from where she stood.

Lindsay watched to make sure he really was going to leave them alone before turning to Than. "What was that all about? A marriage proposal? Why would he do that?"

"First of all, I think he was a little drunk."

Lindsay's eyes widened. "Drunk? At this time of day? In *church*?"

"I don't think alcohol is as regulated here as it is in the US. And as for being in church, I have a feeling he heard there were some pretty *Americanas* here and decided to check it out for himself."

"So what did you say to him?"

Lindsay could see humor glinting in Than's eyes. "Let's just leave it. Suffice to say he won't bother you again."

She frowned. "What did you say to him?"

Than shook his head and sighed. "He took my presence at your side and added it to Barb's comment and came to his own conclusion. I didn't bother to dissuade him."

Lindsay felt warmth rush up her cheeks and looked away. "Oh."

"If you'd like, I could explain to him he was wrong," Than offered.

She jerked her head up to tell him not to do that, but when their gazes met, she saw the humor was still there. "Well, we're even now."

Than arched a brow. "Even?"

"I saved you from the beauty queen, and you saved me from the drunken man."

Than chuckled. "I guess we are. I'd already forgotten about her."

"Ouch. No woman ever wants to hear that."

He smiled at her. "Oh, no worries. You'll never hear that from me."

Not at all sure of his change in mood from earlier, Lindsay found herself warming to him once again. It was an endless rollercoaster of emotion she seemed to be on with him lately. She pulled her gaze from his and once again followed the progress of her would-be suitor. He seemed to be headed in the direction of Amanda and the young teenage girl.

"I wonder why he didn't go to Amanda first?" Given her blonde hair and blue eyes, Lindsay thought she stood out more amongst the predominantly dark hair of most in the church. She didn't realize she'd said the words aloud until Than replied.

"He obviously has good taste and went with the most beautiful first." When Lindsay turned her gaze to him, he held up his hands and said, "Totally unbiased opinion, of course."

She arched a brow. "Unbiased?"

Than shrugged. "I'm not your dad, husband or boyfriend, so I'd say it was unbiased."

"But you are my friend," Lindsay pointed out.

Than's gaze seemed to bore into her. "Am I?"

16

HIS question shocked Lindsay and made her think. He'd been on the periphery of her life for a few years now. She'd heard about him through Adrianne and Melanie Thorpe, but it had always been in passing, and she hadn't thought much about him. Then when he'd stepped forward to help find Lincoln, he'd moved from the outer edges of her world into an inner circle. Maybe she'd never considered him a personal friend, but certainly a friend of the family since he hung out with Lincoln a fair bit and was at the house at least once every couple of weeks. Then he'd become her bodyguard, and now he was smack dab in the middle of her life.

But was he her friend? As she watched Than take in her ponderings, she realized that this answer was important to him. As it was to her.

"Yes," she said with a quick nod of her head. "You are my friend."

When the corners of his lips turned up, Lindsay knew her answer had pleased him.

"It's definitely a step in the right direction," he said, his gaze warm.

Lindsay felt the need to move beyond that moment and glanced back over to where Amanda stood. "Maybe you should go rescue her."

"Nope. I'm your bodyguard, not hers. Besides, she has a real reason to refuse him. She has a boyfriend."

"Yes, I know. She's mentioned him a few times." But a boyfriend wasn't a husband.

Than's brows drew together. "She has?"

Before the conversation could go any further, they were approached again, this time by a small group of girls who seemed to have their sights set on Than. As Lindsay watched him interact with the young women, she recalled what Mark had said in one of their pre-trip meetings about things like mail-order brides. He had been speaking to the single men in the group, pointing out that often women in countries like the Philippines saw marriage as a way out of a life that was steeped in poverty. And it wasn't just because they wanted to escape, but often marriage to foreigners also gave them the opportunity to support their families back in the Philippines.

She wondered what that must be like—to choose to marry for financial security rather than love. It was a scenario she'd never have to consider, but clearly it was something women like those talking with Than did. There was such an innocence surrounding the girls—giggling, hiding their smiles behind the handkerchiefs they held in their hands— that Lindsay wondered how often women like them fell prey to men who were unscrupulous and abusive.

"Lindsay, look who's here," Barb said as she held out her arms.

Marissa approached with her family in tow and quickly placed the baby in Barb's arms. Lindsay bent over to peer at her and smiled when her namesake looked back at her with big round dark eyes. To think that she'd played even a small part in bringing this little one into the world was amazing to her. A bright light in the midst of the scary darkness of the storm.

They chatted with Marissa for a few minutes before Than touched her elbow and told her that Elliot was getting ready to take the first group back.

"Can we go on the second one?" Lindsay asked. "Unless there's not enough going the first trip."

"No. It's fine. I'll let Elliot know we'll take the second trip."

By the time they returned to the mission center, Lindsay was feeling lighter and more encouraged than she had since arriving almost a week ago. The damage from the storm was being cleaned up. The people of the town were resilient, not letting it get them down. Those who had shared in the church service earlier had proved that.

The lively conversation over the dinner that was ready for them shortly after they returned seemed to show that she wasn't the only one feeling that way. Once they were done, Elliot said they were setting up a volleyball net if anyone was interested in playing.

Feeling in the mood for some lighthearted competition, Lindsay changed into a pair of capris and a T-shirt. She gathered her hair back into a ponytail and grabbed the BlackThorpe Security ball cap and shoved it on her head. When she got back down to the large open area beside the dining room, she could see that the volleyball net was up and blankets had been stretched out on the grass in the shade of the building.

Than stood talking to a couple of the guys. He'd changed as well and now wore a pair of black cargo shorts and a white T-shirt. The shirt fit him in such a way as to remind her of the job this man had taken on for her. His broad shoulders and the strength revealed in his arms and chest were all part of the protector he was. For now, her protector.

The thought tripped her up as she walked across the grass toward him. Toward the group of people gathered there.

"You know how to play?" Than asked when he spotted her at his side, his dark eyes alight with humor.

Lindsay crossed her arms and tilted her head. "I think I can figure it out."

"Figure it out?" Than chuckled. "I think you need to be on the other team while you figure it out."

"A bit competitive are we?"

"I don't lose," Than said. "Ever."

"Fine." Lindsay made a show of stomping over to the net and ducking under it to get to the other side. "Guess you guys are stuck with me."

Her team was made up of the two teens, the teens' dad, Amanda and one of the single guys. Lindsay sized up the teens and motioned them close. "Either of you play volleyball in school?"

They both grinned at her. "We're on the school teams."

Lindsay couldn't help but grin back. "I was too when I was in high school. I might be a bit out of practice, but I have a feeling it's going to come back in a rush. We need to beat the other team. We need to beat Than."

The teams fumbled through the first few points. Than was definitely the best player on the opposite team. Lindsay could see that the teens were deliberately hiding their skill until they could size up the opposing players. She did the same thing until it was time for her to serve.

"You need to get it over the net," Than called to her. "Do you want a practice shot?"

"Only if I can aim for your head," she muttered under her breath. The twins, who were in the back row with her, chuckled. "You two ready? Let's put on a show."

"Go for it," the teenage boy said with a thumbs-up.

Lindsay took a position like she was going to serve from her hand but then she tossed the ball into the air, jumped and hit it with a sure strike. It landed exactly where she'd been aiming...in the space between Than and one of the other single guys. As the guy scrambled to get the ball, Than stood with his feet braced, his fingers splayed across his hips, staring at her.

"Hey, Than," Lindsay called over to him. "I think I've got it figured out."

There was a swell of laughter at her comment.

Even though the opposite team now knew of her serving power, she still managed to get them a couple more points before it went back to them. Now that Lindsay had shown what she was capable of, the teens also stepped up their game. It was clear the brother and sister practiced together because they had some pretty fierce moves with one of them setting the ball for the other.

Though Than tried valiantly to keep his team alive, Lindsay's experience—along with the teens' skill—pretty much guaranteed their win. When they made the teams for the second game, they made sure to separate Lindsay from the teens so she ended up on the same team as Than.

"So where'd a rich kid like you learn to play like that?" Than asked, his upset at having been beaten evident in his tone.

She lifted her chin and arched a brow at him. "You don't think we have competitive volleyball teams in private schools? I was on the team all four years in high school. Even played a couple of years in college. Did you play in high school, too?"

Than nodded. "I was also on the team through high school and college."

"Not sure we can beat the wonder teens over there, but let's give it a good old college try."

With the teams a little more evenly balanced, the next game was closer in score. Than's competitive streak strengthened Lindsay's and soon it had basically turned into a game between the two of them and the teens with the other team members standing in their spots watching.

As the ball sailed over the heads of the front row, Lindsay made a dash for it, calling it at the same time Than did. Coming from opposite sides of the court, they collided and Than's height and bulk guaranteed that she was the one on the bottom when they fell to the grass.

"Oof!" Lindsay felt the wind leave her lungs as she hit the ground with Than landing on top of her.

He immediately rolled away and then bent over her. "Linds? Are you okay?"

Lindsay lay with her arms out, staring up at the clouds and tried to draw breath into her lungs. Than's face blocked out the sky, his dark gaze filled with worry.

"Lindsay? Did I hurt you?"

She felt his hands quickly running over her arms and then cupping her face. "Lindsay, sweetheart, say something!"

"Let me have a look at her." Barb's calm voice washed over Lindsay. "I think she's likely just had the wind knocked out of her."

"Help her!" Than demanded, an edge of panic to his voice. "Help her, please. I didn't break any of her bones, did I?"

"Help me sit her up. Bend her knees."

Lindsay felt Than's arm go around her shoulders to support her as he slipped an arm under her knees to bend them as Barb had instructed.

"C'mon, Lindsay," Barb said. "In through your nose. Out through your mouth."

Slowly the paralysis that had seized her diaphragm lessened, and she was able to draw air into her lungs. The panic that had been threatening to overcome her eased away with each breath she was able to take.

After she'd taken a few deep breaths, Lindsay said, "I'm okay. I'm okay."

Than still knelt beside her on the grass, one hand rubbing her back. "I'm so sorry, sweetheart. Are you sure you're alright? If I broke a bone in your body, Lucas is going to kill me and demand his money back. I'm supposed to be protecting you, not hurting you. Are you okay?"

Lindsay watched as Barb reached across her to give Than a light slap on the cheek.

"Snap out of it, son. She's fine." Barb looked down at her. "Tell him, sweetheart."

Lindsay took a deep breath, let it out, then looked up at Than. The emotion in his eyes momentarily robbed her of words. She swallowed and said, "I'm fine, Than. A little winded but nothing broken."

"Are you sure?" Though the panic had eased, there was still a lot of emotion in his eyes—some she couldn't identify.

Not sure she could handle everything that was swirling between them, Lindsay looked away and held out her hand. "Help me up, please."

Than took both her hands and pulled her up. He kept a tight grip on them even after she was steady on her feet. Refusing to look at him, Lindsay gave his hands a squeeze then tugged. "Thanks."

With apparent reluctance, Than let her hands slide from his grasp. He took a deep breath and stepped back from her. Telling herself she was foolish to miss his hands holding hers, Lindsay focused on her breathing.

"How about we call the game and let Than and Lindsay's team take this one?" the teens' father suggested. "I think Than is a little traumatized. Maybe a win might help him recover."

Lindsay couldn't help the chuckle that escaped. Than traumatized? She glanced over to see him standing in his normal pose, feet braced, hands on his hips. She couldn't read anything on his face. Any emotion from their fall had disappeared behind a serious expression.

Suddenly he shrugged, and one corner of his mouth lifted. "Hey, I'll take the win any way I can get it."

With that, the tension that had followed their collision slipped away. They decided to continue to play, but Lindsay had had her fill of the game and settled onto a blanket next to Barb. Sitting in the shade was a nice break from the sun, especially when a soothing breeze kicked up. She pulled off the ball cap—which had somehow survived her crash—and set it on the ground next to her.

Though she kept her gaze on the game, Lindsay found her thoughts going to the moments following the fall. Unable to do anything—even breathe—her world had narrowed to

Than's face as he'd hovered over her. The emotion in his eyes would have taken her breath away if it hadn't already been slammed from her lungs. Fear. Panic. And then there had been the gentleness in his hands as he'd touched her face and her arms, searching for any damage that may have come to her.

Lindsay wasn't sure she remembered ever seeing someone so concerned about her. Was it possible he really did feel something more for her than she'd thought? Did he want more than *just* a second date? And if he did? What was she going to do about that?

Than pulled the sweat-soaked T-shirt over his head and dropped it onto the pile of dirty clothes he had going next to his suitcase. Though the relaxed afternoon had been a nice break from the tense week they'd just come through, Than found he couldn't keep his mind from going to those few minutes following him crashing into Lindsay.

It had taken him by surprise to such an extent that he hadn't even reacted like he should have. He should have gotten his arms around her and twisted them so that his body took the brunt of the fall instead of her. Should have done what he could to protect her from injury. That was his job.

His hands clenched even as his mind told him that there hadn't been enough time. That he'd done the next best thing by rolling off her as soon as they'd hit the ground. But never in a million years would he forget seeing her lying so still, her arms spread wide. And then when he'd bent over her and stared into her eyes that were open, but she didn't seem to be breathing, he'd just about lost his mind.

Him. Mr. Calm, Cool, and Collected. He'd been shot at. He'd had clients get shot at. He'd even had a client get shot because they'd done something stupid. And then there had been the time his nephew had taken a bad spill on his skateboard. Even though his sister-in-law had freaked out at the blood and odd angle of his arm, Than had been able to deal with the situation calmly and get the boy to the hospital.

But nothing—absolutely *nothing*—had ever totaled his emotions like that run-in with Lindsay.

Than sank down onto the bed and ran a hand through his hair. This really wasn't good. He didn't need that second date with Lindsay Hamilton to know that she was far more important to him than he'd ever known someone could be. He swore his heart had stopped beating from the time he'd bent over her until she took that first breath.

And more telling than anything else had been the thought going round and round in his head. *This can't be happening. I haven't had my forever with her yet.*

Forever?

That had never been in his vocabulary when it came to women until that moment with Lindsay. And surprisingly enough, it didn't instill in him the panic it might have at one time with anyone else.

But Than knew that the situation they were in right then wasn't the place to test the waters with her. He needed to just get through this next week and then figure out what to do when they got back to Minneapolis. It was just a feeling in his gut, but he was pretty sure that her attitude toward him— which had been getting more open and relaxed—would change when they got back home. Whatever he wanted to have with her had to be grounded in their real life. Not this one where the full spectrum of emotions from fear to joy had pushed them together in a way they never would have been in Minneapolis.

He just hoped that she would remember everything they'd experienced together. That she'd remember the man she knew here and realize that he was still that man when they got home. And recalling Barb's words about his faith, Than knew that he had a few things he needed to work on there, too.

Than bent forward, his forearms resting on his hands, fingers intertwined. He closed his eyes and...waited. He wasn't sure how to pray. He didn't know *what* to pray. Finally, he just voiced what was currently in his heart.

God, please open Lindsay's heart to me. Help me to be able to show her that I can be the man she needs. And help me be that man. I'm confused. Please help me.

For someone who was used to relying on his own abilities and talents, asking for help felt awkward to Than. Did God really hear his prayer? Would it make any difference?

Than pushed to his feet and braced his hands on his hips as he stared out at the trees beyond the window. This next week he would keep to his job and give Lindsay the opportunity to get used to him being around when things weren't falling apart. No pressure for anything more than that. He'd already gotten to friend-level in the first week. Now he just needed to strengthen that and hope it would move to something more once they got back.

For the remaining five days of the trip, Lindsay and the rest of the team spent most their time on the mission center. They were able to focus on the things that had been initially planned for them to do. They had also helped to repair the damage to the second floor of the school where the roof had blown off.

Lindsay wasn't sure what she expected from Than after that intense moment they'd shared, but he'd gone on like it had never happened. Was he embarrassed by it? Or did he think she might misinterpret what had passed between them?

She told herself she should be glad things hadn't changed between them, but the sad truth was, for the first time in her life, she'd felt a real connection to a man. The emotion she'd seen in his eyes had burrowed its way deep into her heart. She wanted to see his eyes alive with emotions just for her again.

Instead, she got nothing more than anyone else on the team got. Smiles. Laughter. A bit of teasing. But beyond that? Nothing. She tried to act the same because there was no way on earth she was going to wear her heart on her sleeve if he apparently didn't care. At least he was still holding up his end of the wager. No flirting of any kind was going on.

Lindsay let herself into the orphanage on the evening of their last night on the mission center. She'd still made time each day to come and hold Maya. Because they'd been focused on repairing the damage to the buildings, her visits had occurred in the evening. She'd been allowed to bathe and feed Maya and then rock her to sleep. She'd told Than each night where she was going, but he hadn't come with her. Lindsay assumed that he figured she was safe enough on the center.

And she agreed with him on...one level. She was certainly in no danger physically, but the same could not be said for her heart. She was supposed to have been guarding her heart while he guarded her body, and while he'd done his job very well, she had failed miserably.

"Hello," one of the workers called out to her with a smile. "She's waiting for you."

Lindsay moved to take Maya from the woman. She lifted her to press a kiss to her soft cheek. "Hello, baby."

As she went through the motions of giving Maya her nightly bath, all she could think was that it was the last time she'd do this for her. Would it be the last time she'd ever bathe a baby? For some reason, she just couldn't imagine ever having a baby in her arms that didn't have big brown eyes and olive skin.

Giving her head a shake, Lindsay pulled her thoughts back to the little girl kicking her legs on the change table as she put a diaper on her. She smiled as she thought of what the people back in her life would think of her changing diapers and burping babies. She'd gotten pretty good at it, too.

"Here's her bottle."

Lindsay took the bottle and settled into the rocking chair in the corner of the dimly lit room. As she'd done on other nights, she softly sang while she rocked. Maya's rosebud mouth worked the nipple of the bottle, her gaze locked onto Lindsay's. It wasn't until she saw the drop of moisture slide down Maya's fisted hand where it lay against the bottle that Lindsay realized she was crying.

She lifted a hand to wipe the wetness from her cheeks, but the tears kept coming. Even taking a couple of deep breaths didn't stem the rush. She hunched her shoulders and gathered Maya close to her chest.

This little girl would be holding a piece of her heart when Lindsay left early the next morning. She wished that going back would mean being able to put aside the pain she was feeling right then. That she'd be able to go back to all-business Lindsay. That her protective shell would be in place and she'd be able to slip back into her life as if nothing had changed.

Except everything had.

She lifted the baby to the cloth covering her shoulder and rubbed and patted her tiny back until she was rewarded with a burp. When another one didn't follow the first, Lindsay returned Maya to the cradle of her arms and continued to rock her. Slowly her eyelids dipped... opened... dipped... opened... and then finally they dipped and settled, her dark lashes fanning out over her cheeks.

Knowing that once Maya was asleep her time was growing even shorter, Lindsay bent her head to press kisses to the soft thatch of hair, inhaling the scent of baby shampoo. She held her longer than she normally would have before finally standing up to put her in the crib. Though she longed to linger, she still had some packing to finish up. They were leaving early in the morning, and she wanted to not have to do much except dress and get on the bus.

Than knocked on the open door of the room Lindsay shared with Barb and Amanda. "Is Lindsay here?"

Barb straightened from where she stood putting clothes into the suitcase on her bed. "No. She's over with the babies."

Than frowned. "Still? Usually, she's back by now."

Barb moved closer to him, her brows drawn low over her green eyes. "You might want to consider going over there."

"Why? Is something wrong?"

"Really, Than?" Barb sighed and gave her head a shake. "She's saying goodbye to Maya tonight."

As he realized what Barb was saying, Than wondered how he could be so stupid. "Of course. I'm going there right now."

"Good boy." Barb's voice followed him as he moved quickly down the hallway.

He was halfway to the orphanage when he saw a figure step in front of the screen door lit from behind by the lights in the house. The door opened, and he knew it was Lindsay. Her head was bent and her arms were crossed over her middle.

Than slowed his steps as she headed in his direction. As she moved into the shadowed area where the porch lights of none of the buildings reached, he said her name.

She came to a halt but didn't lift her head. Than stopped in front of her and reached out to grasp her shoulders. "You okay, sweetheart?"

He heard the sniffle as she leaned toward him, gripping the front of his shirt. His resolve to keep things on a friendly level dissolved as she seemed to be seeking solace from him. Than gathered her into his arms, tucking her head under his chin as sobs shook her body. He pressed a kiss to her hair, inhaling its fragrant scent. As he held her, all he could think about was how perfect she felt in his arms. He wanted to hold her through all her tears.

He rubbed his hand up and down her back. "It's going to be okay, sweetheart. They'll take good care of her. She's got lots of love here, too."

Her grip on his shirt tightened, and he could feel the heat of her tears as they soaked through to his skin. There seemed to be no words that would offer comfort to her, so Than just held her close until the heaving sobs settled into mild shudders then a few deep breaths.

Then, still clutching his shirt, Lindsay's head lifted. In the darkness, he had no way of reading her expression, but she wasn't pushing him away so he kept his arms loosely around her. He felt her grip on his shirt loosen and prepared to release her, but suddenly he felt her hands on the back of his neck. She shifted onto her tiptoes as she drew his head down. Unerringly, she pressed her lips to his and kissed him.

For a moment, Than froze in shock, but when she didn't immediately push away from him, he kept one hand around her waist while the other slid into her hair.

17

THAN took control of the kiss, pouring everything into it that he'd tried to keep within him this past week. Her lips were soft beneath his as she followed him into the maelstrom of emotion that had descended on them.

Though the kiss seemed to go on forever, when Lindsay moved back from him, it felt like it had lasted only a heartbeat. He didn't try to hold her when it was clear she was coming to her senses. He let his arms fall to his sides, shoving his hands into the pockets of his shorts.

She took one step back and then stood there for a moment.

"Lindsay?"

Without a word, she spun and began to walk toward the dorm. Than watched her walk away, trying to figure out what on earth had just happened. He would have understood completely if he'd been the one who had initiated that kiss since he'd thought about it more than once. But it had been *her* that made the move. She'd drawn his head down and kissed *him*.

But why?

Had the emotion of the moment been the only reason she'd kissed him like that? He sure hoped not because even though he'd seen other layers shedding from Lindsay, this one had been most unexpected. The passion that had sparked between them had just added one more dimension to what he already felt for her.

And yet he had a funny feeling that come morning, she'd be acting as if the kiss had never happened. Than sighed as he trudged toward the dorm. He sensed that just like she was leaving the baby behind, she was going to leave behind that kiss and whatever else had passed between them over the past ten days.

His heart hurt at the thought, but he'd come to realize that he wanted Lindsay to come to him on her own terms. It was the only way for it to work. She knew who he was. She had to decide on her own that he was what she wanted. He didn't want to flirt, cajole or plead for her to give him that second chance anymore.

The ball was in her court now.

Not that it had ever really been in *his* court, Than realized with a wry grin. From the moment she'd dictated what type of date he was going to take her on and what he'd wear, she'd been in control.

Lindsay was surprised her legs didn't give out from under her as she tried to make it to the dorm before Than caught up with her. She was still trying to catch her breath, too. Who would've thought a kiss could be like that? She hadn't experienced anything like that with any of the guys she'd previously kissed. Not that there had been that many of them, but even her most serious relationship—the one that had gotten as far as an engagement—hadn't held that kind of spark.

She had always thought Than was attractive physically—that had really never been in question—and recently she had come to see he had a lot of other attractive qualities, but this had been totally out of the blue. And she didn't quite know what to do with it. She'd been looking for an escape from the pain of having said goodbye to Maya, but she hadn't expected that.

When she reached the room, she slipped inside, shut the door and leaned back against it, her palms flat on the smooth wood surface. Barb was sitting on the edge of her bed, and her eyes widened.

"Something chasing you?" she asked.

Lindsay looked around the room and noticed that Amanda wasn't there. She pushed away from the door, dropped down on her bed and stared at Barb. This was so unlike her. Lindsay Hamilton did not get shaken up like this. She might have controlled the start and the end of the kiss, but everything in between had been in Than's control.

"I kissed him."

Barb's brows rose. "I suppose I don't really have to ask who *him* is."

Lindsay lifted her hand to her lips. "It was way more...than I expected. Is that wrong?"

Barb didn't reply right away, almost as if she was trying to figure out what to say. Finally, she said, "No, it's not wrong. God created us with emotions, feelings, passions. Experiencing that passion isn't a bad thing either, but you have to realize it can lead to places you need to steer clear of if you're not married."

Lindsay nodded. "I don't even know what made me kiss him and then *bam*, it was like a match had been tossed on dry kindling." Her cheeks flushed at the memory. "I didn't expect anything like that."

Barb chuckled. "Well, dear, you must be the only one who hasn't seen the chemistry between the two of you. You just have to be sure that a relationship isn't based solely on that. Physical attraction can be a good thing, but it's only one part of a relationship because if it's based only on that, it can burn out."

Lindsay knew what Barb was saying, but she wasn't sure she was ready to look that far into the future with Than. That kiss had just served to complicate things more than anything. But if she was honest, it had started even before the kiss. That he'd come to her, held her and offered her comfort had already touched her heart. The kiss had just kind of been the icing on the top of a very emotion-filled cake.

"If you want a little advice..." Barb began but then didn't continue.

"Sure. When it comes to this stuff, I think I need all the advice I can get."

"Don't rush into anything until we get back home. This has been a very unusual set of circumstances that has pushed us all together in ways things might not have at home. Give yourself a little time to get back into life there and then see where things go."

"Say yes to that second date?" Lindsay asked.

"Yes. I think you'll find that just as this trip has changed you, it has also changed Than. Pray about it and then spend some time together."

Lindsay bit her lip and frowned. "What if he's decided he doesn't want a second date?"

Barb laughed. "Oh, honey, I don't think that's something you need to worry about."

Taking a deep breath, Lindsay stood up. "Okay. I'll figure it out once we get home. Now...packing."

If Than had been a betting man, he would have said it was a sure bet that Lindsay would ignore what had happened between them with that kiss. And he would have been right.

When he'd seen her at breakfast the next morning, she'd said hi and smiled, just like normal. If the kiss hadn't been seared into his memory, he might have questioned if he'd dreamed the whole thing.

The kiss had actually confirmed something he'd suspected from the moment he'd felt a spark of attraction for

Lindsay. Yes, it was true he'd been attracted to her physically first, but he could honestly say that there was so much more to how he felt about her now. And he had a feeling that was why the kiss had packed the punch it had for him.

He could have sworn Lindsay had been as impacted as he had, but watching her act as if everything was the same between them had him wondering. Than had always prided himself on being able to read women, but Lindsay definitely confounded him. Just when he thought he'd figured her out, she threw a curve ball at him like that kiss. But then he *had* known that she'd ignore it just like she had, so he wasn't completely clueless.

After they had loaded up the bus that had returned to take them back to Manila, Than hadn't bothered to try to sit next to her. He had thought maybe he'd try to talk to Mark a bit about some of the questions he had, but in the end, Than realized he felt more comfortable with the idea of talking to Eric or even Lucas about them. They knew enough about him to know where he was coming from.

As the bus left the center and wound its way through the streets to the highway that would take them back to Manila, the damage done by the typhoon was still evident in places, but more apparent was the resilience of the Filipino people who had picked themselves up and moved forward with their lives. He was proud to be able to claim his Filipino heritage even if it only made up half of who he was.

The trip back to Manila took longer due to damage on the road, but they finally pulled into the mission house compound shortly after two o'clock. Than knew from the announcements that morning at breakfast that they had set aside time that afternoon and evening to do some shopping if people wanted. He wasn't surprised at all when Lindsay told him that she wanted to do a little shopping, which meant, of course, he was also doing a little shopping.

After dropping their bags in their rooms and grabbing a quick lunch, they were taken to a huge mall. Than hoped that the women didn't plan to hit every store or they'd for sure miss their plane the next day. Thankfully, the driver who dropped them off arranged to meet them at seven.

Than half expected Lindsay to ask him to give her some space to shop—which he wouldn't have been able to do—but instead, she asked his advice on a few things she was considering for her brothers and Danny. In return, she offered some thoughts on the things he was looking at for his nieces and sisters. Lindsay had insisted that Barb join them, and Than enjoyed seeing the two of them interact.

After having completed their lists, they found a restaurant and Than was as glad for the food as he was to be off his feet for a little bit. He was surprised that neither Lindsay nor Barb was complaining, but then he'd been the one carrying all their bags. If he'd had to go for his gun at any point, he would have definitely been slowed down by the mountain of plastic bags he'd been carting around. They were all piled up in the booth next to him as they ate. He hoped there was enough room in the vehicle that picked them up since he was pretty sure Lindsay and Barb weren't the only ones who'd bought out a store or two.

Once they got back to the mission house, Than had hoped to have a little time to talk to Lindsay, but she took off with Barb to their room and then he had to wait for his aunt and uncle to stop by again. This time he'd be returning the items Alberto had gotten him. His aunt came with a bag with things for his mom and sisters. And thankfully there had been no beauty queen in sight.

Knowing they'd be up early the next morning, Than decided to call it a night. He'd have a good stretch of time during which to talk to Lindsay on the plane, so he figured he'd just leave her be for the evening.

Eventually though, she'd have to talk to him.

He hoped.

To say Lindsay was relieved when the plane landed in Minneapolis would have been an understatement. Almost twenty-four hours of trying to keep the conversation from veering in the direction of the kiss had just about stressed her out of her mind. But planes and airports were the last places she wanted to have the conversation she knew they needed to have. And Lindsay knew Barb was right when she'd said that she needed to allow herself to process everything from the trip before jumping into anything.

Than's frustration had been very evident, but she'd just ignored it. And the one time he had dared to ask outright if they could talk about it, she had just said, "Not right now."

Thankfully, they'd gone through customs in Detroit so it was just a matter of deplaning and getting their bags once the plane landed in Minneapolis. She was thrilled to see her mom waiting for her along with Lucas, Brooke, Danny, and Lincoln. When she wrapped her arms around her mom, she thought she'd never let go. She couldn't wait to share everything with her family.

As they moved to the baggage claim area, her gaze drifted around to see who else had come to meet the team members. Her gaze snagged on Than as he stood with a woman Lindsay was sure was his mother. He'd mentioned she had been a beauty queen back in her day, and Lindsay could see that she was still a beautiful woman. A large man stood on the other side of her and, even though his coloring was Caucasian, Lindsay knew immediately that it was Than's dad.

She looked away from him when Lucas asked about her bags. When she spotted her first bag, she pointed it out to him and then pointed out the other one when it appeared a few bags behind the first. As Lucas and Lincoln loaded them onto the cart, it dawned on Lindsay that for the first time in two weeks, she wouldn't be seeing Than on a regular basis once they left the terminal.

Her gaze went back to him as he reached for a bag, his shirt stretching taut across his shoulders.

"Ready to go?" Lucas asked once the bags were on the cart with her carry-on.

With one last look at Than, she nodded. "Just let me say goodbye."

She quickly found Barb and moved in her direction. She was surrounded by two young women and a young man. The older woman held her arms out to Lindsay as she approached. Lindsay went into her embrace without hesitation. Her heart was aching as she realized she was being unplugged from this great group of people who'd shared experiences with her that no one else in her life in Minneapolis had. She was going to miss them. Particularly Barb and Than.

"Thank you for everything, Barb. This trip wouldn't have been the same without you." Lindsay smiled and blinked rapidly to keep the tears from falling. It was silly really, since they lived in the same city and attended the same church. It wasn't like she was saying goodbye for a long time.

"I feel the same way, honey." Barb reached out and cupped her cheek. "I'll be praying for you and for Than. Let me know what happens."

Lindsay nodded. "I will."

Barb introduced her to her children and then Lindsay looked around for Mark and Mel. When she found them, she gave them both a hug. "Thank you for taking a chance and letting me come with you. The things God has shown me on this trip have been life-changing."

"You touched lives, too" Mel said with a wide smile. "And we've all experienced things on this trip I don't think we'll ever forget."

Mark reminded her of their final mission team meeting on Sunday after church. "Food will be provided."

"I'll be there," Lindsay assured him and then headed back to where her family waited.

They were walking to the exit when Lindsay heard her name. She turned to see Than jogging toward them. He greeted her family before looking at her. "Can I talk to you for just a minute?"

When Lindsay nodded, he laid a hand on her back and led her away from her family to a spot that wasn't as crowded with people. Keeping his back to both their families, he looked down at her. "We need to talk."

"I know," Lindsay said. "I just need a little time."

His brown eyes seemed to look right into her heart. "I can give you that as long as it's not a no."

"It's...not."

Then, before she knew what was happening, his fingers lifted her chin, and he bent to press a soft kiss to her lips. Though it was nowhere near as intense as their last kiss, Lindsay reached for his waist to steady herself.

He lifted his head and stared down at her. "I know I lost the bet, so the ball is in your court now, sweetheart." His gaze darkened. "Please give me...us a chance."

Lindsay couldn't seem to make her vocal cords work. Her hand slipped from Than's waist as he stepped back. Feeling bereft, she could only watch as he turned and headed in the direction of his mom and dad. She quickly became aware of the fact that they had been the subject of curious gazes from both their families.

Taking a deep breath, she headed to where her family waited. All of them were looking at her expectantly, but all she said was, "Ready to go?"

"Anything you want to share with us?" Lucas asked as they headed for the exit.

"No," Lindsay said as she noticed Than's mother turn around to look at her as they walked out of the terminal. She wondered if she would be telling Than he could do better than her. After all, she didn't have any Filipino blood in her, even though she did have a profound love for the Philippines and its people.

Lucas had brought his large SUV so after loading her bags, they all climbed in and headed for the mansion. As she stared out at the city that had been her home for her whole life, Lindsay braced herself for the return to her old life and all that would mean.

With a sigh, Lindsay shoved back from her desk and walked over to the window that looked out over the sprawling metropolis. The clouds hung low in the sky as they dumped heavy rain across the Twin Cities. As the rain ran in streaks down the large glass window, a bolt of lightning shot across the sky. These were the kind of storms she liked. Although she did prefer to view them sitting on the porch of the cabin at the lake.

The rumble of thunder reminded her of the noises that had come with the typhoon. Not for the first time since returning home, her thoughts went to the people she'd met there. Marissa and her family often came to mind, along with Maya and Benjie. She'd asked Mel if there was any way to get news about the center and was pleased when the woman had directed her to a blog that one of the missionaries kept updated with news of what was happening on the center.

The first time she'd visited the blog, she'd been surprised to find pictures of the mission team trip even though she remembered a couple of people with cameras, and they'd had a couple of posed photos of the team members. Her breath had caught when she'd seen the picture of her holding Maya with Than seated near her with Benjie. She'd saved that one to her computer along with the one someone had taken of her flat on her back with Than kneeling next to her after their collision. Than had taken plenty of ribbing about that throughout the week that had followed. Lindsay was pleased that they'd identified him as part of the team, because in every way that had mattered, he had been.

She pressed a hand to the glass and sighed again. Somewhere out in that wet city was Than. She'd asked him for time. There had been so much to process after the trip. Not just what she felt about him, but also her outlook on life in general. She'd wondered if she'd slip back into her old ways once immersed in her life again, but from the responses of her family, she'd have to say that wasn't the case.

Her mom and Brooke had both commented that she smiled more often and more easily. Lucas and Lincoln had mentioned that she seemed a lot less uptight since her return. Danny was the only one who hadn't said anything about the changes in her. At first she'd wondered about it, but then she'd realized that he was already used to seeing her that way because she was always like that with him. That made it easier for her to hold onto those changes and now, a week after her return, it felt more natural to be this way.

Lindsay had never realized how stressful it was to keep so much of herself hidden from the world. Or even more stressful was trying to keep parts of herself from certain people while sharing them with others. Letting go of the masks had been incredibly freeing. The emotions that had risen to the surface while in the Philippines had stayed there and she relished having them there. Laughter, tears, joy and sadness...giving herself permission to experience each of the emotions as they came was so much better than trying to keep everything bottled up until she could process it when she was alone.

The only thing missing now was Than, and she really couldn't explain why she hadn't gone to him yet.

When her cell phone rang interrupting her thoughts, Lindsay left her place by the window to pick it up. She smiled when she saw Barb's name on the screen. She had called her several times since their return, and Lindsay didn't know what she would have done without those conversations.

"Hi, Barb."

"My last patient of the day cancelled so I thought I'd give you a call and see how you're doing. Is this a good time to chat?"

Lindsay sank into her chair and turned it so she could still watch the storm beyond the window. "It's perfect. I'm working late so I could use a break."

"Still catching up from being gone?"

"A bit, but I'm also trying to learn a more about the foundation Hamilton Enterprises has. I told Lucas I want to join him in running it."

"That's great news! Sounds like you're going to be busy."

"I've decided to hire an assistant to help me with my job so I'll have more time for the foundation. Lucas said he thought that was a great idea."

There was a beat of silence before Barb said, "Have you talked to Than yet?"

Lindsay knew from previous conversations that Barb had kept in contact with him, but she'd never volunteered anything about what they discussed. "No. Not yet."

She wasn't sure how to explain why she hadn't called him yet. At first she'd held off because she wanted to work through what had transpired on the trip in the light of her "real" life. The week had been more than enough time to figure out she liked the changes and that they were necessary for continued joy and happiness in her life. She knew that though she'd been looking for a new outlook on life when she'd gone on the trip, the changes God had wrought in her heart were beyond what she could ever have hoped for.

"What is holding you back, hun?" Barb asked. This was the first time she'd asked for an explanation for why Lindsay hadn't called Than yet.

Lindsay smoothed her fingers over the fabric of her skirt. "I told him at the airport I needed some time before we talked."

"Yes, you mentioned that when we first talked. Do you still feel like you need more time?"

"Not really. I've thought and prayed a lot about what has gone on between us, about me needing to be able to accept the type of person he is and trust him. I'm at peace about that now, but I'm not at peace about calling him. It's almost like now I need to give him time. Does that make sense?"

Barb gave a soft laugh. "More than you know. Listen to whatever it is that's telling you that."

Lindsay felt her stomach knot at Barb's comment. Had Than told Barb he was having second thoughts about her? Did he need time to figure out how he felt about her? She knew she'd given him a lot of mixed signals on the trip. Maybe he'd decided that he didn't need someone that complicated when all he really wanted was a second date.

"Just give him a little more time, Lindsay," Barb said, obviously reading her silence correctly. "He has his own things he's dealing with right now. Clearly God has put it into your heart to wait for now. Rushing into things will never be as good as waiting on God's timing. I'll be praying for both of you and that you'll feel a clear sense of peace about the right time to make contact with Than again."

They talked for a few more minutes before Barb ended the call. Lindsay lowered her phone to her lap and stared at the sky that was even darker than it had been just a few minutes earlier. The unsettled feeling in her stomach made her queasy. What if Than *had* changed his mind about her? Would she be able to survive the hurt without closing herself off again?

Emotions made her vulnerable. Being vulnerable meant being more easily hurt. Could she handle the hurt that might be headed her way? Somehow she knew that the pain that would come if Than didn't feel the same about her as she did him would be far worse than what she'd felt when she'd discovered her ex-fiancé had been after her money.

Lindsay closed her eyes. *Okay, God, I have no idea what's going on with Than, but I know that You do. Please help me to trust You and to believe that all things will work out for Your glory. If that means that Than and I aren't to be together, give me strength to get through that hurt.* She paused as verses tumbled through her mind. *Help me to find my peace and joy in You no matter what else comes my way.*

Knowing there was nothing more she could do until she felt that peace to contact Than—if that time ever came—Lindsay slowly turned back to her desk and the work that waited there for her.

Lindsay was surprised at the ease with which she was granted entrance into the BlackThorpe office complex. The guard at the gate had asked for ID and the purpose of her visit before waving her through with instructions on where to park. Then when she'd entered the large main building, the men at the desk had again asked for ID before giving her a visitor badge and directing her to the elevator.

They obviously controlled the elevator because she hadn't needed to press any buttons to close the door or to start its ascent. She smoothed the skirt of the dress she wore. She'd left work early and gone home to change before coming to the BlackThorpe building. No one had said Than had already left when she'd said she was there to see him. Nerves fluttered in her stomach at the thought of seeing him again. It was Friday, so she hoped that he'd be available to go out for dinner with her.

Their second date.

She'd spent a lot of time over the past two weeks thinking about everything that had happened and had prayed for wisdom to know what to do. It had been strange that every day since her return, she'd had a strong sense that she needed to put off seeing Than for another day in spite of the fact. She had had no clear message, just a feeling that she needed to wait and pray. So she had. She hadn't called, texted or sent him an email.

But when she'd awoken that morning and thought of him, for the first time it was like she had been released from whatever had been holding her back. And the rightness of the decision to see him hadn't lessened throughout the day. She was a bit nervous, and she hoped he wouldn't be angry with her for having taken so long to make contact with him. But he *had* said he'd give her time.

She lifted her head to watch the floor numbers slide by without any idea of where she would end up. Lindsay just hoped Than was waiting for her when she got there.

When the elevator doors opened, Lindsay stepped out, hoping she was on the right floor. The woman seated behind a large desk smiled as she approached.

"You must be Lindsay Hamilton," the woman said as she stood up. "Security said you were on your way up to see Than."

Lindsay nodded. "Is he available?"

"I haven't been able to get him on his phone, but you can go to his office and wait for him if he's not there." The woman's smile widened. "I doubt he'd have a problem with that."

Before she could stop herself, Lindsay wondered if many women dropped in to see Than. Pushing the thought from her mind, she returned the woman's smile. "Can you tell me where his office is?"

After the woman pointed her in the right direction, Lindsay walked down the plush carpeted hallways, her stomach slowly knotting. Was this a mistake? She thought she'd finally felt peace about coming here, but now she wasn't so sure.

As she neared the door the receptionist had told her was Than's, she heard his phone ring.

"Miller." The sound of his voice as he answered it—even just that one word—washed over her and anticipation built inside her.

Lindsay paused outside the door since she didn't want to interrupt him if it was business related, but she quickly realized—thanks to the speakerphone—that it was a personal call.

"Well hello, handsome!" The sound of a husky female voice started an uneasy ache in her gut.

"Hey there, beautiful. How's it going?" And Than's response made her want to throw up.

"Excellent! But you're a hard man to get hold of. I called three weeks ago but they said you were out of town on a job."

"Yeah, been a bit busy," Than replied.

"Well, I'm calling to collect on the rain check for the dinner you owe me."

Lindsay knew she should turn around and walk away, but she wasn't sure her legs would cooperate. At this point, she was surprised they still held her upright.

"When were you thinking?"

"Tonight?"

"Are you in town now?"

"Yep. And I want that dinner."

"Can't do tonight. I already have plans, but I'm free tomorrow night."

Lindsay reached out and braced a hand on the wall. She'd finally felt peace to come to Than and this was what she got? *God, help me.*

"You're seriously available tomorrow night?"

"Yeah, I am." His response was edged with laughter. "Do you want the slot or not?"

"Oh, I want." The woman's soft laugh was the last straw.

Praying that she could make it back to her car before falling apart, Lindsay turned around and focused on putting one foot in front of the other. Thankfully, the receptionist was no longer at her desk and didn't witness her confusion and pain. The elevator doors slid open almost immediately. It wasn't until the elevator began its descent that she exhaled and drew in another shuddering breath.

Her heart felt shredded by the realization that Than hadn't changed. Whatever he'd been working through hadn't involved her. That much was pretty clear. She'd been so, so stupid to think she could be special enough to him that he'd change into a one-woman man. This...this was why she protected herself. No one person—one man—should have the power to hurt her this much.

Pain clouded her thoughts but she managed to hand back the visitor's badge with a smile at the two men who'd let her in just minutes earlier. Hurt dogged her steps as she left the building and headed for her car. But in the midst of the pain, she prayed for clarity from the confusion that had gripped her. She just needed to understand.

"Text me where to meet you guys," Than said.

"Will do," Emma said. "It will likely be a buffet place since Frank always eats enough for two and, of course, I am too these days."

Than laughed. "How long 'til the baby arrives?"

"Too long," Emma said with a groan. "I'm huge!"

"But still beautiful, I'm sure."

"Ah, you know how to make a lady feel good. I knew there was a reason I let you be my friend all these years. Be sure and tell me that again when you see me in all my glory tomorrow night."

"I'll make sure to do that." After ending the conversation, Than quickly closed up his briefcase and shut off the light in his office. The thought of spending time with his friends had buoyed his spirits. He had a lot to share with them.

He lifted his briefcase onto his desk and slid his laptop into it, then turned out the light to his office. It was hard to believe it was two weeks since they'd gotten back from the Philippines. The days since he'd last seen Lindsay had been filled with emotion and upheaval. Though he hadn't liked the idea of giving her time after saying goodbye to her at the airport, he knew now that it had been the right thing. He'd had a lot of stuff to work through, and he wouldn't have been able to focus on her the way he should have.

"Good night, Kelsey," Than said to the receptionist as he passed her desk on the way to the elevator.

"Hey, did she find you?" Kelsey asked.

Than hit the button to call the elevator then spun around. "Did who find me?"

"Lindsay Hamilton," Kelsey said. "She arrived a few minutes ago. I tried to call you when security let me know she was on her way up, but you weren't in your office."

18

THAN glanced back down the hallway toward the offices. "You didn't see her leave?"

Kelsey shook her head. "After I told her where your office was, I popped into the bathroom to get ready for my date."

A sick feeling crept over Than. If she'd heard his conversation, she'd no doubt jumped to the conclusion that he hadn't changed at all. He turned back around as the elevator doors slid open. Though his car was parked underground, he hit the button for the main floor. Once there, he approached the security desk.

"Did Lindsay Hamilton come by here?"

"Yep. That was a fast visit, man."

"Can you ring the gate and tell them to hold her car when she gets there?"

"Will do."

Than pushed open the glass doors and looked toward the visitor parking. The tightness of his chest eased just a bit when he spotted Lindsay. He started to run toward her but then slowed to a jog when he realized she wasn't moving. She was standing next to her car, head bent, but not making any move to get into it.

Letting out the breath he'd been holding, Than walked toward her. When he was within a few feet of her, he stopped. "Lindsay?"

He saw her shoulders tense, but she turned around to face him. Than drank in the sight of her like a man who'd been without water for fourteen days. The sunlight brought out the different shades of her brown hair as its soft curls lay on her shoulders. She wore a sundress similar to the one she'd worn to church during the trip. This one had swirled shades of pink all over it. She'd never looked more beautiful to him.

Then he noticed how tightly she gripped the purse she held and the furrow of her brow. Her gray eyes regarded him with wariness and...hurt. Though Than tried to take encouragement from the fact that at least they weren't sparking with anger, uneasiness in his gut still lingered because of the hurt.

"Were you going to leave without letting me know you had stopped by?" Than asked, fighting the urge to explain everything.

"I was." Her voice was soft but steady. However, the expression on her face was indecipherable.

"But?" Than prompted. He saw her take a deep breath.

"It hasn't felt right to come see you until today." Her brow furrowed even more as she frowned. "I thought I was coming for one reason, but maybe God wanted me to come for a completely different one."

The tightness that gripped Than's chest robbed him of his breath. "A different reason?"

He could see confusion on her face now. "To say goodbye?"

"No." There was absolutely no way he'd waited this long only for her to tell him that. His heart was not prepared to say goodbye when they'd barely said hello.

He wished he could read Lindsay's mind because clearly she was having some sort of internal conversation. Her gaze met his. "No. It doesn't feel right."

"What doesn't feel right?" He tried to prompt her gently, afraid if he said the wrong thing she was going to bolt. He would chase her if she did, but his feeling that she needed to come to him of her own accord hadn't changed.

She tilted her head. "Saying goodbye."

He let out a quick breath. "What *does* feel right?"

Her brows drew together again as if she was still not sure about saying the words. Almost as if she needed to convince herself. "Being with...you."

Joy exploded within Than. He wanted to reach out and grab her into his arms, but there was just enough uncertainty still on her face that he knew it wasn't the time.

"But..." She looked toward the main building behind him.

"Let me explain." Than wished he didn't have to, but something told him that he needed to this time and once they got over this, she'd be more willing to give him the benefit of the doubt.

She pressed a hand to her stomach and looked back at him. "I wish I could tell you I didn't need an explanation. I thought I'd gotten to the point where I felt like I didn't."

"It's okay. I understand how it appeared to you. I would have felt the same if I'd heard you have a conversation like that with a man." And Than knew that was true. As he replayed the conversation with Emma in his head, he knew he'd have felt he was owed an explanation, too. He set his briefcase down and stepped closer. "Emma is a really good friend from high school. We never dated or were close in a physical way, but she was kind of like the female version of me. She moved to Chicago a few years back, but she's in town with her husband, Frank, and they wanted to get together. They're expecting a baby actually."

"A baby? She's married?"

"Yep. Married to a guy bigger than me. If I put the moves on her, I would likely end up with a cast on at least one limb."

Lindsay looked up at him. "I'm sorry."

"For what?"

"For needing that explanation."

"It's fine. There's no need for an apology." Than smiled at her then. "I'm just so thrilled you're here."

A smile spread across her face, too. "I'd ask you if you wanted to go out for dinner, but I also heard you already had plans tonight."

"Yes, I do, but you're welcome to come with me. In fact, I'd love it if you would."

Lindsay slipped the strap of her purse over her shoulder as if she no longer needed to hold onto it. "Come with you?"

"Yep. It's my dad's birthday, and my mother has been cooking up a storm for a family dinner."

Lindsay's eyes widened. "You want me to go with you to a family dinner?"

Than shrugged, trying not to show how important it really was that she agree to go with him. "Hey, your family knows me already. It's only fair mine knows you."

"But...that's different. They know you as Lincoln's friend."

Than arched a brow. "Clearly you weren't there when I stopped by to hang out with Lincoln last weekend. They were looking at me a bit differently."

"Are you sure it would be okay?"

"Most definitely. My mother would be thrilled if I actually brought a woman home to meet the family." Than paused then said, "It would be the first time. Ever."

As his words sank in, he saw comprehension dawn on her face. "The first time? Ever?"

"Ever." He held out his hand toward her. "Come with me?"

He wasn't about to tell her that him bringing her to his parents' home was akin to saying that this was the woman he planned to spend the rest of his life with. But something told him that she already knew that. Still, she reached out and slid her hand into his.

He pulled her toward him, wanting to kiss her but he held back. They needed to talk first—really talk. "We'll take my car and come back for yours later, okay?"

She nodded, her grip on his hand tightening. "Let's do this."

Lindsay leaned back against the seat and let out a long breath. She'd survived. It had actually been a fun evening once Than's family had gotten over their shock that he'd brought a woman with him. She hadn't missed the glances they'd shared as he'd slipped his arm around her waist when he introduced her.

His mom had been a bit standoffish at first, and Lindsay could see how much she doted on her *Nathaniel*. But once she complimented the woman's cooking and backed it up by eating healthy servings of the dishes she'd prepared, Than's mother had warmed right up to her. His siblings were all friendly as was his dad, but it had been his nephew and nieces that she'd felt most comfortable with. They reminded her a lot of Danny as well as the kids they'd run into in the Philippines on their trip.

"So was it as bad as you'd feared?" Than asked as he took her hand in his.

"Not at all. Your family is lovely. And it was great to be able to have more Filipino food."

Than's thumb rubbed back and forth over her hand. "You definitely won my mom over when you showed her how much you appreciated the dishes she'd prepared."

"I hope she knows I wasn't just saying that. It really was terrific."

"She knows." He lifted her hand and kissed it. "If she'd had any doubts, she would have told me, but instead, when she hugged me goodbye, she told me she liked you."

Lindsay smiled. "Your mom is sweet, and I see where you get your good looks from."

Than chuckled. "I like to hear you say that."

"That your mom is sweet?"

"Well, yes that, but also that you think I'm good looking."

Lindsay scoffed. "Like you've never heard that before."

"Ah, but you're the only one I want to hear it from now."

Lindsay felt her heart clench at his words. She squeezed his hand. It was odd to consider how deeply she felt about him, but she supposed that in a way, they'd had fourteen dates while in the Philippines. Each day they'd been together, she'd learned something new about him. And given the situations they'd been in, they'd learned more about each other than they would have going on nice fun dates in Minneapolis.

After two weeks apart after such intense times of being together, Lindsay was certain that this man was meant for her.

As Than pulled into the parking spot next to her car, Lindsay felt disappointed that their evening was coming to an end. Even though she'd enjoyed the evening with his family, she'd been looking forward to spending time with him...just the two of them.

Than released her hand to put the car in park, but then he picked it up again. In the darkness of the vehicle, Lindsay couldn't see his face and she really wanted to.

He lifted her hand to his lips again and then said, "I'm not quite ready for this night to end."

Lindsay smiled. "Me, either."

"How about you drive your car back to the mansion, and I'll pick you up there."

"Sounds good to me," Lindsay said.

"But first." Than reached out and slid his hand along her neck and pulled her toward him.

Lindsay lifted her hand to grip his wrist as his lips settled against hers. She felt flickers of the passion that had flared to life during that kiss outside the orphanage. But instead of kissing her with the intensity that he had then, Than kept the kiss soft and gentle.

When the kiss ended, he rested his forehead against hers. "I have missed you so much."

The emotion in his voice brought tears to Lindsay's eyes. She cupped his cheek in her hand, enjoying the feel of his five o'clock shadow against her palm. "I've missed you, too. More than I had thought I would." She paused, swallowed. "So much it scared me."

"Scared you?" Than asked, his voice soft.

"Missing you that much meant that you were more important to me than anyone else has ever been. And it was scary not knowing if you felt the same way."

"Oh, I did. I do. The only reason I stayed away was because I promised you time. And I did cheat a little when I went to see Lincoln. Only you weren't there."

"I was there," Lindsay said. "My bedroom window looks out over the pool."

Than pulled back a bit from her. "You were watching me at the pool?"

"Sure. I couldn't resist. Did they tell you I wasn't there?"

"No. I just assumed you weren't because you didn't make an appearance. Why didn't you?"

Lindsay sighed. "Like I said earlier, there was something stopping me from contacting you. Today was the first time when I woke up that I felt a sense of peace about talking with you again."

Than nodded. "I have lots to tell you. Let's go drop your car off so we can talk. I want to be able to see you. After so long apart I've missed your beautiful face."

Lindsay felt a rush of warmth at his words. "Okay. Meet you there."

She pressed one last kiss to his lips before climbing out and getting into her car.

Thanks to the lighter evening traffic, Than had no problem following Lindsay back to her place. She didn't even bother going into the house once she parked. When Than pulled up behind her car, she was waiting to get back in.

"Do you have a curfew?" he asked as she climbed into his car.

Lindsay laughed. "I have no idea. It's been so long since I've been on a date, but I'm going to say no."

"Good."

He hadn't been sure where they should go. He wanted to be able to talk to her without interruptions, but knew that going to his apartment was out of the question. Instead, he went to the next best place.

Before she could comment on his choice of Denny's, he said, "They're open twenty-four hours so we're not going to get kicked out. The other option was my place, and I think that's probably not a good idea."

When the hostess took them to a booth, Than waited until she'd settled in one side before he slid in next to her.

"Sorry," he said with a grin. "I don't want to be sitting across the table from you."

After they'd placed the order for drinks and a dessert, Than slid his arm around her waist and pulled her close to his side.

"How has your return to life here been?" he asked, wanting to know everything he'd missed the past two weeks.

Lindsay shrugged. "There are times I get so engrossed in my work and such that I forget, but then when I remember again, I get so angry. I feel like I should never be able to forget what all we went through there. The good and the bad."

"I know how you feel, but I think that's normal, too. You do have a life here that's very different from there. I think your heart will always remember, even if your mind might forget for a time."

"One good thing is that I've become more involved with the charitable side of Hamilton Enterprises with Lucas. Sometimes it feels like it's just a drop in a giant bucket when I think of all the needs out in the world. But I know that every little bit helps, even if it doesn't completely solve the underlying problems." She glanced over at him. "You said you had lots to tell me. What's been going on with you?"

Than glanced down at Lindsay, still not quite used to seeing her look at him without a trace of reserve. He doubted that she had even a clue of what that did to him. He wanted to know more about how she'd gotten to that point, but first, he needed to share his own story.

He told her how he'd been able to spend time with Eric and Trent and get the answers he needed. They had been patient with him as he'd tried to work through everything he'd experienced and learned while in the Philippines. Both men had told him they'd been praying for him and had asked God to reveal Himself to Than while in the midst of the mission team.

And God had indeed done that. His moment of clarity had come when Eric had explained he needed to only accept the gift God offered in order to gain salvation and eternal life. That no matter how good of a guy he was, he needed to accept that Jesus had died for his sins. Four days ago, he'd done just that. Barb's words from their trip came back to him. He understood now in a way he hadn't on that day.

"I'm so happy for you, Than," Lindsay said as she slipped her arms around his waist and gave him a tight hug. "You know, I'm about at the same point you are. Oh, I've been attending church for years and at one time made the decision just like you did, but I haven't grown." She sat back a little from him. "I wonder if Eric, Stacey, Trent, and Victoria would be willing to meet with us. Kinda like a couples' Bible study."

"I think that's a terrific idea," Than said. "Maybe even Lucas and Brooke would like to be involved."

Their conversation over the next two hours ranged from serious and emotional to lighthearted and humorous. Around two in the morning, they ordered a plate of smothered cheese fries to share. As they talked and laughed together, Than realized that while there were things that had changed in Lindsay while they were on their trip, some of the things he was seeing in her now weren't a result of those changes. They were parts of herself that she kept from people she didn't trust. From him.

Feeling a rush of emotion, Than bent down and pressed a lingering kiss to her lips. Sliding a hand to the back of his neck, Lindsay leaned into him. If his heart hadn't been completely gone by that point already, he'd surely have lost it right then.

When the kiss ended, she sat back a bit and tilted her head. "What was that for?"

"Do I need a reason to kiss you?" Than asked, trying to interject some lightness into the emotions he was feeling.

Lindsay grinned. "No, you most certainly don't, but it just felt like that kiss was prompted by something."

Would he scare her away with his observation? He didn't think he could handle it if she shut down on him now. Still, he wanted to communicate with her in ways he never had with anyone else.

He looked down at her, allowing his expression to go serious. Her gray eyes were soft, her gaze open and expectant. "You trust me."

She blinked once at his words, and her gaze slipped away for a moment, but then she looked back at him and nodded. "Yes, I do. Did this just come to you now?"

Than thought about that. "I think it's been a kind of gradual thing, starting when you shared about your dad during the flight to the Philippines. But it just struck me now because you're acting the way you only seem to act when you're around people like Danny or Lucas. I've seen it before but always understood that it was only because I happened to be there, not because I inspired that response in you. But now...it's just me here. You trust me not to hurt you."

Lindsay stared at him and then nodded. "On the trip, I had no choice but to trust you with my safety. It took a while longer to get to the point where I felt I could trust you with...everything else." Her gaze dropped as she trailed a finger down the front of his shirt. "But that's not to say I won't ever struggle with jealousy. I know there are a lot of women out there who would gladly take you off my hands."

"They could only do that if I were looking for a way out." Than placed his hand over hers and moved it to cover his heart. "And I'm not. I know your concerns. And they are...were valid. At one time, I would have balked at focusing on just one woman for any length of time. And anything more permanent was definitely not in my future. I mean, how did I know that the minute I tied myself to one woman, a better one wouldn't come along? But that all started to change after our date. I tried to continue on as usual once you turned me down, but after three dates with other women, I just couldn't do it anymore."

Lindsay arched a brow at him. "You've only been on three dates in the past eight months?"

Than nodded. "And those all occurred in the month following our date. So technically, I haven't had a date at all in seven months. And in that time I realized that I didn't need to worry that a better woman might come along because I'd already found the best one for me. I just needed to be patient and wait for you to accept that I was the best one for you." Than pressed his hand more firmly over hers, wanting her to feel the beat of his heart. "I know that technically we haven't even had a real second date, but I don't need that in order to tell you that I love you, Lindsay."

He felt her hand jerk beneath his and then curl into a fist, gathering the fabric of his shirt into her grip. "You love me?"

Than stared into her eyes that had turned to liquid silver and smiled. "I certainly do. And you're the only woman— aside from the ones in my family—that I've ever said that to. A year ago I would have laughed at anyone who said I'd be professing my love to you sitting in a booth in Denny's in the middle of the night, but right now there's no place else I'd rather be and no one else I'd rather be with than you."

"Oh, Than." Lindsay leaned closer to him, her eyelashes spiky with unshed tears. "I love you, too. Sorry it took me so long to get with the program."

Than shook his head. "It's God's perfect time. Anything sooner might have resulted in a relationship that would have floundered. Right now, I'm confident in God's plan for us, and the timing for this is part of that."

He bent to press another kiss to her lips, knowing that this time she'd understand what prompted it. The kiss was soft and sweet, full of the love and promise they had for each other. And as they kissed, Than pledged to guard Lindsay's heart and their love like they were the most precious things on earth.

Because they were.

EPILOGUE

LINDSAY tried not to feel sad and alone, but it was hard not to since Than had been away for over two weeks. She'd known that there would be stretches of time like this when he would be away because of his job. And so far they'd dealt with it one other time. This time was different though. It was her birthday, and he hadn't even called to wish her happy birthday. Nor had there been a card or any type of acknowledgment of her special day from him.

Her family had made it special for her though. Her mom had taken her out for breakfast and then to do some birthday shopping. She'd ended up with a new dress which she was wearing for their family dinner at Thom and Amanda's restaurant. It would have been a perfect end to the day...if only Than were there to share it with her.

"I'm so hungry I could eat everything on the menu," Danny said, slipping his hand into hers as they walked from the parking lot to the restaurant.

They were trailing behind Lucas, Brooke, Lincoln and her mom, but Danny didn't seem to be in any hurry to catch up.

And neither was Lindsay. She loved her nephew beyond words and spending time with him ranked second only to spending time with Than. In fact, being with both of them together was one of her favorite things.

Danny was the one who'd first broke through the walls around her heart. He'd offered her affection and love almost from the first time they'd met, and it had only grown from there. And she'd quickly learned she could be completely herself with him because he never held back anything when he was around her. She thanked God every day for bringing Brooke and Danny into their lives.

"Hey! There's a plane, Auntie!"

Lindsay stopped and looked up at the sky, shading her eyes. Danny had a fascination with planes, and she wouldn't be surprised if he ended up as a pilot one day. The fact that his father had almost died in a plane accident didn't seem to be a deterrent at all. Lindsay just looked at the plane wishing it was bringing Than home.

"C'mon, you guys!" Lincoln called from where he stood holding the door to the restaurant open.

"They're such spoilsports," Lindsay said with a grin at Danny as they jogged the last few feet to the restaurant.

They had just stepped in the door when there was a resounding *SURPRISE!* Lindsay froze in shock while Danny danced around her, obviously beyond delighted that they'd truly surprised her.

She looked around the room for that one face she longed to see. But he wasn't there. Pushing aside her disappointment, she focused on those who were there because their presence touched her more than she could say. Barb. Mark and Mel. Eric and his family. Trent and Victoria. A group from BlackThorpe. Several of her co-workers. And Than's family. She was so glad to see them all there, too. If Than couldn't be there, she was glad they were. In the six months they'd been dating, she'd grown to love them as if they were her own family.

She felt an arm slip around her shoulders and looked up to see Lucas standing there, a big smile on his face.

"Well, I wasn't sure we could actually surprise Lindsay, but it looks like we pulled it off!" There was a round of cheers and applause. "Why don't you all find seats so we can get this party started?"

Lucas led her to a seat that had balloons attached to the back. On the table beside the chair was a vase with three roses. One white. One pink. One red. She knew that they were from Than and blinked back tears as she reached out to touch one of them.

"Than is the mastermind behind this whole evening and has been a pain in the butt trying to make sure everything was perfect." Lucas touched her shoulder as he looked down at her. "And he wanted to be here. We had planned a Skype session, but then his plans changed *again* and he has been out of contact. Thankfully, we knew that might happen so he took the time to make you a video in case this was how things ended up."

Lindsay looked around and realized that several people had their phones out and were videoing her. She was overwhelmed with love for these people who had chosen to spend their evening celebrating her birthday with her.

"We've set up a screen here so we can project his message for you, Linds."

Her eyes widened when Than's face filled the screen that sat at the end of the room. It was frozen for a second and then he smiled, his brown eyes warm. Lindsay felt a rush of tears as she reached out toward his image. She loved this man so much—even more than the night they'd professed their love for each other.

"Hi, sweetheart. Happy birthday! I wish I could give you this message in person, but..." His broad shoulders lifted and fell as a rueful expression flitted across his face. "I want you to know that these past six months with you have been the best of my life. All I'd hoped for when Lucas asked me to be your bodyguard for the mission trip was to get you to go out on a second date with me. Instead, I found a faith that has turned my life around and a love that's filled my heart." He leaned forward and Lindsay had to gather her hand into a fist to keep from reaching out toward him again. "When I told you that night in Denny's that I knew I didn't need to keep looking for the perfect woman for me, I meant it. You might drive me nuts on occasion. And yes, I know I've driven you crazy, too. But at the end of each day, I have gone to bed knowing I love you even more than I did the day before. You are my forever, Lindsay. So..." He relaxed back and a smile lifted the corner of his mouth, his eyes sparkling. "The next time I see you, I'm going to have a question for you. And I expect you to have your answer ready."

Lindsay felt her mouth drop open as her heart pounded in her chest. She wanted him there *now* because she already knew her answer. Had known it from the moment she'd told him she loved him.

"Because when I see you, I'm going to ask you..."

Suddenly, the fog of emotions that had swirled around her as the video had played evaporated. She knew his scent— felt his presence—even as her hand was lifted in a familiar grasp. Lindsay looked to her right and saw him there, down on one knee, all teasing gone from his expression.

It was just him and her as he finished the sentence his videotaped image had started. "Will you marry me, sweetheart?"

Lindsay stared at him, almost afraid that this was a dream. But it didn't matter. Dream or reality, her answer would still be the same. She reached out to touch his cheek, her heart pounding at the love she saw in his beautiful brown eyes. "Yes! Yes, I will."

There were whoops of joy as he got to his feet, pulling her along with him. He wrapped his arms around her and drew her close for a kiss. Lindsay gripped his shoulders, the feel of which reinforced just how real this was. When the kiss ended, he pressed his forehead to hers.

"I love you, Lindsay. And you've made me the happiest man on the planet today."

"Then I must be the happiest woman because I love you, too, Than, and spending the rest of my life with you is exactly what I want to do."

"Hey, buddy!" someone in the crowd called out. "What about the ring?"

Than looked a little sheepish as he moved back from her. "I can't believe I forgot that."

"You forgot the ring?" Lindsay asked, fighting the urge to laugh.

"No, I didn't forget the ring. I forgot to give it to you." He reached into the pocket of his pants and pulled out a small velvet box. "I was just so excited to see you again and to pop the question, I forgot about giving this to you."

Lindsay watched as Than lifted the ring from the box. He reached for her left hand and slid it onto her finger. After lifting it to his lips for a kiss, he let her have a look at it.

"Oh, Than, it's perfect." And it was. There was nothing super flashy about it, but it was something she would have chosen herself if she'd had a say in the matter.

He bent his head to hers as he curved her fingers over his. "The large stone represents God and the smaller stones on either side represent you and me, because I know now that it's the only way to be in this relationship with you."

They kissed one more time and as they turned from each other to face the crowd of loved ones gathered there with them, a cheer went up. "To Than and Lindsay!"

Than slid his arm around her, pulling her tight against his side. Lindsay put her arm around his waist and rested her hand with its new ring on his chest. They posed for a few pictures and then were encircled by their families offering them congratulations.

When Lindsay thought back over the year, she knew that it had been only by surrendering her heart to God's will that she'd been able to find joy in her life. And she knew the same was true for Than. She was looking forward to what the years ahead held for them, but first she was going to have to convince her mother *and* his that a long engagement and a big wedding weren't necessary.

THE END

OTHER TITLES BY

Kimberly Rae Jordan

Marrying Kate

Faith, Hope & Love

Waiting for Rachel (*Those Karlsson Boys: 1*)
Worth the Wait (*Those Karlsson Boys: 2*)
The Waiting Heart (*Those Karlsson Boys: 3*)

Home Is Where the Heart Is (*Home to Collingsworth: 1*)
Home Away From Home (*Home to Collingsworth: 2*)
Love Makes a House a Home (*Home to Collingsworth: 3*)
The Long Road Home (*Home to Collingsworth: 4*)
Her Heart, His Home (*Home to Collingsworth: 5*)
Coming Home (*Home to Collingsworth: 6*)

This Time With Love (*The McKinleys: 1*)
Forever My Love (*The McKinleys: 2*)
When There is Love (*The McKinleys: 3*)

A Little Bit of Love:
A Collection of Christian Romance Short Stories

For news on new releases and sales
ign up for Kimberly's newsletter

http://eepurl.com/WFhYr

Please visit Kimberly Rae Jordan on the web!
Website: www.kimberlyraejordan.com
Facebook: www.facebook.com/AuthorKimberlyRaeJordan
Twitter: twitter.com/KimberlyR Jordan